BISHOP

BY

L. ANN

BISHOP

Cover design by A.T. Cover Designs

Interior Formatting by Crow Fiction Designs

Edited by Teresa Smith

Blurb by Tami Thomasson

First Edition: April 2023

ISBN: 9798392282913

L.Ann Online -

www.lannauthor.com

THERE ARE CHANCE MEETINGS
WITH STRANGERS
THAT INTEREST US FROM THE FIRST
MOMENT
BEFORE A WORD IS SPOKEN

Fyodor Dostoevsky

Dedication

Special thanks must go to my Alpha readers, without whom this book would probably have taken a lot longer!

As always, thank you to all my readers who indulge my need to explore all the shiny what if's my mind points out to me.

Be Aware

Bishop contains talk of domestic violence.

1

Bishop

rip ... splash ... drip ... splash ...

My eyes focused on the water as it formed small-tear-shaped beads on the ceiling. They stretched down, detached, and fell, hitting the floor with quiet slaps of water against cement. After each tiny ball exploded, my eyes lifted and sought out the next.

Drip ... splash ... drip ... splash ...

The noise was enough to drive a person insane, which I'm certain was the point.

The man seated on the other side of the table hadn't said a word in thirty minutes. His head was bowed as he thumbed through the folder in front of him, occasionally grunting and glancing over at me.

I said nothing. I recognized what he was doing. It was a ploy, a means to get me to speak, to break the silence, and offer up the

1

information he was looking for.

Drip ... splash ... drip ... splash ...

Beneath the table the fingers on my left hand twitched, the only outward show of irritation I allowed myself. My time was being wasted, *purposely*, and I didn't like it.

I also didn't like how the hair was standing to attention on the back of my neck.

Or the way my instincts whispered that I needed to be aware, be *ready*.

Something about this entire situation was a little ... *off*.

I swallowed a laugh. *Off?* Had I become so immune to the hazards of my life that being dragged out of my hotel room at gunpoint in the middle of the night and locked in a room with someone *claiming* to be FBI was only a *little* off?

"Something funny?" The man seated opposite broke the silence and glared across the table at me.

I lifted my hand and held my thumb and finger an inch apart. "Little bit."

"Care to enlighten me?" He dropped the papers he'd been reading to the table, and I caught a quick glimpse of a photograph before he tucked it away inside a folder. The face was unrecognizable to me. I had a photographic memory. If I'd met the woman in the image, I would have remembered her.

"Not really." I checked the time on my watch. "I have somewhere to be. Can we speed this up?"

"I don't think you understand how much trouble you're

in right now, Mr. Chambers." He leaned back in his chair and looked at me.

"Enlighten me." I threw his own words back at him.

"Do you know why you're here?"

"I'd have to be a talented mind reader to answer that since I was on my way to bed when you broke into my room and *insisted* I come with you."

"We know you were hired to make Eden Marshall disappear."

"Is that so?"

He flipped open the folder, took out the photograph and slid it across to me. I glanced down at it but didn't bother picking it up.

"Am I supposed to recognize that woman?" I feigned disinterest and boredom. "I hate to disappoint you, and I don't know who's been telling you otherwise, but I've never seen her before."

"To be clear, you're saying you've never met Eden Marshall or taken money to build her a new life."

"Never met her, never spoken to her, never taken money from her."

"Yet we have eyewitnesses who say they saw her outside your hotel room earlier this evening."

I snorted. "I find that very unlikely."

That wasn't how I ran my business. I rarely met with my clients in hotels. It was usually in a public place in the middle of the day, far away from where I was staying or lived. This was a fishing expedition and one that was going to be unfruitful.

"If that's all you've dragged me here for …" I stood.

He jumped to his feet. "This is a criminal investigation. *Sit down, Mr. Chambers.* I'm not done with you."

My eyes dropped to the gun at his hip. It *wasn't* a government issue, and I was pretty confident he *didn't* work for the FBI or any other agency. I checked the time again. I needed to be at the airport in less than an hour.

"I don't have time for this." A quick look around the room accompanied my words.

There were no cameras. Nothing other than *him* and *me.* I placed my palms on the table and leaned across it.

"Do you *really* want to know where Ms. Marshall is?" I dropped my voice and cast another furtive look around.

He bought the action and stooped closer to listen to me. *That* was his mistake.

I grabbed his tie with one hand and yanked *hard.* As he staggered forward, I flattened my other hand on the back of his head and slammed his face into the table. Before he could react, I was across the table and had his gun out of the holster on his hip and pointed at his head.

"We could have kept this civil, but you called me a liar." I thumbed the safety off the SIG P365, and he froze at the audible click it made. "I don't like being called a liar."

"If you kill me, you'll have the entire FBI after you."

I laughed. "You're no more FBI than I am. My guess is someone has hired you to find Ms. Marshall. Did she steal something from your employer? Or maybe she's related to them?

It doesn't matter." My finger moved from the gun's grip to the trigger. "I don't know who she is, nor do I care. What I *do* care about is why someone is trying to involve me. But since you don't have the answer to that question ... Well, too bad, so sad for you." I squeezed the trigger.

The gunshot was a muted sound, courtesy of the suppressor attached to the muzzle. Not silent, but not loud enough to draw outside attention. Blood and brain matter exploded outward, and I grimaced when some landed on my sleeve. Blood was such a bitch to get out of silk.

Pushing the body to the floor, I did a quick search of his pockets and came up with no I.D and no badge, but there was a set of keys. Whoever he was, he didn't work for any government agency.

I checked the time. Fifty minutes until I needed to be at the private airstrip. If I was late, Wade would never let me forget it. I needed to leave.

I checked the gun's magazine for ammunition, then opened the door and stepped out into the hallway.

The guard outside scrambled for his gun a second too late. His brain took a moment to catch up with his body, and his eyes widened as he fell to the floor, blood dripping down his face. I stepped over him. I was certain there should be at least one more. When they burst into my hotel room, I heard three distinct voices.

So where was the last one?

I moved along the hallway, gun held steady while I listened for movement or voices. Silence greeted me.

Where was he?

I stopped, head tilting when I heard the flush of a toilet. Moving to the side, I turned until my back was against the wall so I could see in both directions and waited.

Two minutes passed before a shadow heralded the arrival of the missing man. From the lack of urgency in his pace, he clearly hadn't heard any of the gunshots or knew his partners were dead. He had his head bowed over his cell as he walked and didn't see me step out to face him.

Lucky for him, I didn't want him dead. I needed him to take a message back to whoever his employer was. I waited until he was less than a foot away, then cleared my throat. His head jerked up. He dropped his cell and reached for his gun.

"Touch it and I'll kill you."

He froze.

"Hand me your gun ... *slowly*." I held out one hand and kept my gun trained on him as he reached for the gun in its side holster. "That's it. Nice and easy. You don't want to die tonight. That won't benefit either of us."

"Where's Henry?" His voice quivered, and I gave a mental headshake. He was clearly green, new to the business of kidnap and killing.

"Henry is meeting his maker." I leaned forward and took the gun from his shaking hand. "Now listen carefully ..." I cocked a brow in query.

"Tom."

"Okay, Tom. Listen carefully now. I want you to go back to your boss and tell him that Bishop Chambers said if he tries this again, I'll be paying him a visit."

It wouldn't be difficult to find out who was behind the order to grab me. A few well-placed questions and I'd have the answer within twenty-four hours.

"Whoever employed you to find the girl needs to understand that it has nothing to do with me, and I'd like to keep it that way. Think you can do that, Tom?"

"Y-yes sir."

I nodded. "Good. Then I'll head out. I have a flight to catch." I stepped past him. "Oh … one more thing …"

As the young man turned, I hit him with the grip of the gun, and he dropped to the floor like a stone.

"I'd say I'm sorry about the headache you'll wake up with, but it's better than being dead."

2

Bishop

utside the building were three cars. I pushed the button on the keys and walked to the one whose lights flashed. Once in the driver's seat, I leaned across the center console and opened the glove compartment. Inside was another handgun, a driver's license, and a packet of wet wipes. I took the gun, checked the mag, and placed it on the passenger seat next to the two I'd taken from inside. The driver's license was next.

Sandro Trebuni. The name meant nothing to me.

The photograph was of the man who had tried to interrogate me. I put that with the guns, then checked the time. I had less than thirty minutes to get to the airport, but I needed to go back to the hotel first. It was going to be tight, so I had to be fast if I wanted to make it.

Jamming the key into the ignition, I started the car. Just before the engine roared to life, there was a muffled thud from the back of the car.

I cocked my head.

What was that?

I cut off the engine and listened.

Nothing.

As I was about to start the engine again, there was another muted bang. I frowned. It definitely seemed to be coming from the back of the car. I grabbed one of the guns and climbed out.

Skirting around to the back of the car, I looked down at the trunk. Another thud sounded. I popped the lock ... and revealed a body hogtied inside it.

Face down with a hood covering their features, their hands and feet had been pulled behind their back and tied together, it was hard to say whether the figure was male or female, especially in the dark. The shape wriggled while I watched, and muffled moaning reached me. At a guess, I'd say their mouth had been taped closed.

Rubbing the muzzle of the gun across my jaw, I considered my options. I could leave them there and drop an anonymous call to the police once I was at the airstrip ... *or* I could find out who they were.

Could they be something to do with why I'd been grabbed? If so, they might know who was behind it, which would save me the hassle of tracking them down.

I checked the time again. Wade was going to fucking shoot me. There was no way I could avoid being late. I needed to find a phone and let him know. Slamming down the lid of the trunk, I rounded the car and climbed back in. Whoever they were, they'd keep for another fifteen minutes. I'd get my shit together and *then* deal with it.

I drove out of the abandoned trading site, and followed the roads until I started recognizing the sights, and then found my way back to the hotel. I didn't park there, though. I found a deserted side road, wiped down my fingerprints off the car and left it there, walking the block back to the hotel.

The hotel lobby was silent and empty when I entered, and I got back to my room without being seen. Once inside, I found my cell where I'd left it beside the bed and called Knight.

"Bishop." As always, my youngest brother was wide awake.

"Run a search on the name Sandro Trebuni for me. I want to know who he worked for."

"Worked?"

"He met with an accident a little while ago."

My brother laughed. "Was the accident six five, temperamental and named after a chess piece?"

"Might have been." I dragged my suitcase out of the closet and tossed clothes into it." He was asking after someone called Eden Marshall."

"Oh? Do you know who she is and why they were asking?"

"I'm guessing she pissed someone off. *That's* where you come in. I want to know who is looking for her and why. I should be back home tomorrow night. Tell me what you find then. I have to go." I cut the call before he could respond.

Once I had everything packed, I went into the bathroom and

grabbed the toiletries I'd left there, tossed them into the case, and then pulled on fresh clothes. I wiped down all the surfaces in the suite to remove my fingerprints, then picked up my case, the bag containing my laptop, and walked out.

I'd already paid my hotel bill, so there was no reason for me to linger and I made my way to my car. I tossed my stuff into the trunk, then checked the time. Fifteen minutes. Glancing back down the block, I sighed, locked the car, and set off toward the side road where I'd left the other vehicle.

When I arrived, I unlocked the trunk, threw it open, reached into my pocket for my switchblade, and leaned over.

"Don't move."

A muffled yelp sounded, and the body tried to wriggle toward the back of the trunk.

"I'm holding a knife. I want to cut the hood off your head. If you keep moving, I might accidentally stab you. While I personally don't care either way, I doubt *you* want to bleed out in the trunk of a car."

The body froze.

"Better. Now *stay still*." I cut a hole through the material, then grasped each side with my fingers and ripped it apart. Dark red hair spilled over my hands. I pushed it away and got my first look at the person lying there.

Female, for sure. It was hard to tell much more than that. Blood and a purple bruise marred one cheek. Tape covered most of the lower half of her face. Eyes wide and full of ... was that *anger?* ... stared up at me.

Tossing the hood to one side, I moved to the duct tape around her wrists.

"Hands now. I don't know how long you've been like this, so be aware that when I release you and the blood returns to your extremities, it might hurt." I sliced through the tape, and straightened her arms and legs as best I could in the confines of the trunk of the car.

"Can you sit up?" I reached in, ignored her when she shrank back, and wrapped my hands around her arms to haul her upright. She glared at me and lifted one hand to pull the tape away. I caught her wrist, stopping her. "It looks like there's blood dried to the tape. Let me check you're not going to rip away a scab or something first."

Her eyes continued to shoot fire at me, but she dropped her hand. I pressed a finger beneath her chin and tipped her head up, letting the glow from a nearby street light shine on her face.

I picked at the edge of the tape with one fingernail, ran along the edge of it and then gave a sharp tug and ripped it off.

Okay, so I'd lied about the possibility of ripping scabs away.

But I knew from experience she would have wanted to peel it away slowly, and that would have been worse. My way was better.

She screamed, the sound echoing down the road. I slapped my palm over her mouth and sighed.

"Don't do that. People will come. I'll have to defend myself.

Things will get messy, and then I'll have to deal with *your* body on top of all the other shit I've had to put up with tonight. I don't have time for drama." I lifted the gun with my other hand. "I didn't put you in here, so why don't we try this again? I'm going to remove my hand. If you scream, I'm going to shoot you. Got it?"

Her eyes widened, and then she gave a sharp nod.

I slowly removed my hand. She screamed. My voice was irritable when I lifted the gun.

"What did I just tell you?"

"N-no, please." Her voice was hoarse, probably from all the screaming I'm sure she'd been doing before they gagged her the first time.

"Then do as you're told, or I'll gag you again. Can you stand?"

She eased forward until her feet touched the floor, and then cautiously rose to her feet. She swayed but stayed upright.

"Great. Do you know who grabbed you?"

She shook her head.

"Do you know *why* you were grabbed?"

Another headshake.

Damn it. She was either lying or got caught in the crossfire of something she had no idea about. My gut said she was lying; I just wasn't sure what about.

"Fine. Then you're no use to me. I'll call the police and have them come to collect you." I slammed the trunk shut, narrowly missing her fingers, and strode to the front of the car.

"No! Wait!" She stumbled after me, caught my shirt sleeve

and tugged at it.

And that's when I got my first good look at her face.

"Who are you?" My demand was sharp.

She ignored my question and asked one of her own. "You're Bishop Chambers, aren't you?"

"How do *you* know my name?"

"I've been trying to find you."

3

Bishop

Her words sent me into autopilot. I grabbed her arm and dragged her to the passenger side of the car. She struggled against my grip, so I lifted the gun.

"Don't try me." My voice was flat. "Get in the car." I leaned past her and opened the door, keeping my gun trained on her until she climbed in. "Stay put." I pushed the button on the keys to lock it and stop her bolting while I moved around to the driver's side.

She still attempted to flee when I unlocked it to climb in, but I lunged across and grabbed her arm again.

"I *will* fucking shoot you. Do not make me chase you." The gun touched her temple. "Decide fast. I have to be at the airport in ten minutes."

She stared straight ahead, lips compressed into a thin line.

"You said you were looking for me. *Why?*" I pulled back the safety and she flinched at the sound it made. "Don't make me repeat myself."

My cell blared, and she jumped. Without taking my eyes or gun off her, I reached into my pocket and pulled it out, then tapped connect. "What?"

"Are you running late?" My friend, Wade, asked. "We have to be in the air within the hour, Bish. What's keeping you?"

"I'll be there in ten minutes. I had to make a slight detour, but I'm on my way."

Thankfully, we had a little bit of leeway on the flight schedule. But not much. I stared at the woman, who refused to look at me.

"If I brought company with me, would that be a problem?"

"Company? *You?* No, it's not a problem."

"Okay, good. See you soon." I ended the call.

"Guess you're coming with me." *That* got a reaction.

She twisted in the seat and swatted the gun away from her face. "I am *not*."

"You said you were looking for me. Well, congratulations, sweetheart. You've *found* me. But I have somewhere to be, so if there's something you want from me, you're going to have to spit it out or tag along."

I started the engine, drove the car back to the hotel and parked up beside mine. The woman beside me didn't speak for the entire drive.

I cut off the engine and glanced at her. "Ready to talk yet?"

She shook her head.

"Then you are giving me no other choice. I can't leave you here. I've just killed two men because they think I'm helping you."

She gaped at me for half a second before rallying and snapping her mouth closed. "You *found* me tied up in the trunk of a *car*!"

I shrugged. "Could be a ploy to lower my guard. For all I know, you're involved with the men who dragged me out of my room in the middle of the night." I lifted the gun. "Let's go."

"No."

"Do you think this is a toy?" I tapped her temple with the gun and her face drained of color. "Or maybe you think I won't use it? If you have been searching for me, like you claim, then you know what I do. Get. Out. Of. The. Car."

Her throat moved as she swallowed, but she stayed put.

"Okay then." My voice was soft. I threw open the car door and climbed out.

She bolted the second my back was turned. Not unexpected. I lifted the gun, took aim, and fired. The bullet hit the ground near her feet. She skidded to a stop.

"That was your only warning. Get in my fucking car."

She turned slowly to face me. "I heard about you from a friend. I wanted to hire you, but I've changed my mind. I thought you were just a ... a middleman ... I didn't expect someone to jump me when I was walking to your hotel room. I want no part of whatever it is you're involved with." The words merged together in her haste to share them.

"Three."

"What?"

"If I get to one, and you're not in my fucking car, I'm going to stop being nice … Two."

"You're *not* being nice." She hurried toward me. "I don't want to go with you."

"If you were looking to hire me, you'd end up going *somewhere* with me." I threw open the passenger door of my car. "In."

She shot me a dark look but bent and scrambled into the passenger seat. I slammed the door and went around to the driver's side.

"Why were you looking to hire me?"

"I need to disappear. Just for a little while."

"The people who hire me disappear for life, not just a *little while*."

"My friend said you helped people."

My eyebrow shot up. "Oh? And who is your *friend?*"

If it was someone who'd hired me then they'd broken the one rule I have—*no one* talked about it. The whole point of disappearing was not to talk to anyone about your past life.

"She said you don't know her, but you helped someone she knew disappear."

"Why do *you* need to disappear?" I kept my eyes on the road. I could find out who had been talking another time.

"I … My ex-boyfriend is stalking me."

"Report it. Get a restraining order. That's what the police are for."

"He *is* the police." She blurted the words. "He's a detective. We dated for a year. He was … Well, it wasn't working, so I ended it. He won't leave me alone."

"How long has it been going on?"

"Four years."

Her answer surprised me. I'd expected her to say a couple of months.

"I've moved twice. He finds me every time. He even transferred to a new precinct to be closer to me."

"And ... *your friend* ... how did you meet her?" I turned onto the road leading to the private airstrip.

"I didn't, as such. I'm in an ... ummm ... an online group for people who are dealing with similar situations."

"I see. And this person told you about me? Out of concern for a stranger on the internet?"

"She gave me a number to call and leave a message. She said someone would contact me with a time and location to come and meet you."

"That's not how I work." The fine hairs on the back of my neck stood up. Someone was fucking around. "Did you get a message?"

"Yes. I was to book a room in the Swallow Falls Motel in Dallas and wait for you to contact me."

"And that's what you did?"

She nodded. "I got a call tonight that you were staying at the Dallas Spring Hotel, and I was to meet you at eight in room six-three-two. I got there a little early, and there were three men outside. They grabbed me."

"Hmmm." I'd never heard of the Dallas Spring Hotel.

"Do you believe me?"

"I haven't decided yet." I pulled the car into a space and turned to look at her. "Let's pretend for the moment that I do. What did you think you were contacting me to do?"

"To help me get away from my ex-boyfriend."

"Let's say I'm open to being hired. For me to be effective, I'd need you to do *exactly* what I say without argument. Can you do that?"

"If it means I'll be free from him, *yes*."

I stared at her, making no secret of the fact I was assessing whether or not I believed her. She held my gaze.

"Okay," I said finally. "First thing you have to do is come with me. We'll call this our assessment meeting. You'll fly with me to New York, and tell me everything about the situation you're in. If, at the end of the flight, I decide this isn't the job for me, we part ways."

"New York?" she whispered.

"If this is the point where you tell me you don't have the money to pay for your flight back to wherever you're from, then I should inform you now that you won't be able to afford my fees, either." I climbed out of the car. "I'll give you a few minutes to decide."

4

Eden

I let out a shaky breath once I was alone in the car.

I'd found him.

Bishop Chambers.

And he was nothing like what I had been expecting or imagined. The man had an intensity about him that scared me.

What did you expect, idiot? He makes people disappear.

Well, for one, I hadn't expected to be grabbed, tied up, and stuffed into the trunk of a car by three men. For another, when I was freed, I didn't think it would be by the man I was supposed to be meeting. And *thirdly*, why was he acting like he hadn't expected me?

I rubbed my left wrist. My entire body ached, partly from being manhandled, mostly from … I cut off that thought. The last thing I needed was to break down in the middle of nowhere in front of the man holding a gun.

Where were we, anyway?

I looked around but couldn't see much. The entire area was dark.

He'd mentioned flying to New York. Were we at an airport? It seemed too quiet to be one of the main ones. Could it be a private airstrip? They were a thing, weren't they?

"Clock's ticking." A sharp rap on the window accompanied his words, and I jumped.

I didn't need to think about his proposal. New York was where I lived. My hesitation was down to the fact that it was where my ex lived as well. And he would *know* the moment I returned. I was sure he would already be aware I'd left, and my heart rate increased just thinking about his reaction when I arrived back home. I had to hope I could convince this man that he wanted to be hired.

I took a deep breath, then reached for the door.

He was standing at the back of the car, his hip propped against the trunk, arms folded. When I stepped out, he straightened.

"Well?"

I nodded. "I agree to your terms."

His eyes tracked over my face, paused on the bruise on my cheek. "That's not recent."

"No."

"Are there anymore?"

"Yes." I waited for him to demand to see them. He didn't.

"Alright. Let's go then. I'm already late."

He set off without checking to see if I followed. I scrambled into movement and caught up. His longer strides meant I had to trot to keep up with him, but he didn't slow his pace. After a minute or two, a small plane came into view. I glanced at the man beside me.

He didn't look at me.

"It's a friends. We both need to go to New York for different reasons, so I'm hitching a ride with him."

"Bishop!" A shadow detached itself from beside the plane and came toward us, hand outstretched.

"Wade."

They shook, and the newcomer looked at me. "This is the *company?*"

"Possible new job. I'm multitasking. Need to do an assessment and don't have time to stop, so we'll do it on the way."

"When did *you* start doing the assessment work?"

"When I was given no other choice." He slanted an unreadable look at me. "You have three and a half hours to convince me."

"Speaking of time, we need to get in the air," his friend, *Wade,* said.

The man I'd traveled over one thousand miles to find turned to me.

"After you." He swept a hand toward the steps leading up to the entrance of the aircraft.

I hesitated. This was it. If I stepped onto the plane, there would be no going back. This was the start of erasing Eden Marshall from the world.

"Tonight would be good. Unless you've changed your mind?"

The cool words drove me forward and up the steps.

I'd never been on a private jet before. The interior of the plane was not what I expected. The seats were soft beige leather, set in pairs facing each other with a table between them. A bar was at one end, and a large screen television on the other. Two doors were next to each other beside the bar. I had to assume that at least one led to a bathroom.

A firm hand pressed against my back. "Take a seat."

I took one near a window and clipped the seatbelt into place.

"Would you like something to drink?" the other man asked.

"Just water, please."

He nodded, while Bishop slipped into the seat opposite me. "I guess it's time for a formal introduction." He held out one large hand. "Bishop Chambers."

I took it, masking a wince at the firm grip as we shook. "Eden Marshall."

His brows met in a dark frown, but his voice was level when he spoke. "So, *Eden*, tell me about your situation."

I licked my lips. "Like I told you in the car, I need to disappear. It's the only way my ex is going to stop coming for me."

"Tell me about him. Why isn't he able to move on? Were you living together? Married?"

"We lived together." I took a deep breath. "I was twenty when I met him. My car had blown a tire and he pulled over. He introduced himself as a detective, showed me his badge, and changed the tire for me. He was sweet, *nice*, and asked if I'd get a coffee with him sometime. I said yes." I broke off when Wade placed the bottle of water on the table. "Thank you."

"Bish, I'm going to speak to the pilot. Call me if you need anything." He disappeared through a door at the front of the plane.

"We dated for a while. Everything was good ... *perfect*, even. And about six months into the relationship, he gave me a key to his apartment. Said I spent more time there than at my own place, so I might as well have the ability to let myself in while he was at work." I paused and shook my head. "It was little things at first, barely noticeable. I stopped going out with my friends on weekends. He pointed out that he was at work so much, it was the only time we could spend together. Then I changed my job because it was easier to find something closer to his apartment."

I looked down at my hands, fingers clasped together. "The first time he hit me was because I was late getting home. He said it was because he was scared something had happened to me, and anger and relief made him lash out." My laugh was quiet. "I swallowed it, of course. He'd never shown any signs of aggression before that."

"They never do." His voice was dry.

My eyes darted up to his. "The second time was over a disagreement about where we should go to eat one night. He flew into a rage because I wanted to stay home, and he wanted to eat out. He apologized and promised it wouldn't happen again."

"But it did."

I nodded. "It got worse from there. By that point, my friends had all moved on. I lost my job because I was constantly making excuses and not turning up. How could I, with black eyes and a broken nose? They would ask questions. His job would be at risk. No one would believe me. He was a detective." I pressed my lips together to stop them from trembling. "It would be his word over mine, and he worked in law enforcement. Who would they be more likely to believe? He had a perfect track record."

"How did you find the strength to leave?"

"It was his landlord, believe it or not."

"His landlord? Did he walk in on a situation?"

I shook my head. "No. He walked in on the aftereffect of one." I took a sip of water.

"Tell me about that." He stood and crossed to the bar, poured a drink, and then returned to his seat. "Did he overhear you fighting?"

"No, he came to remind Chester about the rent being overdue. Chester had just left. I was ..." My intake of breath was shaky. I didn't enjoy reliving that moment. "He'd broken my arm when I ... when he ..." I cleared my throat. "Anyway, I was trying to get dressed when he knocked. I thought it was Chester and that maybe he'd forgotten his keys, so I hurried to open the door. But it wasn't him. Greg took one look at me and guessed what had happened. He helped me put on clothes and then took me to his apartment. It took him hours to convince me I had to go to the hospital for my arm, then insisted he drive me there and waited while they checked me out. When I tried to tell the doctor that it had been an accident, he chimed in with what he thought had happened.

"They asked if I wanted a report written up so I could press charges. Of course, I said no. If he found out about that, it wouldn't have stopped with him breaking my arm."

"But once you had it on record, if anything further happened to you afterward, it would have made it clear it was him."

"No, it wouldn't. You don't understand. He's charming, *loved* by the entire team he works with. They wouldn't believe me. I told the hospital I didn't want to go to the police and left."

"Is that when you ran?"

"No. I … It's stupid looking back, but I was *sure* when he calmed down and realized how badly he'd hurt me, he would feel remorse, *guilt*, and try to be better."

"But he didn't." It wasn't a question.

"No, he didn't." I reached for my water again, my hand shaking as I lifted it to my lips.

"Let's fast forward. How long until you left? *How* did you leave?"

"Another two months. He kept a close eye on me after I went to the hospital. I think he was sure I was going to try to talk to someone, so he took time off work, claiming he needed to help me after my *unfortunate* accident. But eventually, he had to go back to work, and once he did, I called Greg and he helped me pack. He owned another building and said I could take an apartment for as long as I needed. It was on the other side of town, and I thought that maybe it would be far enough away."

"For someone who needs that level of control, the other side of the world wouldn't be far enough away."

"I know that now. He found me two weeks later, and... I had to move again. I thought once I'd made it clear we were over, he'd leave me alone, but he wouldn't. I think he has people in the police force watching for me. It doesn't matter where I go. I've moved across the city twice and he *still* finds me."

"And that brings you to me ..."

I nodded. "I've been saving up every bit of spare money I could. My plan was to try and leave New York completely. Maybe move to a different state. Then I was told about you. I didn't call the number they gave me straight away. I needed to be ready. They'd said that contact could be made at a moment's notice, that it could take minutes or weeks after I left a message. So, it took me a couple of months before I called and left a message."

"How long *did* it take to get a response?"

"Three days."

"And they told you to come to Dallas and go to the ... Swallow Falls Motel, you said? And that I'd make contact with you?"

"Yes."

"And then they sent you to the Dallas Spring Hotel?"

I nodded.

"Nothing else?"

"No."

"You're sure?"

"Yes."

5

Bishop

She didn't *appear* to be lying and the story she was telling me was a common one. Her reactions were natural and in line with what I expected from a victim of domestic violence, but in my line of work, you could never be too careful. When she described how her ex treated her, it was clear she was leaving out huge chunks of the story. I could make a good guess as to *why*. She didn't want to relive them. It was understandable, so I didn't push her to tell me.

But, as mercenary as it sounded, no matter how much her story tugged at the heartstrings, I didn't work for free. It set an expectation, one I was not interested in allowing, and I wasn't confident she could afford my fees, regardless of how much she'd saved.

"If he *is* as clever as you think at finding you, then making you disappear won't be easy. You'll need a completely new identity. You might even need to move somewhere off grid for a while. It'll be easier and *cheaper* to hire a hitman and kill him." I wasn't joking. Rook could make himself available. He was retired, sure, but he still took the occasional job to keep sharp. Mostly, though, I just wanted to see her reaction. You could tell a lot about a person by whether they were willing to consider cold-blooded murder.

She blanched. "*Kill* him? That's a thing?"

"It's less costly than the alternative. As good as I am, there's always that slim possibility he'll find you. If he's dead..." I shrugged. "Well, then it's no longer a problem, is it?"

"But—"

"Surely, after what he's put you through, you'd want to see him dead?"

"Maybe ... but I don't think I could do it. He has a family. His mom and dad would be devastated. That would make me just as bad as him."

"Would it?" I swallowed a mouthful of bourbon and eyed her over the glass. "What's worse? Living in fear for the rest of your life, knowing that all it will take is one person to recognize you and inform him or having his blood on your hands? I mean, your blood is all over *his* hands, right?" My voice was flippant. "Quid pro quo. Something for something."

She flinched. "Yes, but..." Her tongue swept out to wet her lips. "No. I couldn't live with myself. Would I like to see him scared? Of course. I'd like him to understand the fear he put me through. But I couldn't do that."

"You understand that by *not* making public what he's done,

you're leaving other women at risk. He could kill the next one." That hit home. Her face lost what little color it had left. "Still not convinced killing him is the best option?"

"I just... that's not who I am."

"Okay." I stood.

"So ... are you going to let me hire you?"

I looked at her. *Would I?* Most of my jobs were for people involved with the criminal underground in some way—hiding weaker or valuable members of mafia families because they were being targeted, or organizing a new life for someone because they took the stand against a powerful crime lord and didn't trust the witness protection offered by legal entities. This woman, while having experienced a very unfortunate thing, didn't meet that criteria. And yet...

"It's three hundred thousand dollars for me to set everything up. That doesn't include any additional expenses that might crop up. The fee covers your new identity and relocation. It comes with a credit history, passport, birth certificate, Social Security number, and everything you will need to continue to live normally." I delivered the details in a clipped tone. "But, on top of that payment, there are occasionally extras, depending on the situation. Do you have that kind of money?" The teeth worrying at her bottom lip told me the answer. "I didn't think so."

"Is there no ... *cheaper* ... option?"

"*Cheaper?* Sweetheart, this isn't a store or website where you can shop around for the best deal. I don't offer discounts.

It costs what it costs. Have you any idea how difficult it is to build someone an entirely new identity? One that stands up under intense scrutiny? This isn't a cheap government witness protection program. It's an entirely new *life*."

Her eyes dropped. "I guess you're right." Her fingers plucked at the label on the water bottle. "I'm sorry for wasting your time."

I jerked my chin toward her face. "The bruise on your cheek. Was that from him?"

"He caught up with me a week ago."

So *yes* then. "Was that why you finally called the number you were given?"

"Yes." she whispered. "He said he was going to kill me if I didn't go back home with him. That I owed him for all the time and money he'd used to find me. That I should never have left him. I ... I played along, waited for him to go out, climbed out of the bathroom window and then made the call. I've been moving from motel room to motel room for days, waiting to hear. When I finally got the contact information, I flew to Dallas."

"*Flew* to Dallas? You weren't there already?"

"No. I was in ..." She swallowed and her tongue snaked out to swipe across her lips again. "New York."

And I was taking her right back to where she'd come from.

There was no accusation in her tone, but I felt a sharp, unexpected stab of guilt all the same. I pushed it down and turned away. I wasn't about to let a pair of pretty green eyes and a sob story convince me to take a job without payment.

When did you notice the color of her eyes?

I drained the rest of my drink, crossed over to the bar and refilled it.

"How much money do you have saved?"

"Fifty thousand."

"In a bank account?"

"No, I drew out the cash. I bought a security box and put it in that. I hid it in my motel room before I flew to Dallas."

"If you can get it and your passport when we land, and meet me at JFK before six am, I *might* be able to help you." The words left my mouth before I even considered them.

"You're going to help me?" The hope in her voice made my jaw clench.

"No promises, but I'll see what I can do." *What the fuck are you doing, Bishop?* "You said you lost your job. How have you survived?"

"Odd jobs here and there. Waitressing sometimes. Filling in for people. Temporary work. Anywhere they would pay me cash. I didn't want to risk using my name because he always finds me."

"But you didn't leave New York? Surely that should have been the first thing you did when you got out of the relationship."

She gave me a helpless look. "You make it sound so easy. I don't have a car. New York is *home*. It's what I know. What was I supposed to do?"

I didn't answer that question. My mind was already puzzling through the situation, looking for answers as to why I'd just killed two men who had a woman tied up in the trunk of their car. A woman they'd accused me of helping. My senses were telling me there was more to this than simply running from an abusive ex.

But this could also work in my favor. I had a situation of my own that I needed to deal with. Those pretty eyes of hers might actually come in useful if I played this right.

I poured a second glass of bourbon, carried them both over to where she sat and sank down onto the seat opposite her. Setting the glasses down, I slid one across the table and studied her for a second.

"The jobs I take aren't usually from … the average public." I took a sip of my drink and waved a hand to the other glass. "Drink up."

She shook her head. "I'm okay. I'll stick with water."

"Drink the bourbon. You're going to need it."

I had an idea. It was a fucking *stupid* idea, but it was the only thing I could think of to keep her safe, temporarily at least.

This is a huge mistake. Don't do it.

I ignored that inner voice. It would help *me* with something I'd been trying to figure out a way to deal with for months.

Her fingers clutched the bottle, squeezing the plastic. "Why?"

I tilted my glass toward her in a toast. "Congratulations. You're getting married."

6

Eden

"I'm doing *what?*" I must have misheard. Had he just said I was getting married?

"You don't have the money to pay for all the things I need to do in order to put together a new life for you. So, as a one-time deal, I can offer you this solution. We'll take a detour once you've picked up what you need in New York."

"A ... detour?"

"Vegas, for a quick wedding, then we'll continue on to my intended destination."

"A wedding ... Intended destination?" My voice rose with each word.

His sigh was noticeably irritable. "It'll be temporary. Long enough to send a message, then we can annul it. Until then, this is the only way I can ensure your safety ... which is what you'll be paying me to do. You'll come with me for a trip I need to take.

That way I can keep you safe while I work on your new identity."

"Wait ... who are you *marrying* me off to?"

His eyebrows drew together into a v above dark eyes. "I thought I'd made that clear already."

"Pretend you haven't!" There was a hint of hysteria in my voice.

He ran a finger around the rim of his glass. "When we land in New York, I'll get someone to arrange another flight. We'll detour to Vegas, say our vows, then—"

"I'm marrying *you*?"

He ignored me. "Once that's done, we'll travel to Glenville, where I have a place. It's secluded and secure. Your ex will not be able to reach you there. No matter how many friends he has."

"Why do we need to be married?"

"Because if your ex catches up with you before we get there, it gives me a valid reason to get between you. Legally, you will be my wife and under my protection. That might send him the message that you're no longer available. It might not." He delivered the words clinically, as though he was describing a job position to a potential new employee.

"But don't you think marriage is a little drastic?" I whispered.

"It's the quickest way to change your name. Sadly, it'll leave a paper trail that can be followed. But you'll be safer with me than you would be staying in a motel room somewhere while you wait for me to arrange things for you. And since you only have fifty thousand, that means I'm also working on a small budget, *far* less than I usually work for."

"But *marriage!*"

"In name only. It's just a means to an end." He pulled out his cell and tapped on the screen, then lifted it to his ear. "Davis, I need you to do something for me." He rose to his feet and strode away without another glance in my direction.

I stared after him.

Marriage? To him? He wasn't serious, surely.

I grabbed the glass he'd placed in front of me, took a large mouthful, and swallowed. It burned the back of my throat, and I coughed, tears springing to my eyes. That had been stronger than I expected.

He was back by the time I'd finished spluttering, frowning at me. "You said you don't have a car, so you'd need to use public transport to … you said you were staying in a motel?"

I nodded. "I paid in advance for a week. I have another two days. I put a Do Not Disturb sign on the door so housekeeping wouldn't go inside."

"How far from JFK is it?"

"A forty-minute bus ride." My fingers returned to the label on the water bottle, picking at it.

"Are you serious about the marriage thing?"

His expression didn't change. "What part of it sounded like a joke to you?"

"But—"

"It's just another contract. People sign contracts for things all the time, without questioning it. Why should this be any different?" He drummed his fingers on the tabletop. "I've arranged for a prenup, which you'll need to sign, detailing the terms of our arrangement. We don't really have time for you to find a lawyer of your own to check the fine print, so I'll get one of my team to explain it all to you. But we're on a time schedule, you'll have to do that while we travel."

"And ..." I licked my lips. "What if I don't like the terms?"

"There won't be anything in it that will cause you problems. It's more to protect my interests and businesses. You need to understand that I have more to risk by doing this than you do."

"Then why suggest it?"

His head tilted, as though it was a question he hadn't expected.

"Buckle up." His friend came out of a door at the far end of the plane. "We're about to land."

Bishop Chambers stared at me for a second longer, then lowered his eyes and secured his seatbelt in place without answering my question.

He didn't speak again until we'd landed and made our way to the exit.

"Watch your step." A hand touching my elbow joined the words as I stepped off the boarding stairs and onto the runway.

We were whisked through a private check-in area away from the main part of the airport and stepped outside less than twenty minutes after landing. Habit made me check up and down, looking for police cars, or familiar faces.

"I'll drive you to your motel. It'll be faster than waiting for you to use public transport. My car is just over here." Bishop's voice drew my attention to him, and I followed as he led the way to a low, sleek sports car.

"Did you leave the car parked here while you were in Dallas?"

He shook his head. "No, I had someone drop it off." He pushed a button on the keys in his hand and the lights on the car flashed. He opened the passenger door. "Hop in."

I took another glance up and down the road, then climbed in.

"What's the motel you were staying at?"

I gave him the name, and he pulled into traffic. I gazed out of the window. The man beside me didn't speak, didn't try to fill the silence, and I was left to my own thoughts.

I was doing this then? In return for this man hiding me, I was going to marry him ... temporarily? This was really happening.

7

Bishop

This has got to be the worst idea you've ever had.

Is it, though?

You're marrying a girl because she can't afford your fees. On what planet is that going to work out well?

Two birds, one stone. She gets protection. I get out of a self-made situation that I should have known better than to get involved in.

You really think that's a good reason to get married?

It's a better reason than most people have. Anyway, it's only for a couple of weeks. Then I'll get her set up in a new life and carry on with mine. Like every other contract, once my part was done, I'd never see her again.

And your mother will lose her shit if she finds out what you've done.

I'll deal with that if I need to.

I eased my foot off the accelerator when flashing red and

blue lights appeared ahead of me, and the car rolled to a stop just before the turnoff into the parking lot of the motel.

"Stay here." I told the girl beside me and climbed out of the car. I pushed the button on my keys, locking the doors, shoved them into my pocket and walked slowly toward the motel.

The lights grew brighter, and I spotted a police car parked at an angle outside one of the motel rooms. The door to the room was open, and voices drifted toward me on the night air.

"It doesn't look like she's been here for a couple of days."

"Is there any clue to where she might have gone?"

I stepped back into the shadows cast by the motel's sign.

"No. Nothing. Her clothes are here. So, she must be planning to come back. The owner said she's paid up for a couple more days."

"Did you manage to get into the security box?"

"Not yet."

"Maybe there's something in there that will tell us where she's gone."

"Maybe … Look, Chester, I thought you guys broke up."

"We're giving it another go."

Hmmm. I'd heard enough to know there was no way I was getting inside to collect the security box *or* any clothes, so I turned and headed back to my car.

She glanced at me when I settled back into the driver's seat.

"Your ex is in your motel room."

She swallowed, paling. "What? How?"

I shrugged and reversed down the road until I could change

direction. "Doesn't matter. We can adapt."

"But my money is in there."

"We'll work that out later."

Truth was, at this point I didn't *need* her money. Fifty thousand wouldn't get her much from anyone in my line of work. She didn't need to know that, though. If word got out that I had done a job for such a small amount, other people would ask. And, anyway, the favor she was doing me, albeit without knowing, would balance out what I'd need to do for her. I'd continue with the plan and work out the fine details later.

It had worked out well for Rook. Okay, granted, it had been Magdalena who was in dire straits and needed a pretend boyfriend, not Rook. But it still worked out. I needed something a little more ... *persuasive* than a girlfriend to get a message across.

"What do we do now?" Her question broke into my thoughts.

"Airport, Vegas, wedding, Glenville."

"I don't have a change of clothes ... or my passport."

"We can get both in Vegas."

"I can't get a replacement passport that quickly!"

"*You* can't. *I* can."

"How?"

"By having powerful friends and money to throw at them." I pulled into the parking lot of a hotel and cut off the engine. "Our flight to Vegas leaves at noon."

"What happened to me meeting you at JFK for six?"

"I've changed the plan. My original flight was leaving at six.

Now we're going to Vegas first, then we'll fly out from there."

"I still don't understand why you think marriage is the best idea."

"I've explained already. It puts you under the safety of my name."

"Do you marry all the women you've helped relocate?"

"Of course not. That would take up far too much time."

"You don't strike me as someone who does *favors*, so how does this benefit you?" There was a suspicious note in her voice.

"And you'd be correct. But you're desperate, and lucky for you, I need a wife for a couple of weeks."

"Will the length of the marriage be in the contract?"

I nodded. "Four weeks. I can work out the details of your new life and have everything ready for when our contract ends."

"Why do you need a wife?"

"That's none of your business." I unclipped my seatbelt. "I've booked a suite here for a few hours. You should make use of the facilities. I don't need questions on why my soon-to-be wife looks like she's been beaten up, *or* a good Samaritan thinking I'm forcing you to marry me and taking steps to stop it."

I climbed out of the car. She didn't move.

I rested a hand on the roof of the car and leaned back inside. "What now?"

"You want me to trust you, put my life into your hands, and marry you. The least you can do is tell me *why* you need a wife."

"It's a personal matter. Nothing that will affect you."

"I'm about to change my name and marry a man I haven't even known for twenty-four hours. You don't think that affects me?"

"The car is not the place for this conversation. Come inside."

"And then you'll tell me?"

"I'll consider it." I straightened, slammed the door, and strode toward the entrance. She'd either follow me or freeze in the car. It made no difference to me. If she didn't come with me, I'd simply be back in the original position I'd been in.

8

Eden

I waited while he picked up the room keycard from the reception desk, ignoring the glances directed at me by the woman. I knew how I looked. Split lip, bruised cheek, hair probably a wild mess. Bishop didn't seem bothered or even appear to notice my discomfort, paying for the room and spinning the keycard between his fingers as he turned to me.

"Elevator is this way," he said. "Let's go." He set off, once again not waiting to see if I followed.

I was beginning to feel like a child, trotting to keep up with an adult who had very little patience. I caught his sleeve.

"Could you *please* slow down?"

His gaze angled down, brows pleating as he stared at my fingers clutching his shirt sleeve, then back up at me. "When did you last eat?"

I blinked. "What?"

"Food. When did you last have some?" The words were clipped, impatient.

"I don't ... yesterday, maybe? Breakfast before I flew to Dallas."

His sigh was irritable. One finger stabbed at the call button and the elevator doors slid open. He strode inside and turned, one eyebrow rising. "Are you coming or just going to stand in the foyer all night?"

I stepped into the elevator.

"I'll order room service, while you shower and change."

"Change into *what?* My clothes are in the motel room."

He pressed the floor number and the elevator started moving. "Tell me your sizes and I'll get some things delivered."

"Just like that?"

His frown didn't smooth out. "It's almost four in the morning. We have to be at the airport at eleven. I told you the flight leaves at twelve. There's not really any time to go clothes shopping."

"So where are you going to get clothes from?"

"I'll make a call."

He made it sound so easy. *Make a call.* To whom, and where would they get clothes?

The elevator doors swished open, and Bishop strode forward into the hallway. He turned left, leaving me trailing behind him. I sighed quietly. He was standing outside a door by the time I caught up to him. Unlocking it, he stepped back.

"After you."

I moved past him and inside the room ... and stopped. This

wasn't a room; it was a suite. A large living room containing a circular cream couch, a giant television on the wall, a desk in one corner, with floor to ceiling glass doors which led out onto a private balcony. On the opposite side, an open door showed a hallway, with three more doors leading off it. I turned in a slow circle.

"I need to go back down to the car. Make yourself comfortable. Bathroom is through there." He jerked his chin toward the hallway. "There's probably a complimentary bathrobe or two in the bedrooms. Clean up. I'll order some food when I get back and organize a change of clothes for you until we get to Vegas."

"Vegas." I repeated the word quietly. Where I'd get married to a man I'd sought out to help me disappear. It didn't even make sense. "And then you'll tell me *why* you need a wife?"

He paused on his way back to the door. "I'll consider it." His hand wrapped around the door handle. "If you want to back out, now's the time to do it. You can leave and—"

"And Chester will find me in a couple of days, and I'll be right back to where I started." I licked my lips. "Or dead." I knew how it worked. I'd researched the statistics about domestic violence. So many women ended up dead at the hands of the men who supposedly loved them. "I think I'd rather take my chances as a temporary wife."

He inclined his head. "Then I'll be back in a couple of minutes." The door closed behind him, and I was left alone in the hotel suite.

I didn't move for a full minute, letting the weight of the

silence settle over me, then I stepped deeper into the room and dropped onto the couch, my head sinking into my hands, exhaustion taking hold.

I'd been running on hope, fear, and adrenaline for the past three days. I traveled to Dallas, found the hotel where I'd been instructed to wait for Bishop Chambers to contact me, and then was grabbed and stuffed into the trunk of a car. A laugh bubbled up my throat and I clamped a hand over my mouth. I wasn't going to let hysteria take over. Now I was about to travel to Las Vegas and *marry* the man I'd gone searching for, *after* he rescued me from the car, shot at my feet, and threatened to leave me in the trunk.

The laugh I'd muffled escaped, shrill in the quiet room.

What was I doing? I was trying to escape a man who wanted to force me to love him by marrying a man who wanted to use a wife to aid him in some way. What way? What did he expect from me?

My eyes darted to the door. Maybe I *should* leave. Escape while there was still time. Run. Leave the city, the *state*. Try and make a new life somewhere else. Except all my money was in the motel room, and Bishop said Chester was there.

Everything I owned was in that motel room.

I sat up straight.

Oh god, had I left anything that could tell him what I'd been planning? Where I'd been going?

What if he had people watching the airport? Would he know I was back in New York? Was he on his way to the hotel now?

My heart picked up speed, hammering against my ribs, and I lurched to my feet when the door swung open. I swayed and flung out a hand to stop myself from falling, when Bishop Chambers came into the room.

He stopped, those dark brows dipping into a frown as he looked at me. "I half-expected the room to be empty when I got back." He set down a black case and kicked the door shut. "I called my lawyer. He'll have a prenup contract ready for when we land in Las Vegas." He crossed the room and picked up the service telephone. "I'll order food. Do you drink coffee or something else? There's also a small clothing store downstairs. If you give me your sizes, I'll get them to bring a selection of clothes as well."

"There's a store *inside* the hotel?"

"The clientele here require access to things outside of typical hours, and sometimes they don't want to be accosted by the general public."

I blinked. He meant rich and famous people. Of which he was one ... because how else could he afford the room ... *suite* ... we were in.

"You were going to tell me why you need a wife," I said, and marveled at how calm I sounded.

That ever-present scowl turned in my direction. "I wasn't, but it's clearly an issue for you." He held up a hand when I opened my mouth to reply. "Penthouse seven. Can you send up a carafe of coffee, a selection of finger foods, and get someone to stop by and pick up jeans, underwear, and t-shirts." His eyes dropped to my feet. "Also, a pair of sneakers and black dress heels. Sizes?" He threw that question at me. "Eden!" My name was an irritable bark when I didn't reply fast enough.

I told him, blushing when I gave him my underwear sizes. He didn't notice, or behaved like he didn't anyway, relaying them to whoever was at the end of the line, then dropped the receiver back down.

"Go and get cleaned up before food arrives."

He strode across to where he'd left the black case and picked it up.

"You're used to people doing what you tell them, aren't you?"

"Yes, so I'd appreciate it if you'd head that way and do as you're told." He pointed down the hallway.

"What if I don't?"

He paused in the process of unzipping the case. "Excuse me?"

"What if I don't do as you say?"

One eyebrow arched. "Is that a challenge?"

"No. I'm just curious."

"I see." He flipped open the lid on the case and pulled out a sheet of paper. "Well, first I'd throw you over my shoulder and dump you under the shower. There's blood in your hair and dirt under your fingernails. Regardless of why we're getting married, I'd rather you didn't look like I've just dug you out of the closest cemetery." He delivered the words calmly without looking at me.

My eyes widened. "You wouldn't."

His head turned, dark eyes gleaming. "Try me."

9

Bishop

"Can I assume by the fact you're still there and *not* in the bathroom that you really are going to see if I'm bluffing?" I straightened.

She took a step backward, caught herself and narrowed her eyes. I walked toward her. She watched me, eyes getting wider as I moved closer. I stopped less than a foot away.

"For the sake of transparency since you're going to be spending at least a month in my company..." In a quick move I caught her waist and threw her over my shoulder, fireman style. "I *never* bluff."

She shrieked, one hand clutching my shirt, while the other slapped my back. I ignored her, adjusted my grip so she wasn't going to fall, and strode through the hallway and into the bathroom.

"Put me down!"

"I intend to." I threw open the shower door and stepped

inside, smacking a hand against the power button. The water hit us both. A cold jet which caused her to throw her head back with a gasp. An unfortunate decision since I was standing with my back to the spray, and it hit her in the face.

She swallowed a mouthful of water, breathed in, choked, and coughed. I swung her off my shoulder and onto her feet in front of me.

She gasped, eyes streaming, water dripping down her face. I folded my arms and stared at her.

"Why did you do that?" she shrieked when she finally caught her breath.

"You're filthy and we don't have that long before we need to leave. Now you have no choice but to get out of those disgusting clothes and clean up." I stepped past her. "I'll bring a bathrobe in for you."

I didn't wait for her reply, and walked out and into the bedroom opposite, stripping out of my shirt as I went. There was a hook on the door, so I tossed my shirt onto it. It wasn't too wet and should be dry before we had to head out to the airport. Glancing around, I found a bathrobe folded up on a shelf in a sealed packet. I tore it open, shook it out, and made my way back to the bathroom.

"Here—"

Her scream cut me off. "Can't you *knock?*"

My eyes swept over the woman in front of me. I dropped the bathrobe and stalked over to her, reaching out to flick a finger over the yellow bruise covering one shoulder. She jerked back.

"Stop it. Turn around."

"Get out."

"Show me the rest of that bruise. Turn around." I didn't wait for her to comply, wrapping a hand around the top of her arm and pulling her into the position I wanted. "You said he hit you. You didn't say he used a weapon. What was it?"

"It doesn't matter."

"It matters."

"Could you *please* leave?" She spun and hurried past me to snatch up the bathrobe and pull it on. "You told me to wash. I'd rather do that without an audience."

"I'm not interested in watching you wash."

She wrapped the robe around her body, and tied it closed with a savage yank. The thought that she'd have liked that belt to be around my neck when she pulled it tight flitted through my mind. That spark was in her eyes again, the one I'd spotted when she was tied up in the trunk of the car. No matter what she'd gone through with her ex-boyfriend, this woman was a fighter at heart.

"If you won't tell me, then I'll guess." I crossed to the tub and leaned down to turn off the faucet, then turned and sat on the edge. "From the shape of the bruising, I'd say he went for the tried and tested method of wrapping a bar of soap in a towel. But he didn't want to cause too much damage, so he softened it by using more than one. He wanted to bruise but not break."

The fire in her eyes was hidden when she lowered her lashes. "Three towels. He experimented until he got the balance right. Three towels wouldn't break my ribs when he swung it but left a nice purple bruise."

I nodded. "But he wasn't content with bruising you in places that couldn't be seen, was he?" I tapped my own lip. "He liked seeing the damage he'd inflicted, which is why you have a split lip and a bruise on your cheek."

"He said that was to remind me of what would happen if I tried to leave him."

"You understand that he's going to kill you if he catches up with you again, don't you?" That brought her eyes back up to meet mine. "I can guarantee your safety while you're with me, but once our contract is over and I've relocated you, I can only do so much. Staying safe once I've put everything into place is up to you. I have people who will ease you into your new life, but eventually you'll be on your own."

"Are you trying to tell me you're not going to help me now?"

"Not at all. I just want you to be clear about the situation."

She gave a slow nod. "Like you said, it's die or try to live. There's only one obvious choice really, isn't there?"

"I want the name of the person who told you about me."

"I promised—"

"I don't care. I'm willing to do this. It's come at a time where I need something in return, so you've fallen on your feet. If there hadn't been something I needed from you, you'd be on your own. But

I want that name. Someone is out there talking about my business. That's dangerous for someone like me. So, since I'm helping you for free, grant me the courtesy of giving me what I want."

"I'm marrying you. That's not free."

"I hardly think the price of taking my name for a month, and a brand-new wardrobe which I'm paying for is something that's costing you, do you?"

She blushed and looked away.

"The sooner you give me what I want, the sooner I'll be leaving the room and you can take your bath."

"I only know the username she used in the online group. *FreedomIsPainful.*"

FreedomIsPainful. What the hell kind of name was that?

"And she told you I'd helped someone she knew."

Eden nodded.

"Did she tell you who?"

"No. But it was a woman. She said they were in a similar situation to me."

My mind sifted through all the jobs I'd taken. I'd *never* relocated someone who was running from a domestic violence situation. "She lied."

"Then how did she know you were in Dallas?"

It was a good question, a *valid* question. I never advertised my whereabouts and my stopover in Dallas hadn't been planned. Wade called me when I was in Chicago and asked for my help. In return, he offered to fly me back to New York. I'd been at the airport waiting for my New York flight and canceled it to purchase a ticket to Dallas instead.

That meant one thing.

Someone was watching me.

10

Eden

I don't know what it was because nothing in his expression changed, but the fine hairs on the back of my neck stood to attention. I glanced around, checking where the exit was from where I stood, and took a step back, putting distance between us. The man in front of me was dangerous. Dangerous in a way Chester wasn't. With his abrasive attitude, and the crazy rush of the past twelve hours, I hadn't really had time to stop and think about it. But standing here, in a hotel bathroom, I realized that Bishop Chambers was more than just a suited businessman who organized paperwork to give people new lives.

Because when he fired a shot that landed inches from your feet, that didn't clue you into the danger?

My inner voice was a dry whisper, and it wasn't wrong. I'd been so fixated on the situation I was in; I hadn't thought about what was going on around me. He'd handled me like he was used to dealing with hysteria. He'd threatened me like it was nothing. And then made a decision to marry me with absolutely no emotion at all.

"Why are you marrying me?" I forced the words out from between dry lips. "Why do we need to be married?"

His dark eyes held mine and I thought, like every other time I'd asked, he wasn't going to answer. But then he sighed and pushed away from the tub.

"Okay, I guess that's fair. You gave me what I wanted, so I'll answer your question." His hand rubbed over his jaw. "In my line of work, I come into contact with a lot of powerful people. So do my brothers. Because of who we are, some of our friends are ... Well, let's just say they're not on the right side of the law. I've been invited to an engagement party. I can't afford to refuse the invitation, but one of the men who'll be there is married to a woman who ... I may have had several interactions with her *before* I knew she was married. She wants to continue them. If I show up with a wife of my own, it'll reduce the number of opportunities she'll have to get me alone and lower the risk of there being an incident between me and her husband."

"An incident? You mean if her husband finds out you're having an affair with his wife?" Why was I disappointed to find out he was sleeping with a married woman?

"As far as I was aware, I *wasn't* having an affair. I ended things when I found out."

"I thought you were all-knowing. How couldn't you know

she was married?"

"Because I ignored one of my rules. Always investigate the people who you're spending time with. I took her at face value."

"I just bet you did," I muttered, unable to help myself.

One corner of his mouth tipped up. "Yes, I let the fact she was beautiful blind me. Go ahead and judge me for that."

"She's never going to believe we're married. We barely know each other. Surely, the woman who finally steals your heart to the point where you'd want to put a ring on her finger would know everything about you."

He shrugged. "I doubt you'll spend enough time in her company for her to issue you with a pop quiz. All we need to do is hold hands a couple of times, maybe a public kiss or two. No one is going to expect us to be going at it like rabbits across the banquet table."

"How are you going to explain my presence?"

"They'll see you as my plus one. What else is there to explain?"

"How about the fact you've never mentioned me or introduced me before?"

"No one will question it. I never advertise my ... liaisons. Just behave like you adore me and it'll be fine. They'll be too busy focusing on the newly engaged couple to worry about what I'm doing."

He walked across the room and stopped by the door. "Take your bath. Food will be here soon."

I didn't stop him when he pulled the door open and walked out.

***

I exited the bathroom in a scented cloud of raspberry and cocoa butter, my body wrapped in the bathrobe and a towel around my hair. The soak had eased the aches from my body, and I was ready to crawl into bed and sleep. But the second I entered the living room, the smell of food hit me, and my stomach rumbled into life.

Bishop looked up from his cell as I walked across to the serving tray.

"Let me take a look at your lip before you eat." He set his phone to one side and stood.

"But—" I cast a sidelong look at the food.

"It'll still be there in two minutes. I want to make sure you cleaned it properly."

"It's not the first time I've had a split lip."

"No doubt, but humor me anyway." He pressed a finger beneath my chin and tipped my head up.

"Why are you so concerned about it now?"

"Because we'll be getting on a public flight in a few hours, and I'd rather not be arrested on suspicion of beating you up." He touched my lip with his thumb. "Does that hurt?"

"No. Won't your friends ask what happened?"

"Maybe. We'll deal with that if it happens." His hand dropped. "Okay, go eat."

"Sir, *yes sir!*" I saluted him and turned to the serving cart.

The husky chuckle he uttered surprised me. I hadn't heard him laugh once in the time I'd spent with him so far. I lifted the lids on the serving trays to see what they hid. There was a mixture of breakfast foods—scrambled eggs, toast, bacon—sandwiches, and ... I lifted the bowl to sniff ... tomato soup. Odd mix, but I wasn't going to argue. I took a plate, piled it with eggs and toast, then sat on a chair at the small table.

"You don't have to sit over there. The couch is more comfortable."

I shook my head, mouth full of food.

"When you're done eating, there's a bag of clothes near the door. Make sure everything fits okay and pick out something to wear for traveling. We'll have time when we land in Vegas to go shopping for anything else you might need. My lawyer will have the prenup ready for when we land, as well. So we'll go straight to the hotel, go shopping, get everything signed, then head for the chapel. We'll fly out from Vegas at four am."

I swallowed and nodded. "You seem to have everything worked out."

"I like to have a plan." He reached forward and picked up a cup from the coffee table in front of him. "I've met a lot of women who have been in a similar situation to you." He paused to take a sip from the cup. "You're very different from them."

I stopped with the fork halfway to my mouth. "What do you mean?"

"They are broken, shadows of their former selves. You, though ..." He shook his head. "He didn't break you."

I lowered the fork back to my plate and turned to face him. "I'm not lying."

He shook his head. "No, that's not what I'm saying. I know you're not lying. I think you were lucky. You got out before he could break you down. The women I mentioned ... they flinch at the slightest movement. You don't. You get ready to fight." There was approval in his tone. It warmed me, made me feel like I'd done something right.

"I've never been someone to just let a person walk all over me. I just wish I'd realized what was happening sooner."

He stood and crossed the room to refill his cup. "That's how they get to you. It's a gradual thing, which is why a lot of women find themselves in a situation they can't get out of. Women who, like you, were never weak to begin with." He filled a second cup and handed it to me. "Decaf. Not my favorite, but you need sleep so caffeine would be a stupid decision right now. Drink up, then go to bed. I'll wake you when it's time to leave."

11

Bishop

I let her sleep until ten and used the time to clean the gun I'd kept hidden out of sight in the suitcase I brought to the room with me. She knew I had one, I'd fired it at her, after all, but I wasn't certain she remembered, and I didn't want to startle her.

I tapped on the bedroom door twice before opening it. She was a blanket-covered bump in the center of the bed. The only reason I knew she was there was because of the dark red hair spilling across the pillow like blood.

"Eden?" I pitched my voice low so I didn't scare her.

She didn't stir.

I moved closer. She was lying face down, an arm thrown above her head and tucked beneath the pillow. One shoulder was bare and uncovered, and the sheets were tucked around her.

"Eden." I spoke a little louder.

She scowled, a small crease forming above her nose, then

turned her face into the pillow. I sat on the edge of the mattress.

"Eden, you need to get up. We're leaving in an hour."

"Lemme sleep ... bit longer," she mumbled.

"If you don't get up in the next five minutes, I'm dragging the sheets away. You remember what happened last time you called my bluff, don't you?"

Her head turned, eyelashes fluttering and then green eyes, still hazy with sleep, found mine. "Has anyone ever mentioned how bossy you are?"

I scratched my jaw. "Maybe. A time or two." I stood. "You didn't try on those clothes last night. I've left them at the foot of the bed. There's a toothbrush in the bathroom, and breakfast waiting in the other room. You have twenty minutes before I come and drag you out of here."

Her sigh was heavy, but she rolled onto her back and then sat up, clutching the sheet against her chest. Her hair tumbled around her face in a fiery mess, and I had a sudden vision of her on her back, lips parted in pleasure. I blinked and shook my head.

What the fuck was that?

"Twenty minutes," I said, my voice gruff.

"Or you'll come and drag me out by my leg. I know, I know. You don't bluff." The words were thrown at me around a yawn. "You could at least bring coffee with your threats."

"Coffee is also waiting for you in the other room. Seventeen minutes, Eden."

"Yes sir, Mr. Chambers, sir."

I found myself chuckling again when I turned to leave the room. "Bishop."

I stopped and glanced over my shoulder at her hesitant tone. "Yeah?"

"Thank you." She bit her lip. "I feel like the next couple of days are going to be chaotic, so I wanted to make sure I said thank you now. For helping me."

Our gazes locked, and then I nodded. "Fourteen minutes, Eden." I masked a smile at her irritated sigh and left the room.

**

"Is that *Cole Spencer?*" We'd been in the air for less than an hour when Eden leaned close to whisper in my ear.

I glanced around the first-class section. "I don't know who that is."

"You don't …" She gaped at me. "How can you not know? He's the biggest action movie star around."

"I don't watch television."

"Or go to the movies?"

I shook my head.

"*Seriously?* How busy do you have to be not to sit down and watch a movie?"

"Busy."

She sighed and sank back against the seat. "I used to love going to the movies. A big tub of popcorn, a large drink and just lose yourself for a couple of hours." There was a wistful note to her voice.

I set down the contract I was reading and half-turned toward her. "When was the last time you went?"

"I don't remember," she said after a moment's thought. "When I first started dating Chester maybe. Once I moved in with him, we rarely went out at all."

"Since you recognized … Cole Spencer, did you say? … I take that to mean you enjoy action movies?"

"Action, comedy, romance, horror. I love it all. I'm a mood watcher."

"A mood watcher," I repeated.

Her smile widened, green eyes sparking to life. "Yeah, you know. You pick something to watch based on the mood you're in, or how you *want* to feel."

I'd never heard of anything so odd in my life. "You're telling me you watch something to make you feel a particular way?"

"Don't you?" She waved a hand. "Don't answer that. You said you don't watch television. What about books? Do you read?"

"I don't have the time for hobbies."

"That's sad. There's more to life than just work, Bishop."

Her words struck home, mirroring something my mother had said more than once. My jaw clenched.

Who was she to criticize how I lived my life?

"If that was true, you would still be locked in the trunk of a car." My voice was clipped.

Her smile faded and she looked away. "If you don't want to have a conversation, all you have to do is say so."

I let out a quiet sigh.

How the fuck did she manage to make me feel bad for telling the truth?

"I never said that, but you can't deny I'm right. If I wasn't invested in my work as much as I am, I wouldn't have been there that night. Maybe I wouldn't have even been suggested to you."

"By that argument, I wouldn't have been in the trunk in the first place. So, in actual fact, I could say that the fact you're a clear workaholic is *why* I ended up in the trunk of that car."

"My work ethic is why I'm the best at what I do."

"Your work ethic is going to kill you. Everyone needs to relax now and then."

"I relax."

"You said you don't have time for hobbies. How do you relax?"

"I work out."

Her eyes narrowed as she stared at me. "You work out," she repeated.

"You have a problem with that?"

"You work out to relax?"

"I need to be in peak condition. My job can be dangerous. If I'm not fit and—"

"So, you're not relaxing, are you?" She pointed a finger at me. "Working out is part of your routine, part of your *job*."

"Can't it be both?"

"Do you stop thinking about work when you do your exercise routine?" There was a challenge in her tone.

"So now I can't *think* about work either?" I arched an

eyebrow, amused despite myself, and curious to see where she was taking this. "My plan was to use this engagement party as a semi-vacation."

"You're going to spend a weekend doing nothing work-related?"

"That was my plan, and then *you* showed up."

12

Eden

"I'd be curious to see the conversation you had about me. I don't suppose you still have it?"

I shook my head. "After she gave me all the details for contacting you, she told me I should delete the conversation to keep both of us safe, in case someone ever got hold of my phone."

"And, due to the position you were in, that made perfect sense." His tone didn't sound mocking, more thoughtful. "Covering your tracks has become second nature, I imagine. But there are always traces, if you know how to access them. My brother is a tech wizard. If you will allow it, I'll ask him to take a look at your phone history and see if he can recover the messages."

My heart plummeted in my chest. "That's possible?"

"Nothing is ever truly deleted."

"I thought things like that only happened in the movies."

"Even fiction has some basis in reality."

"That's terrifying." And it was. To me, anyway. Was that why Chester kept tracking me down? Oh god, was that possible? "I lost my cell when the men grabbed me. I don't know if I dropped it or they took it." I licked my lips. "Would … if deleted messages can be tracked, can people?"

"How do you mean?"

"I've seen in the movies how people can put trackers on phones. Is that a real thing, as well?"

He picked up on my meaning immediately. "You want to know if your ex was using your phone to keep updated on your location. There are apps that will do that. It would make sense. Especially if his last confirmed location was the motel in New York."

"I was told to switch off my cell before I boarded the plane for Dallas." My voice was low. I lifted my eyes to find his. "Is that something you would have requested?"

"No. I'd have told you to ditch the phone completely and would have sent you a burner to use. But it suggests someone knew or, at the very least, *believed* there was a tracker on your phone."

"I'm so stupid. I just thought it was because he was a detective that he knew how to find me."

"You're not stupid, Eden. You just don't live in a world where you expect things like that to happen." He lifted a hand, and a flight attendant came over. "Could we get something to drink?"

And just like that he ended the conversation, and I didn't try to start it back up after drinks had been delivered. Instead,

I picked up one of the magazines scattered around and flicked through it and left him to concentrate on whatever was on the pile of papers he was thumbing through.

***

We took a cab from the airport to the hotel—another suite with two bedrooms—but I didn't get a chance to investigate too deeply before Bishop whisked me out again.

"There's a boutique just down the road. You're going to need enough clothes for the month, as well as something to get married in, and a couple of evening dresses for the engagement weekend. You have two hours to pick out everything you think you might need. I'm going to drop you off. I have a few errands to run, and I'll be back to get you."

His hand touched my back to turn me toward a door. "Here we are."

I looked at the building in front of me. On each side of the door, there were window displays. Mannequins dressed in clothes ranging from jeans to ballgowns.

Bishop pushed open the door and stepped back so I could enter before him. My eyes darted around. This place was *not* the type of clothing store I shopped at. A plush carpet covered the floor, soft music played through hidden speakers, and the shop assistant was dressed like she was about to go for an expensive evening out. She approached us, a smile curving her red lips.

"Mr. Chambers," she greeted Bishop. "We have everything ready. I'll just need your signature." She turned her attention to me. "Ms. Marshall. I have started on a potential selection for you to look through. If you'll follow me, we can get started."

I threw a panicked look at Bishop, who smiled. "You'll be fine. I'll see you in a couple of hours." He turned his back on me and moved across the store to the cashier desk, where he took a pen and signed something.

"Come along." Red nails which matched the lipstick covering her mouth plucked at my sleeve. "We have a lot to do in very little time."

"Bishop said we have two hours." *How long did someone need to buy clothes?*

"Exactly! My name is Delta, you can call me Dee, and I'll be your personal shopper while you're here."

"Personal shopper?" I turned back toward Bishop and her grip on my arm tightened.

"Leave the man alone. He's not necessary for what we're about to do." She stopped and eyed me. "Unless you want him to sign off on what kind of lingerie you're buying?"

"What? No! It's not like that. We're not …"

"Of course, you're not." She gave me a knowing look and my cheeks burned, embarrassment twisting my insides.

What did she think was happening here? Did she think he was buying my affections, so I'd sleep with him? Oh my god, that's exactly what she was thinking.

"He's not … we're not …"

Delta … *Dee* … laughed, tugging me through a curtain and

into another side of the store. "He's not what? Your sugar daddy? Honey, that man must be what ... fifteen years older than you?"

I turned my head, trying to see Bishop through the gap, but he wasn't in view. "No. I don't know. I have no idea how old he is!" Jesus, that made everything sound even worse!

"Sometimes it's best not to ask. Enjoy it while you've got his attention. Men like him never stay interested for long."

13

Bishop

"Are you *sure* you want to do this?" Jeremy Rafferty, my lawyer, asked for the fifth time since I entered his office. "It seems a little extreme, just to send the message to a woman that you're not interested."

"That's simplifying the situation, and you know it."

"But marriage, Bishop?"

"It's not just for me. It'll help Eden as well. It gives her some security while I arrange what she needs to disappear."

"If that was the case, this wouldn't be the first prenup I'd have prepared for you. What makes this girl different from all the others who have hired you?"

I ignored the question. "Have you done it? I'm on a time schedule."

"Of course, I have. But I wouldn't be doing my job if I didn't express my concern over it."

"Your concern is duly noted. As long as you've covered everything in the prenup, I don't see the need to be worried."

"I have. Four weeks where you'll take responsibility for any financial needs, within reason. In return, she'll play the role of a doting wife in public and will not give any hint that it's anything but real. At the end of the time period, you'll set her up with a new identity, enough money to give a year's buffer, a house, and a job. She has no claim on anything of yours, other than your agreement to give her a new life at the end of your four-week marriage."

"Perfect."

He handed me the three-page document. "I've put an X where you both need to sign, but I'll be there to make sure you do it *before* the wedding.

"Of course." I slid it into the envelope on the desk and stood, holding out my hand to shake his. "Thanks, Jeremy. I appreciate it."

"I wish I could talk you out of this."

"It'll be fine."

"Famous last words."

***

I detoured to my tailor before going to pick up Eden and picked up a new suit. Thankfully, I'd been for a fitting only a couple of weeks earlier, so I had new suits for the engagement party. If I was going to get married, regardless of how short term it was going to be, I was going to look the part, so I planned to wear one to the chapel. Once I picked those up, I returned to the hotel to shower and change, checked the time, and set off to the clothing store I'd left my soon-to-be-wife at.

The quiet chime as I opened the door and entered was the only noise in the store. An assistant came through the curtain, which divided the store into two halves. She greeted me with a smile.

"Mr. Chambers. You're just in time. Would you like to come through?" She didn't wait for me to reply and turned to hold the curtain open.

I walked through into the section of the store that was kept solely for high-paying customers. Those who wanted to buy entire wardrobes, have clothes modeled for them, and possibly spend an entire day on the premises. There were comfortable chairs, mirrors, snacks and drinks and a small replica of a model runway.

"Please take a seat." The assistant pointed to one of the armchairs. "Can I get you anything to eat or drink?"

"No, thank you."

I thumbed through messages on my cell while I waited. There was a couple from Rook, confirming he was going to be at the engagement party as well.

ME: Did David and Susannah confirm their attendance, do you know?

ROOK: Yeah. Crosby thought about not inviting them, but since you, me and Knight are invited, it would have been an insult not to invite David.

ME: It's fine. I'm bringing a date to protect me from Susannah's advances.

It was a joke that ... wasn't really a joke. I'd hooked up with

Susannah quite a few times, to the point where we were in a semi-relationship. And then I found out she was married. To a crime lord. One who would not appreciate discovering his wife had been stepping out on him. I'd ended things immediately. And she wasn't happy about it.

"Bishop?" Eden's voice pulled my attention from my cell, and I lifted my gaze to search her out ... and immediately reconsidered my plan.

Fuck.

The dress she was wearing followed the shape of her figure and ended just above her knees. There was nothing risqué or revealing about it. In fact, the cut of it ensured that the bruising on her shoulder was hidden. The color was a deep red, the material silk. It was long-sleeved, with a scooped neckline that revealed the barest hint of cleavage. Someone had done her hair and makeup, making the cut on her lip hard to see, and the bruise on her cheek invisible. Curly tendrils of red hair fell artfully around her face.

She looked stunning.

"It's too much, isn't it?"

Her question broke through my thoughts, and I realized I was staring.

"I said it was too much. I'll go and change." She turned away, and I was out of my chair before I even thought about it.

"No. You look perfect."

14

Eden

I read through the legalese on the prenup as best I could and signed in the places Bishop indicated. I wasn't a lawyer, but it *seemed* to make sense. I could make no claim on anything Bishop owned, or his money and he would make no claims on me, other than I behave like his wife in public for the next four weeks. In return I'd get the freedom to live my life without fear of Chester finding me.

It seemed like four weeks being married to the man standing quietly beside me was a small price to pay for the lifelong freedom that would hopefully result from it.

"All done." I straightened and handed the pen back to the man standing on the opposite side of the desk.

The man who had been introduced as his lawyer frowned at me, then directed his glare at Bishop. "I hope the pair of you know what you're doing."

"We do. Have you got everything else?" Bishop answered for us both.

He pulled an envelope out of his jacket pocket. "New passport. Do *not* use it until after the wedding. I put her married name on it."

"That's the plan." Bishop took it, tore it open, flicked through the pages of the passport inside and nodded. "Perfect." He slipped it into his pocket and turned to me. "Ready?"

Was I? It seemed a simple question on the surface of it. *Was I ready? Was I ready to marry a man I've known for twenty-four hours and continue to trust him with my safety?* I curved my hand around his arm and nodded.

"I'm ready."

His fingers covered mine, warm and calloused, and he moved toward the door. His hand secured mine in place, and I had no choice but to follow him. The doors to the chapel swung open at our approach, and the Wedding March began to play as we stepped through.

The next fifteen minutes passed in a blur. Words were spoken by the officiant. Bishop produced two rings from seemingly out of nowhere and slipped one onto my finger, before handing me the other to do the same for him. And then the final words were spoken.

"By the power invested in me, I now solemnly declare you husband and wife. Let no one put asunder those that have been joined together today in the presence of almighty God. You may now kiss the bride."

My eyes darted up to his. "You don't really—"

He lifted a hand to curve over my cheek. "Oh, never let it be said that I don't play my role to the utmost of my ability."

His head dipped and he brushed his lips against mine, drew back slightly and frowned.

"Hmmm." The noise rumbled up from his chest and then his mouth was on mine again, only this time it was no chaste kiss.

His tongue found the seam of my lips, licked along it while his hand slid into my hair and tipped my head back. The move parted my lips and his tongue delved inside, stroked along mine once, before retreating. He raised his head and one corner of his mouth lifted.

"You taste like trouble."

***

I spent the journey back to the hotel room after the ceremony in a daze. Bishop ordered room service and left me to change out of the dress I'd worn. The flash of gold on my finger caught my eye more than once and I paused in the middle of pulling on a pair of jeans to stare at the ring.

I was married.

Married to a man I barely knew.

A man who'd kissed me as though it was the most natural thing in the world.

I was no longer Eden Marshall. I was Eden Chambers, wife of Bishop Chambers. The man I had sought out to give me a new life.

A quiet laugh escaped me.

Well, he'd definitely done that. Just not in the way I'd imagined.

I studied my reflection in the mirrored door of the closet. The bruise on my cheek was hidden by makeup and the cut on my lip was barely noticeable. My hair had been tamed into a braid, although the curls were already starting to escape.

I looked different. I wasn't sure if that was due to a decent night's sleep and not waking up every hour in fear that Chester had found me or just my imagination. But I *felt* different. Stronger, more in control.

"Eden?" Bishop's voice broke through my musings, and I turned toward the bedroom door. "Food's here."

I smoothed a hand over the t-shirt and jeans I'd changed into and headed out to join him.

"Won't your friend be annoyed at you bringing a stranger with you?" I sat on the chair he pulled out, and watched as he rounded the table to sit opposite me.

"No. I told you, my invitation has a plus one. I've already let him know I'm bringing you."

"Will you tell him we're married?"

When he didn't reply, I lifted my gaze from the plates spread across the table and searched him out. His fingers were drumming against the tablecloth as he looked at me.

"Bishop?"

"Maybe. We'll see how it plays out. It might not be necessary."

I nodded. "Okay." I ate a mouthful of pasta. "You said it was an engagement party."

"Correct. An old friend. His family loves to celebrate everything. If we can keep the fact we're married quiet, I'd prefer it, but I find it unlikely. Especially if Susannah pushes."

"Susannah. That's the woman I'm to protect you from?"

His lips twitched at my words, as though he was trying to hold back a laugh. "That's right. I need you to be a buffer, so she doesn't try and climb into my bed and cause a war."

"A *war?*"

"Her husband would not be content with an apology if he discovered she was fooling around with someone else."

"But a war?"

A smile flitted across his face. "You've just married into a dangerous family, Eden."

L. ANN

15

Bishop

Eden pushed the pasta around the plate with her fork, and I waited for her to process what I'd told her. It only took a minute before her fork clattered down onto the plate and her eyes lifted to find mine.

"Dangerous, *how?*"

"How is a shark dangerous? Or a tiger? I come from a family of hunters."

"You hunt animals?" Her eyebrows dipped into a frown.

I laughed quietly. "In a way, I guess you could say that. Only the animals we hunt usually run on two legs instead of four."

"I thought you just helped people make new lives."

"*I* do. Sometimes it involves bloodshed."

"You kill people?" She half-rose from her seat.

"Sit down, Eden." My voice remained calm. "I'm not hunting you, so you have nothing to worry about." I placed my silverware down and held her gaze. "You're not naive enough to think that a new life, a new *identity*, can be built without any consequences. Sometimes, my clients are found before we can put their new life into action. When that happens, we have to take ... precautions."

"By killing people."

"Are you trying to claim that if your ex-boyfriend turned up right now, you would expect me to just let him drag you out of here? Or would you want me to do what you've hired me for ... what I'm *contracted* to do ... and protect you, even if that means putting him down for good?"

Her bottom lip dropped, and her eyes widened as my words hit her.

"I told you on the flight to New York it would be easier to hire someone to take him out than it would be to build a new life. You opted not to take that route, which is why you're sitting here now with my ring on your finger. But just because you decided not to hire a hitman, that doesn't mean I won't arrange his death if I feel it's the only way to fulfill my obligation to you."

"Your obligation ..." Her voice was little more than a whisper.

I reached for my glass of water and took a sip. "There's still time to change your mind. We can annul the marriage right now if you want to and we can go our separate ways. But hear me, if you come with me then I need you to understand that I will do whatever I think is necessary to ensure your new identity is protected when the time comes for our contract to end."

"But you're talking about murder." Her tongue swept over

her lips.

"Only as a last resort. It rarely comes to that. But with the position he holds and the fact he's found you every time you've run so far, you have to be aware of the possibility that he might find you again before I have your new life organized." I shrugged. "Sometimes the simplest answer is also the tidiest."

She stayed where she was, half out of her seat and staring at me across the table.

"Finish your dinner." I flicked a finger toward her plate. "We have another long flight ahead."

"Where are we going?"

"My home. We'll spend a couple of nights there, and then we'll set off for the engagement party. We'll arrive Friday evening and stay until Sunday."

"And where is *that* going to be?"

"About an hour's drive from Glenville. Little place called Trojan Peaks. The party is Saturday night, and I'd rather not rush there and then drive back all in the same day."

She lowered herself back to her seat and slowly picked up her fork. "Is your ... *friend* ... in the same line of business as you?"

I snorted. "Christ, no. Crosby is an investment banker. Dana is a model. They're total opposites, yet they work somehow."

"How do you know them?"

"I was at school with Crosby." I smiled at the memory. He'd been a weedy kid with glasses, bullied by the jocks ... until me and my brothers happened upon him curled into a ball while three boys kicked the shit out of him. By the time we were done, they understood never to touch him again and we had a new friend.

Eden propped her chin on one hand and looked at me from across the table. "And you expect him to believe you got married?"

"It'll probably be the least weird thing I've done for a client."

"Oh?" Her head tilted, eyes sparkling with interest.

"Or maybe not." I leaned back on my chair and took a sip of water.

"What about his fiancée?"

"What about her?"

"Do you know her well? What's she like?"

"Nice enough, I guess. Crosby seems happy. I've only met her a handful of times."

She gave a slow nod. "So, she won't have any preconceived ideas about the kind of woman you might marry? Women are usually harder to fool about relationships than men."

"My lifestyle doesn't really include double-dating or social events. This party is something I wouldn't usually attend."

"Because you never take time off."

"Already getting into the role of a nagging wife?" I arched an eyebrow, and laughed at the impish smile she tossed in my direction.

"Wouldn't it make sense for a newly wedded couple to want to spend as much time together as possible? It's the honeymoon period, after all."

"True. We'll see how it plays out. The only people you really need to fool are Susannah and her husband." I stood and stepped away from the table. "I need to make some calls. The television remote is on the coffee table. If you want anything, call down for room service. Make yourself comfortable. Our flight out is at eight am."

"Where are you going?"

"Into one of the bedrooms."

"Because you don't want me to hear what you're talking about?"

"Exactly." I didn't see the point in lying. "You might have my ring on your finger, but you're still a client. And I don't share the details of my work with my clients."

16

Eden

I didn't see Bishop for the rest of the evening. I watched television for a while—reruns of an old nineties' sitcom—and ordered a hot chocolate from room service because I didn't want to drink coffee. I was already going to find it difficult to sleep, coffee would just make it worse.

The television was mostly background noise to my thoughts. Mainly, how had I become so desperate that marrying a virtual stranger in return for the safety he promised was my only option? Sitting in the hotel room, looking down at the gold band on my finger, I couldn't believe I'd gone through with it. After everything I'd lived through with Chester, why did I trust Bishop not to behave the same way? He could very easily be just as violent as my ex-boyfriend. He was bossy, domineering, clearly used to getting his own way, and yet he didn't scare me. He *should* but ...

I glanced toward the door he'd disappeared through.

I wondered about the woman he'd been seeing. The one that had sent him to the extreme decision to offer marriage in return for safety. From the way he'd talked about her, it didn't *seem* like it had been a serious relationship, so why couldn't he just say it was over and walk away? Why did he need to present the woman with a wife? Why couldn't he have just taken a girlfriend to the party?

You've married into a dangerous family, Eden.

His words whispered through my head. What did that mean? *How* dangerous? Had I moved from one dangerous situation into one that could be worse?

I stared down at the ring, willing it to give me answers, but it just shone under the light. Gold, cold, and silent.

Another two hours passed of me sitting, thoughts swirling around in circles, while the television went through one episode after another.

How long would it be before Chester caught up to me? While I was still married to Bishop? After? Would he be able to see through whatever new life Bishop built for me? Or was he really as good as I was told?

And *that* took me right back to the fact I had just married a man I barely knew.

When one a.m. rolled around and Bishop stayed firmly in his room, I pushed up off the couch, made my way to the other bedroom and crawled into the bed. One of the last thoughts I had before sleep took hold was that very soon, I would have to play the role of a woman in love … and I wasn't sure if I could do it.

***

"I don't think I've ever flown as much in my life as I have since meeting you." I followed Bishop through the airport and out into the chill Baltimore air.

He turned his head to glance at me but didn't say anything. I was beginning to learn that Bishop didn't really talk unless he had something to say. Small talk wasn't part of his makeup, and the longer we were in the air, the more I wanted to fill the silence with nervous chatter to stop myself from telling him I'd changed my mind. Marrying him was a bad decision and I wanted to get out of it.

If I did that, I'd lose my one shot at escaping Chester, and it was the only thing that stopped me.

"Isn't there an airport closer to Glenville?"

"No." He stopped beside a sleek black sports car. "Get in while I put the suitcases in the back."

"I can help".

"I don't need your help. Get in the car, Eden."

I glared at him for half a minute, while he ignored me and set about piling the suitcases in the trunk. When I reached for one of them, he shot me a glare. I rolled my eyes.

"Fine. Let the big macho guy do all the heavy lifting." I muttered the words beneath my breath as I made my way to the front passenger door, pulled it open, and climbed in.

When he joined me a few minutes later, he settled in the seat and clipped on his seatbelt before turning to face me.

"My mother raised me right. I hold open doors, pay for

meals, and do the *heavy lifting*."

My cheeks heated up.

"I also have perfect hearing." He turned to face the front of the car and fired the engine. "It's an hour's drive to where I live. Can I expect you to talk the entire time?"

My lips parted, jaw dropping. "Do you *ever* think about what you're going to say before you say it?"

"Always."

"So, you're rude on purpose?"

One dark eyebrow lifted. "You think I'm being rude?"

"You just said I talk too much."

He didn't reply until he'd reversed out of the parking lot and joined the traffic heading out of the city.

"I said no such thing. I simply asked if you were going to talk all the way to Glenville. If you're not, I'll put music on. If you are, I won't. I just wanted to know which way the journey was going to go."

"Put music on, if you want to."

"I have no preference. You're uncomfortable with silence. If you wish to talk, talk. If not ..." He waved a hand toward the stereo. "Have at it."

17

Bishop

I think she changed the radio station five times during the drive to my place. She must have taken my comments about talking as a challenge because she barely said five words to me. When I pulled up outside my house, I reached out and switched off the music.

"I've been away for three weeks, so I doubt there's anything edible inside. There's a nice restaurant on the other side of town. I need to go out for an hour, so I'll give you a quick tour of the house and leave you to unpack. I'll make a reservation for ..." I checked my watch. "For eight. It's six now. Do you think you can hold out that long, or are you going to starve to death?"

"I think I can manage. I ate on the plane, anyway."

I nodded and unclipped my belt. "Let's go inside, then."

She was already out of the car by the time I rounded it and had the trunk open.

"Remember what I said about the heavy lifting?" I placed my hands on her shoulders and moved her to the side. It was hard to miss the way she tensed under my touch. "Relax, Eden. I just need to get to the cases." I reached in and took out two of the suitcases. Placing them on the ground, I pulled a set of keys out of my pocket and handed them to her. "Go and unlock the door. The alarm is on the wall to the right. The code is 9637485. Punch in the numbers, then hit the green button. Repeat it back to me."

She blinked. "I..."

"9637485," I repeated slowly. "Tell me."

"9637485."

I nodded. "Good girl. Go inside."

I took out the third case, loaded myself up and followed her up the steps to the front door. She was punching in the number when I entered, and I caught her sigh of relief when the alarms didn't go off.

"Got it right first time," she said in response to my smile.

"Gold star for you." My voice was dry.

She rolled her eyes, and I bit back a chuckle.

"The kitchen is directly ahead, living room to the left, my office to the right." I jerked my chin in each direction, hefted the cases, and moved toward the stairs. "I'll show you to your room."

I could hear her close behind me as I moved along the hallway to the bedroom at the end. Nudging the door open with my foot, I stepped through and dropped two of the cases at the foot of the bed. "There's a bathroom through that door. Walk-in closet on the other side of the room. Make yourself at home. I'll pick up a new cell phone for you while I'm out, but there is a landline connected in the house. You'll find phones in the downstairs hall near the door, the kitchen, and one in the living room. I'll write my number down. Do *not* open the door to anyone while I'm out. No one knows you're here and I don't have guests."

I straightened and turned to find her hovering in the doorway. "Eden?"

She blinked and refocused on me. "Sorry." A small frown creased her brow. "I think everything is catching up with me." Her eyes met mine, and her teeth sank into her bottom lip.

I crossed the room and stopped in front of her. "Four weeks and you'll have a new life far away from New York and your ex-boyfriend."

Her nod was jerky.

"Eden, look at me." I reached out and tipped her head back with one finger beneath her chin. "I'm the best at what I do."

"I'm not worried about that."

"Then what's the problem?"

"What if your friends don't believe we're really married?"

"They will. They have no other relationship to compare it with. I've never introduced anyone to my friends or family before. All you need to do is help me sell the lie."

"But what if I can't?"

Her real question hung silently between us.

"I'm not going to just dump you on the street to fend for

yourself. I gave you my word I'd help you, and that's what I'll do. The only person who needs to believe the lie is Susannah."

"But what if—"

"Don't borrow problems that don't exist." I dropped my hand and stepped around her. "I'll write my cell number down and leave it beside the phone in the kitchen. You shouldn't have any need to use it, but it's there just in case. I'll be back at seven-thirty. The restaurant I'm booking a table at is formal, so no jeans. Feel free to explore, just stay out of my office."

She followed me along the landing and down the stairs.

"Where are you going?"

"I want to check in with my brother. He's had some drama of his own recently. I'll be back." I pulled open the door and walked back to my car.

She still hadn't gone back inside by the time I was in the seat and had the engine running. I slid down the window. "Go inside and lock the door."

I caught the flash of her smile before the door swung shut, sealing her inside.

**

After a quick detour to the closest cell phone store, I parked outside Rook's place, climbed out and rapped on the door.

It took him ten minutes to answer. When the door opened, it was to reveal my brother in a partial state of undress. Trousers unbuttoned, shirt open, hair sticking up. I arched an eyebrow.

He shrugged. "Wasn't expecting company."

"Is Magdalena presentable, at least?"

Rook grinned. "No, she's cursing up a storm over your timing. She'll be down in a few minutes. I thought we were meeting at Crosby's."

"I came home instead of going straight there. My plans changed. I might need you to do something for me."

18

Eden

I waited by the door until the sound of the car engine faded, then turned and took a slow walk down the hallway. There was an archway at the end leading into a large kitchen. The countertops were black, the cabinets beneath and on the wall burnished chrome. Everything looked brand new and untouched, which couldn't be right. Maybe he hired someone to come in and clean for him. I didn't want to touch anything for fear of leaving smears and fingerprints, so I backed out and found my way to the door he'd said was the living room.

The interior surprised me. I'd expected something as crisp and cool as the kitchen, but what I found was a room designed for comfort. I toed out of my sneakers before stepping inside. The couch was curved and covered with large cushions. Two throws were folded across the back. The dark-gray carpet was thick beneath my feet as I walked across the floor. In front of the couch was a rug, a deep red stain against the darkness of the carpet, and on top of it was a glass-topped coffee table. A large screen television was on one wall, framed by bookcases stacked high with well-worn paperbacks. A trio of framed photographs adorned the wall to the left of the door. I moved closer to look at them.

In the first were three boys standing in front of two adults—a woman and a man. The boys were in shorts and kneeling on the sand. The woman was leaning against the man and laughing up at him. His arm was wrapped around her shoulders while he shielded his eyes and looked toward the camera. The boys appeared to be in the middle of building sandcastles, holding spades and buckets. I couldn't say for sure, but I guessed one of them must be Bishop.

The second photograph was of three men, dressed in suits and dark glasses. Bishop was immediately recognizable in the center of the trio, and the two either side of him were obviously related. They had the same hair color, the same build, and the same jawline. I couldn't see their eyes behind the dark glasses. Two of the three were unsmiling, while the third grinned, revealing a small dimple in one cheek.

The last one wasn't of a person, but a dog—I thought it was a German Shepherd. It was sitting, head cocked, eyes bright and tongue lolling out. There was a tiny plaque beneath the frame with one word etched into it—Hope.

I touched the image gently with one finger. Was that the

dog's name? Where was it now? Was it a childhood pet? Bishop didn't strike me as the type to be attached to any kind of pet, let alone have a photograph of one on the wall. What did it mean?

Moving away from the photographs, I explored the rest of the room, looking through the books on the bookcase. Most of them were thrillers, but squashed at the end of one of the lower shelves I found a copy of 'Good Omens' by Terry Pratchett and Neil Gaiman. I pulled it out and flicked through it. It was just as worn as the other books on the shelves.

What happened to his claim of having no spare time to just relax? When was the last time he'd read a book? I placed it back in its spot, straightened and turned back to the door.

I needed to go and pick something to wear for dinner. He'd said the place was formal, so staying in the jeans and t-shirt I'd worn to travel in was not going to work. I needed to wear one of the things he'd bought in Vegas. But what? A dress? A skirt? Pants? And how much did I need to take with me when we went to his friends for the weekend?

I retraced my steps back to the bedroom and pushed open the door to the bathroom. Chrome and marble greeted me. The bathtub sitting in the center of the room was designed in the style of an old iron bathtub from years gone by. Beyond that was a shower surrounded by glass panels. My eyes moved between them.

Shower or bath?

A shower would be faster, but unless there was a way for me to dry my hair, it'd turn into a frizzy mess of curls.

Returning to the bedroom, I threw open the door to the closet and looked inside. It was completely empty with enough space for me to step right inside and close the door if I wanted to. But there was no hairdryer. Not in the closet, or in any of the drawers of the dresser.

A bath it was, then.

***

I was putting the finishing touches to my makeup when there was a soft tap at the door. Screwing the top back onto the mascara, I placed it beside the rest of the makeup kit and stood, smoothing my hands down over my thighs.

"Come in."

The door swung open at my words to reveal Bishop. His hair was slightly damp, and he'd changed out of the clothes he'd traveled in and was wearing a dark gray suit, with a white shirt. He propped one shoulder against the doorframe.

"Ready to go?"

"Almost." I crossed to where I'd left the low-heeled shoes I'd paired with the dress and slipped them on. "Am I formal enough?"

One corner of his mouth tipped up while his eyes slid down over my form, from head to toe and back up again. Nothing about the look suggested he was admiring me. It was purely assessing.

"Perfect. My brother, Rook, and his girlfriend are meeting us there." He straightened and held up one hand when I drew breath to protest. "I thought it would give you an easy start. They're going to be at Crosby's party. Meeting Rook now gives us a chance to set our story in motion."

"He knows about me?"

His hand dropped until it was flat in the air, and he waggled it from side to side. "Kinda, sorta."

"What does *that* mean?"

"I told him I'd met someone, and the attraction had hit me hard. So much so I didn't want to lose you, so I brought you home with me."

"The attraction ..."

The hint of a smile teasing his lips solidified. "Yes, the attraction. He met his girlfriend through a pretend date, so there's reason for him to believe something similar might happen to me. So, they're both coming to dinner, and you'll get to meet them and have some faces you'll recognize when we get to Crosby's place."

"Does he know why we're married?"

"No. If I'd told him the truth, he would have told Magdalena. He won't keep secrets from her. The less people who know the truth, the better. He just thinks I used my natural charm to convince you to take a risk and jump into marriage with me."

"This sounds crazier every time you talk about it. There's no way your brother will believe we're together."

"We'll *make* him believe it. The weekend depends on us being able to sell the lie." He turned away. "If you're ready, we should go."

Ready for what? Dinner? The pretense to really begin? To meet his brother?

The answer to all of those was *no*. I wasn't ready. But what choice did I have? I'd already signed the contract and agreed to the terms.

19

Bishop

I strode around to the passenger side of the car, opened the door, and stooped to offer my hand to the woman seated inside. Her green eyes blinked up at me briefly, and then she slowly slid her fingers over mine and allowed me to help her out.

"Open doors, pay for food, and—"

"Heavy lifting, I know." Her soft voice was wry. "I'm still not convinced this is a good idea."

"You'd rather go to the party without any confidence in being able to convince everyone we're married and in love?"

"I'd rather not go at all."

"It's not like I didn't give you all the information before you signed on the dotted line."

"You *didn't*. I'm pretty sure you still haven't told me everything."

I hit the button on the key fob and locked the door, then offered Eden my arm. She hooked her fingers around it and kept pace beside me.

"I've told you everything you *need* to know. This is not a normal situation for me, either. Normally, I take a fee and do the job. I'm not usually *part* of the assignment. You just happened to appear at a time when it was useful for me." I glanced at her. "It's a win/win really, for both of us. You get something that you would never have been able to afford. I get a way out of something I never should have started."

I placed my hand on top of hers and stopped just before the entrance to the restaurant.

"If you really don't think you can pull this off, now's the time to say something. Once we go in there, we're committing to following this through to the end." I ignored the little voice in my head that pointed out how a couple of days ago, I'd have told her if she didn't play her part, then the deal was off.

She lifted her head and looked me in the eyes. For a moment, I thought she was about to call a halt but then she nodded.

"You're the oldest of three brothers. Rook is the middle child, and ... *Knight*? That's right, isn't it? Knight is the youngest?"

"That's right."

"We're meeting Rook, and his girlfriend, Magdalena tonight. They've been together for five months."

I nodded.

"Okay." She took a deep breath, then stepped forward toward the doors.

I caught her hand as it fell from my arm and tugged her back beside me. "We really should walk in together."

A blush colored her cheeks. "Right ... of course."

"Take a breath. Treat this evening like it's the first day of your new life."

She slanted a look at me. "Easy for you to say."

"Isn't that what it is, though? The last couple of days have been laying the foundation, now it's time to put it into action." I tightened my grip on her hand and led her inside the restaurant.

An usher stood to one side, and he murmured a low greeting when we stopped in front of him.

"Reservation for four, Chambers."

"One moment, sir." He looked down at the tablet in his hand and scrolled through the list. "Your guests have already arrived. If you'll follow me ..."

He led the way through the tables toward a corner at the far left of the restaurant. The back of Rook's head came into view, a familiar brunette beside him, and we stopped beside the table.

"Bishop." My brother rose to his feet, his eyes moving from me to the woman beside me.

"Rook, this is Eden. Eden ... Rook and Magdalena."

"Pleased to meet you." Eden held out a hand.

Rook quirked an eyebrow in my direction but accepted it and shook.

"Bishop!" Magdalena stood and wrapped her arms around my waist, leaning up to kiss my cheek.

"Forgiven me for the interruption earlier, then?"

She turned pink, then laughed and bumped my arm with her shoulder before turning to greet Eden with a warm smile. I moved to the opposite side of the table and pulled out a seat. When Magdalena returned to her place beside Rook, Eden took the seat I was holding, and I sank onto the one next to her.

"I ordered a bottle of wine for the girls," Rook said into the silence, waving a hand toward the bottle on the table. "Is that okay?" He directed the question at Eden, who nodded. "I'm curious about how you met. Bishop isn't known for his charming personality." He filled two glasses, handed one to Eden and the other to Magdalena.

"She was having car trouble," I replied before Eden could. "I stopped to help."

"Really?" Rook drew the word out. "And then what? You were struck by lightning?"

"No, I tried to leave, and he shot the ground by my feet." Eden answered his question.

Magdalena choked on the sip of wine she'd taken. "He did *what?*"

"We met in Dallas; he wanted me to fly to New York with him. I said no. When I walked away—"

"You *ran* away," I pointed out.

"You were trying to kidnap me."

"I'm fairly confident I wasn't *trying* to do anything. I'd already done it."

"When I *ran* away, he fired his gun at my feet."

"If I'd meant to fire at your feet, I'd have hit your feet."

Magdalena was shaking her head.

"What?"

"You and Rook are exactly the same." She smiled against her glass.

"I didn't try to shoot you." Rook draped an arm across her shoulders.

"Yes, you did! When I came to your place that night. You held a gun to my head!" She looked at Eden. "He held me at gunpoint for an hour. I thought he was going to kill me."

Rook snorted. "Then you shouldn't go creeping around people's backyards without invitation."

20

Eden

My eyes bounced back and forth between Magdalena and Rook as they bantered with each other. When she caught me watching, she smiled.

"Yes, he really did threaten to shoot me. Don't let him claim otherwise."

"Were you trying to break into his house?"

"No!"

"Yes." Rook spoke over her.

"I was *not*."

"Our other brother, Knight, put the idea into her head. He was matchmaking." Rook leaned back on his chair. "Which brings us nicely to the two of you. So, you met in Dallas, sparks flew as well as bullets... then what?"

I waited, hoping Bishop would answer, but he seemed intent on flicking through the menu.

"I guess he just wore me down until I agreed to come here with him." The answer sounded lame to my ears.

"I see. Just like that?"

"I'm very persuasive." Bishop's voice was rich with innuendo, and my cheeks heated.

Magdalena laughed quietly. "If Bishop's persuasion skills are anything like Rook's, I understand exactly why you're here."

"They're better," the man beside me drawled.

I stared at him. He stared right back.

"Are you ready to order?" The stand-off was broken by the server coming up to the table.

"Steak medium rare." Bishop didn't look away from me.

"Same." That was Rook. "Dall? Do you want the chicken?"

"Yes, please."

I tore my eyes away from the man staring at me and looked down at the menu. "I'll have the same. The chicken, I mean."

"Anything to drink?"

"No, we're good for the moment. Thank you." That was Rook again.

Silence fell across the table once the server left. I cleared my throat and plucked at the napkin in front of me.

"So, is anyone going to explain why she's wearing a wedding ring or are we just going to ignore it for the entire evening?"

The bottom fell out of my stomach at Rook's words.

"You know the saying… if you like it, put a ring on it?" Bishop shrugged. "I liked it."

Rook looked shocked. His jaw dropped and he stared at his brother for a full minute before visibly pulling himself together. "That's *your* ring?"

"Yes. Is it a problem?" Bishop's voice was cool.

"You got married? After knowing her for how long? A couple of days?" Rook shoved to his feet. "We need to fucking talk *right now*."

Bishop's sigh was irritable. "If you'll excuse us, I need to go and remind Rook who's the eldest brother." He stood and followed his brother outside.

I looked down at the table.

"I don't know why Rook is so surprised by Bishop's actions." Magdalena's voice was soft. "I accidentally hired him to be my date for a birthday dinner with my parents."

Her words brought my head up. "How do you *accidentally* hire someone?"

She laughed. "I'm dyslexic. I misread the table numbers at the diner I'd arranged to meet my soon-to-be pretend boyfriend, sat myself down in front of him, and didn't really give him a chance to say no."

"And he went along with it?"

"He claims he was bored." Her bright smile faded into a more serious expression. "I'll never be able to thank him enough for that. If he hadn't gone along with my crazy plan, I'd be dead now."

I gaped. "What?"

Magdalena shook her head. "It's a long, depressing story … aside from the parts Rook was involved in. Let's just say I found out that true family isn't always the people who are related to you by blood." She took a sip of wine, pulling a face. "I never used to drink alcohol. I always felt it'd make me look stupider than I already appeared, because of my dyslexia. I still don't drink it often, but sometimes I'll have a glass of wine or two with dinner if we're out." Her smile was soft. "Something else Rook helped me with."

"Does Rook do the same thing as Bishop?"

"Oh, no. Rook's mostly retired these days. But his ... skill set is different from Bishop's."

Her tone of voice made it clear that she wasn't going to tell me what he did before retiring, so I didn't ask.

"They both seem very ..."

"Bossy?" She laughed. "They are, but I think that's mainly because of the lifestyle they've lived. They've had to be forceful and make split-second decisions. But I will say this. If you married him for something other than love, you couldn't have picked a better person to help you with whatever trouble you're hiding from."

"I'm not—"

Magdalena lifted a hand. "You might be able to fool everyone else, but not me. I can see the same desperate look in your eyes that I had when I found Rook. Don't worry, I won't say anything and I'm not going to ask why you really got married. But if you do ever want to talk, I'm here to listen."

21

Bishop

"What's going on?" Rook spun to face me the second we were outside.

"Why must something be going on?"

"Do you remember when I told you I was pretending to be Dally's boyfriend and you asked if I'd lost my mind?"

"I never said that."

"You insinuated it. You don't date and now you're married? You'll have to forgive me for not buying the *I liked it, so I put a ring on it* story."

"I don't know what you want me to say. She keeps me on my toes, and I like that. I never know what she's going to say or do next."

"You like that so much you *married* her? At least tell me you got a prenup."

"I'm not a complete idiot."

"I'm beginning to wonder." My brother shook his head. "You

gave me shit when I hooked up with Dally—"

"No, I didn't. I just asked you if you knew what you were getting into." I turned back toward the entrance. "Are we done here?"

"You're set on sticking with the love at first sight lie?"

"I never said that, either."

"So, you're *not* in love with her."

I sighed and turned back. "Look, just go with the story that I *really* liked what I saw, otherwise you'll have to tell Magdalena what you know when she asks you or lie to her. And we both know you're not going to lie to her about this."

"And you need your marriage to be convincing when we get to Crosby's …" He blew out a breath. "Fine. I don't like it, but I'll roll with it. And then when it's over, you can tell me the fucking truth."

"Deal."

We headed back inside and arrived at the table just as the server was placing our food down.

"Is everything okay?" Magdalena lifted her head and Rook kissed her cheek.

"Fine. I just needed to speak to Bishop." His gaze met mine, and one side of his mouth lifted into a smirk.

I rolled my eyes and took the seat beside Eden.

"Can I get you another bottle of wine?" the server asked.

Both women shook their heads.

"I'll have a bourbon, neat," I said.

"Make that two," Rook added.

"*Please*!" Magdalena tossed us both a frown.

Rook chuckled. "Two glasses of bourbon, *please*."

"Better." His girlfriend bumped his arm with her shoulder.

"Are you looking forward to the weekend, Magdalena? Have you met Crosby before?" I drew my plate toward me and cut into the steak.

"We went to dinner with Crosby and Dana a couple of weeks ago," she replied. "She's nothing like what I expected a supermodel to be." Her gaze moved to Eden. "She has a wicked sense of humor."

"Keeps Crosby on his toes, that's for sure," Rook added.

The conversation turned to the newly engaged couple, and I admit I tuned out. It was small talk, a way to fill the silence and didn't interest me. Rook was the same, and we let the two girls talk while we ate.

The main course was followed by dessert and then coffee. Magdalena and Eden were chatting up a storm, like they were old friends who hadn't caught up in years, leaving me and Rook to hold our own quiet conversation about our youngest brother, Knight.

"Have you seen him recently?"

Rook shook his head. "I asked him to join us tonight, but he made some weak excuse about being on a deadline for a job."

"We've all cut deadlines close. It could be true."

My brother snorted. "If it was the first time he'd used it, then sure. But he's said the same thing the last three times I've invited him to visit."

"Is he coming to Crosby's party?"

Rook shook his head. "He RSVP'd as a maybe. I'd put money on him being a no-show."

"Maybe one of us should detour to his place and pick him up."

"Do you have the key to Fort Knox … because I don't. You know no one is getting in there without his prior agreement."

I laughed quietly. *Fort Knox*. Knight's apartment was likely harder to get into than that place.

"I'll call him. Maybe he'll listen to me."

"Sure. Because you're the eldest brother and all that." Rook's voice made his thoughts clear on how well I'd do.

"It's worth a try. When was the last time he left his apartment?"

"I'm not sure. He picked Dally up from Baltimore that one time, and then came out for dinner with us to meet her. That was what … Five months ago? I've only spoken to him on the phone since then. When did you last see him?"

"I spoke to him a couple of nights ago. I wanted him to check something out for me." I paused to think. "I don't think I've seen him since dinner that night, either. I've been out of the country for most of it."

"If he doesn't show up at Crosby's, we'll go and see him. He gets lost inside his own world sometimes. I doubt he's even considered how long it's been since we saw him. He might have been outside. Just because it wasn't with either of us, doesn't mean he's cooped up inside all the time."

We traded looks. We both knew that was bullshit. Knight needed to be dragged out of his apartment forcibly. He wasn't a fan of people or the outside world and preferred to stay inside his apartment with his technology.

"Next week, then. We'll take a drive out to his place."

Rook nodded. "It's a date."

L. ANN

22

Eden

It was late when we left the restaurant. Magdalena tugged me to one side just before we parted ways to go to our cars.

"Give me your cell number. If you're not busy tomorrow, we could go shopping."

I glanced over at Bishop. "I lost my cell in Dallas. I haven't had a chance to replace it yet." I already really liked Magdalena, but I couldn't give her the reason why I'd lost my cell, not while we were pretending we were married out of a crazy attraction.

"Bishop," Magdalena raised her voice, and he looked around from where he was talking with Rook. "I want to take Eden shopping tomorrow. Could you drop her at our place around ten?"

His lips pursed, but after a brief hesitation he nodded. "I don't see why not. She bought a new wardrobe in Vegas, but I'm sure you can convince her to buy more."

There was nothing in his voice to indicate anything other

than wry humor. There was a distinct difference in the way he talked to his brother's girlfriend and how I'd heard him talk to anyone else. A gentleness, slightly less brusque than his usual tone. It made me question whether the reason he'd offered me marriage was the one he'd given me. Did he have feelings for his brother's girlfriend?

Rook patted his brother's shoulder and stepped closer to Magdalena, draping one arm across her shoulders, and tugging her closer into his side. "Ready to go?"

She smiled up at him, then looked back at me. "I'll see you tomorrow. Wear comfortable shoes. We're absolutely going to shop 'til we drop."

I couldn't stop a small laugh from escaping at the smile she flashed at me. "I'll definitely keep that in mind." I wouldn't be doing much shopping. I didn't have any money, but I wasn't going to tell her that.

A heavy weight settled across my shoulders, and I looked up at Bishop in surprise. His smile warmed my insides. It was the smile of a lover, of someone who had intimate knowledge of my body, and I had to remind myself it was an act, a means of convincing his brother that our marriage was real.

"I'm sure Eden will take great delight in spending my money." His hand squeezed my shoulder. "And I wouldn't have it any other way."

He sounded credible; I couldn't deny that. Was that how he'd been with the woman he'd had an affair with? I summoned up another smile, hoping it looked as intimate as the look he was angling down at me.

"Whatever I buy, I'll make sure you reap the benefits of it once I'm home." I injected a husky note to my voice and the spark of surprise that lit up his eyes made me want to laugh.

Maybe this was going to be a lot more fun than I thought.

"What time are you heading to Crosby's?" Rook's voice made Bishop turn his head, breaking our eye contact.

"Early. I told him we'd be sometime after lunch on Friday."

"So, you're not traveling on the day of the party?"

Bishop shook his head. "No. I don't want to rush around. We'll go Friday and leave Sunday morning."

"Alright. We're not getting there until Saturday morning. I'll call you when we're on our way."

He turned to the left, then stopped. "Welcome to the family, Eden."

"Thank you."

We moved to the right and walked across the parking lot to the car in silence. It wasn't until we were both inside and he was reversing out of the space that I spoke.

"They seem nice."

"They are."

"What excuse are you going to give Magdalena for tomorrow?"

He glanced over at me, a frown drawing his brows together. "Excuse?"

"For me not going shopping with her."

"Don't you want to go?" The frown deepened. "I thought you just said she was nice."

"She *is*."

"Then what's the problem?"

A short, sharp blast of a horn stopped me from answering immediately. Bishop raised a hand and waved at the sleek black sports car that pulled up beside us. I could see Magdalena through the window. I waved to her, and she grinned, waving back.

"The problem is this isn't a real marriage, and I don't have any money to spend."

"Part of the contract we signed was that I'd supply you with everything you needed to make this marriage look real to anyone outside of it."

"I don't think an impromptu shopping spree to buy clothes I don't need comes under that."

"It does if I say it does."

"Just like that?"

"Don't you want to go shopping? The clothes you bought in Vegas aren't going to be enough for the next month. You're going to need more practical things." His eyes were on the road as he spoke. "Anyway, it solves the problem of me having to take you shopping. I can get on with some work while you spend the day with Magdalena."

"The *day*? A couple of hours, you mean."

He laughed. "Magdalena doesn't have a lot of female friends.

Trust is hard to come by when you're living with a retired hitman, and his family all come with their own special set of skills that can't really be talked about with the general public. So, she's going to want to make the most of being with someone who she feels she'll be able to talk to without having to worry about what she's saying."

"That's crazy. He seems so nice."

"He's nice to his *girlfriend*. There's a difference. You should have met him before he got together with her."

I turned my head to look out of the window. "I imagine he was a lot like you."

"A lot like me," he repeated softly. "And what does *that* mean, exactly?"

"Well, you're not the friendliest person, are you?" I hid a smile. I had no idea what it was about this man that made me want to push his buttons and see him react. After everything I'd been through with Chester, I never thought I would even *think* about teasing someone, but here I was.

"I can be friendly when the situation requires it."

"But you prefer businesslike and bossy."

"It gets the job done."

I laughed quietly. "I guess it does."

23

Bishop

After returning to my house, I left Eden to go to her room and went into my office. While I'd agreed with Rook that we would wait until after Crosby's party to reach out to Knight, my gut was insisting I shouldn't wait.

I called his number while I poured a glass of bourbon and sank onto the chair behind my desk. He picked up on the second ring.

"Two calls in a week, Bishop? What's the occasion?"

"No occasion. Just checking in."

"Is that code for you've just got home from dinner with Rook, and he bitched about the fact I said I wouldn't come out to play tonight?"

"Something like that."

"You asked me to do some digging into Sandro Trebuni, so *that's* why I didn't come along."

"Have you found anything?"

"A number of things, actually."

"Care to share?"

"I'm still putting the pieces together, but it looks like he has links to one of the families, loose links but they're there, nonetheless. It's not something I want to discuss over an unsecured line."

"You think someone might be listening?"

"I always think someone is listening. What I will tell you is a deposit was made into one of his accounts for seventy thousand a couple of days before you came into contact with him. I'm currently tracing where that came from. Did you know your girl was living with a New York detective?"

"I did. My gut thinks that's who the money will lead you to. He's been hunting for her since they broke up."

"One of those types?"

I grunted and took a sip of bourbon.

"Something interesting did come up in my search …" His tone was light.

"Oh?"

"Seems Ms. Marshall got herself married yesterday and has a brand-new husband and name now."

"Oh, that."

"Right … *that*. Want to share with the class?"

"She wanted to hire me. I needed a way out of a jam. Seemed like a win all around."

"Yet the text I got from Rook suggests you told him you

married her because you fell madly in love."

"Magdalena was with him, and you know he won't keep things from her."

"So … you lied to him?"

"I prefer to say I managed the truth."

Knight laughed. "Of course, you do."

"Do you have anything else for me?"

"Nothing concrete. Give me a couple of days to chase down some loose ends."

"Okay. Onto the next reason for my call."

He sighed.

"You're doing it again, Knight."

"I'm fine."

"When did you last leave your apartment?"

His silence was answer enough.

"It's not healthy."

"Bishop—"

"You know it's not. We've done this before."

"It's healthy for *me*. It's better this way, believe me."

"You're turning into a recluse."

There's the hint of a smile in his voice. "That's not a bad thing. There are people out there. And we both know I don't play well with people."

"I'm coming to see you next week. You can give me your update in person."

"Only if I let you in."

"If you don't, I'll shoot your alarm system."

"You know that won't unlock my door, right?"

"I know, but it'll make me feel better."

"Fine. Give me a couple of hours' warning before you arrive, and I'll let you in."

"Excellent decision."

"Not like you're giving me much choice, is it?"

"You're the one who said you'd prefer not to discuss things over an unsecured line."

"Ahhh, using my words against me. That's uncool, Brother."

"I could have sent Mom over instead."

"That's just fucking uncalled for, Bishop."

I laughed. "Whatever it takes, Knight."

"Fine. Okay, I'm hanging up. I have shit to do."

"I'll see you in a few days."

He ended the call without replying. I set my cell down on top of the desk and stared down at it. My youngest brother had always had issues with being outside and around people. He went through phases where he would lock himself away from the world completely and the current signs were signaling that we were fast approaching one of those phases. Sometimes we were able to snap him out of it. Other times, we had to ride through until he was ready to reach out again. All we could do at this point was watch the cues and respond accordingly.

A soft tap at the door brought my head up.

"Come in."

The door swung open, revealing the redheaded woman I'd married. She was still in the clothes she'd worn for dinner but had removed her shoes. She stood in the doorway, one hand holding onto the handle.

"Is everything okay?" I asked when the silence lengthened.

She blinked, as though she'd been lost in thought, and took a step forward. "I just wanted to say thank you."

"For what?"

One shoulder lifted. "For hearing me in the trunk of the car. For not shooting me. For not tossing me out of the plane when I couldn't afford your fees."

"Don't think for a moment that if I didn't need something in return, I'd have taken your case." My words were clipped. A little voice whispered *liar* in the back of my head.

She nodded. "I know. But I'm grateful, all the same. And I … I just wanted you to know that."

"You're welcome." I pushed the power button on the laptop in front of me and waited for it to fire up.

"Bishop?"

I lifted my eyes and found her still standing just inside the room.

"I was going to make a hot drink before bed. I found some instant hot chocolate in the kitchen." A small smile curved her lips up. "And it's still within date. Would you like one?"

"A hot chocolate?"

She nodded.

"I don't really drink—" Her smile dropped away, and I sighed.

This clearly wasn't about a bedtime drink. "Okay, yeah, sure. Why don't you go and make them, and I'll meet you in the kitchen in a few minutes? I just need to check my emails."

24

Eden

I don't know what possessed me to offer Bishop a hot chocolate. I'd been sitting on the bed in my room, thinking about getting undressed and trying to sleep. But I wasn't tired, my mind was already thinking about spending the day with Magdalena, so I decided to see if there was anything to drink in the kitchen.

The hot chocolate had been hidden at the back of a cabinet; the seal still intact. I checked the date, recalling Bishop saying he hadn't been home in a while, and found there were still months before it expired.

Before I even considered it, I was outside his study door. I don't think I really expected him to accept my drink offer, but he did.

I was mixing the second drink when he walked into the kitchen. His steps were silent, and he moved with a grace I hadn't noticed before. Pulling out a chair, he sank onto it. I placed a mug in front of him.

He peered down at it, a look of almost confusion crossing his features, and then he looked up at me. "I can't remember the last time I drank hot chocolate."

I took the chair opposite him. "Well, you must have thought about it at some point, otherwise you wouldn't have it."

"Or my mother bought it, which is more likely." A smile flitted across his lips. "When we all lived at home, her favorite thing to do was gather everyone in the kitchen for a hot chocolate before bed. She claimed it would help us sleep." He chuckled. "We were a handful as boys. It took a lot to settle us."

"Considering the line of work two of you took, I'm sure she still thinks you're a handful now."

His lips twitched. "All three of us do jobs that wouldn't be considered *normal*. But then, so do our parents." He stopped then, frowning.

I sipped my drink and eyed him over the rim of the mug. "You sound like a very close family."

"We are."

"Is there anything I should know, for when we go to your friend's?"

He shook his head. "I doubt you'll need to have a conversation that requires such an in-depth knowledge of my childhood."

"That will make things easier. What about the woman I'm protecting you from?" I purposely kept my voice light.

One corner of his mouth lifted. "Susannah? Her husband is more dangerous than she is, but you should be prepared, just in case she decides to force a confrontation. I don't think she will. She omitted the fact she was married when we met. I have never had any dealings with her husband."

"You don't like the fact she managed to keep it from you." It wasn't a question. It was clear from his expression that he was angry with himself for not realizing he was involved with a married woman.

"I shouldn't have ignored my gut. It told me something was wrong and that I should investigate her before getting involved."

"Is that what you usually do?"

"In my line of work, you can't be too careful."

"I can't imagine having to investigate everyone I wanted to have any kind of relationship with."

"And look where that got you."

I couldn't hold back a flinch at his words. He wasn't wrong. Maybe if, instead of expecting a police detective to be a genuine person and taking him at face value, if I had been more cautious, I wouldn't have had to deal with the consequences.

I shook my head. "You know, even with everything Chester did and what I'm having to do now, I still think it's a sad way to have to live."

"Not everyone cares about your best interests, Eden. You, of all people, should know that."

"I know that. I *knew* that before Chester. But you can't run a background check on every person you interact with."

"You can't. *I* can."

"You know what I mean."

He lifted the mug to his lips and took a mouthful, eyes on me. His throat moved as he swallowed, and his tongue came out to sweep across his bottom lip. The action had me mimicking it with my own.

"I do know what you mean. It shows the difference in our lifestyles." He lowered his gaze to the mug between his cupped palms. "But when you deal with the kind of people I meet on a daily basis, lowering your guard and taking people as you find them could get you killed. There's no justification for me dropping the ball with Susannah. Like you pointed out, I allowed myself to be distracted by a beautiful woman. I guess that makes me human."

"Is that really why you offered marriage, though?"

"What other reason is there?"

"Magdalena." I bit my lip, waiting to see how he reacted to her name.

"Magdalena?" He repeated her name. With careful movements he set down the mug, then lifted his head to look at me. "You think I married you to stop Rook thinking I was lusting after his woman?"

"Aren't you? I saw the way you spoke to her. The way you treated her. You have feelings for her."

"I don't want to sleep with my brother's girlfriend."

"Maybe that's why you let yourself get involved with this Susannah."

"Eden—"

"Are you telling me you *don't* have feelings for her?" I pushed on. I'd seen what I'd seen.

"I *like* her, sure. But I'm not fantasizing about taking her away from Rook. Or trying to distract him by bringing another woman into my life."

"You treat her differently to anyone else."

"Not for the reasons you appear to be dreaming up." His voice was dry.

"Then why? You don't strike me as the kind of person who worries about other people's feelings. In fact, you've admitted as much already. So why are you so much different with her if you're not in love with her?"

"In love with—" He threw back his head, his laughter echoing around the kitchen.

I gaped at him. Of all the reactions I'd expected to my accusation, laughter hadn't been one of them. Denial, anger even, but humor? That I hadn't expected.

When his laughter faded, he returned his gaze to me. "Eden, I'm not in love with Magdalena. She's sweet, funny and, yes, she's very beautiful. But I can assure you, my feelings for her reside firmly in the realm of brotherly. I'm careful with her because she was kidnapped, hurt by those closest to her, and then taken as payment by a mafia son for her brother's transgressions. She is still getting over the trauma of it, and I don't want to set her back on her recovery."

"Oh." There wasn't much I could say to that.

Bishop nodded. "Oh, indeed. When I explained my reasons to you for requiring a wife, I was honest. There are no secret nefarious reasons behind it, other than a need to prove to Susannah that I have moved on and have no interest in rekindling anything we had."

"I'm sorry." I looked away.

"Don't be. I can understand why you considered it. But I swear to you, of all the things I've done in my life and all the things I will possibly do in the future, coming between my brother and the woman he loves is not one of them."

He stood. "Thank you for the drink." He smiled, eyes glinting with suppressed humor. "And the entertaining conversation. You should get some sleep. Magdalena will expect you before ten. I have some work to do. I'll see you in the morning." He took his empty mug to the sink and rinsed it before setting it on the drainer. "Leave your mug on the counter and I'll put it in the dishwasher in the morning." He walked to the door. "Goodnight, Eden."

BISHOP

25

Bishop

I spent most of the night working on the first stage needed to start the ball rolling on setting up Eden's new life, jotting down notes and questions I needed to ask her. Things like whether she would be comfortable changing her first name to something else or whether she would find that hard to adjust to, and if she had any preferences on living locations or jobs she'd be willing to take.

I also arranged to have a credit card assigned to her, under her newly married name, and added her to one of mine so she could use it for her shopping trip with Magdalena.

By the time the sun rose, I had everything I needed to start finetuning the details ready for when we went our separate ways. I crept out of the house at six and took a quick trip into town to the local grocery store which I knew opened early and picked up breakfast options.

By the time seven-thirty rolled around, I'd restocked the kitchen. There was no sign of Eden, so I walked up the stairs to her room. A gentle tap on the door received a grumbled response that caused my lips to curve.

Definitely not a morning person, then.

I ignored the random memory of how much she'd made me laugh over the last couple of days, or how anticipation of seeing her pout and mutter about me waking her up so early unfurled in the pit of my stomach.

"Eden, you need to get up," I called through the door.

The muttered response could have been an acknowledgement. It could also have been a request I leave her alone. I couldn't quite tell, and that gave me the excuse I needed to open the door.

"Up. It's a twenty-minute drive to Rook's place. I've been out and bought food, so you can have breakfast and coffee before we go."

"Coffee?" She surfaced from beneath the sheets, red hair falling like a fiery explosion around her face and shoulders. She shoved it away from her face with one hand, clutching the sheet to her chest with the other.

"So coffee is the key to waking you. I'll keep that in mind." I propped my shoulder against the doorframe. "You look like you slept well."

"I'd still be sleeping if *someone* wasn't insisting I get out of bed." She gave me a pointed look.

"You can sleep in once the weekend is over. If you want to be a lady of leisure for the next four weeks, you can. Call it a vacation before your life restarts. But today, you need to get up, eat, and then go shopping."

A serious expression crossed her face. "Is it safe?" Her voice was soft. "I mean ... he's found me everywhere I went so far. Why will it be different here?"

I pushed away from the doorframe and stepped inside the room. "Well, for one we're no longer in New York." I didn't tell her my suspicions about the guy who'd bundled her into the trunk of the car I'd found her in. "Two, Glenville is a small town. Strangers are noticed. And three ... if he turns up, I'll kill him."

I wasn't sure if it was my words or the matter-of-fact way I said them that caused her jaw to drop.

"You can't kill him, Bishop. He's a police detective."

"He won't be the first I've had to remove." I sat on the edge of the bed. "I'm not going to lie to you, honey, but there is every chance that's going to be the only outcome that works."

Honey? Where the fuck did *that* come from?

"You don't think he'll ever stop? Even if I change my name?"

"Like you said, he's a detective. That means he has resources available to him that most don't. Maybe he won't see through the new life I build for you. Maybe he will. We won't know for sure until we have you settled in place. I'm good at what I do. The best, in fact. But I can't guarantee someone won't see and recognize you and pass the information over to him. I'll do my best to place you somewhere that won't happen, but there's always that slim possibility. But don't worry about it right now.

Once you're situated, you will have access to a panic line, which is set up for anyone I hide, in case their new identity is breached."

"How many times has it been used?"

I smiled. "None."

She bit her lip, then nodded. "Okay."

"Good, then come downstairs and eat." I stood and walked out of the room, closing the door behind me.

I was placing bacon onto a plate when she finally appeared, dressed in a pair of jeans and a t-shirt. That incredible hair was still falling loose around her shoulders, and my fingers twitched with the desire to touch it and see if it was as soft as it looked. I squashed the urge, glaring at the frying pan until the temptation faded away.

What the fuck is wrong with you? It's the red hair. There was something about it that drew my attention.

"I wasn't sure what you'd want. Bacon, eggs or cereal."

"Bacon is good. And that coffee you promised me." She sent me a smile when I placed the plate in front of her. "Thank you."

"How do you take your coffee?"

"With milk and sugar, please."

"Coming right up." I poured two coffees, added milk and sugar to hers, then picked up my own plate and sat at the table, sliding one mug over to her.

"Rook lives on the other side of town. I'll drive you over. Magdalena doesn't drive, so one of us will drop you into town, and then pick you up when you're done." I reached for a box I'd placed on the table before she came down. "Here."

"What's that?" She took it from me.

"Open it. There's a cell phone and a credit card inside. My number, Rook's and Magdalena's are programmed into the cell. The credit card is in my name, but has you listed as a joint user. Use it for whatever you want to buy today. I have your own card coming, but it won't be here until Monday at the earliest."

"I don't think I'll need—"

"Yes, you will. It'll look suspicious if you don't spend any money, so make this lie easier for both of us by spending my money like it's your own."

She chewed on her lip for a second before nodding. "I'll keep my spending small."

I sighed. "Eden, I don't know if you've just not realized it yet, but money is not a problem for me. Buy whatever you like. There's no way you can max out that card in a few short hours in a small town."

"But—"

"But nothing. Call it payment for helping me out of the jam I've gotten myself into. There are not many people who find themselves with such an opportunity."

"Because you don't make mistakes."

"That's right. I *don't*. So, this fuck-up of mine has opened up a way for you to benefit. Use it."

Her lips parted, and I could see she was going to argue with me further. I cut her off before she even began to speak.

"Don't bother. If you don't do it, I'll call Magdalena and tell her to make sure you buy things."

She glared at me. I ignored her and turned my attention to breakfast. Eventually, she quit glowering at me and did the same, and we ate in silence. When our plates were both cleared, she rose to her feet.

"You did breakfast, so I'll clean up. Would you like another coffee?"

I leaned back on my chair. "Yes. Thank you."

She took my mug and moved across to the coffee machine, where it bubbled away quietly on the countertop. I let my gaze drift over her. She'd picked a t-shirt with fuller sleeves, hiding the bruises that covered her shoulder and stomach. I guessed leaving her hair loose also helped draw eyes away from the bruising on her face, although makeup would also hide most of it. The bruising was fading now and would be clear in the next few days, but not quick enough to hide it while we were at Crosby's.

I made a mental note to come up with a story on what might have happened to cause them and discuss it with her later.

"What?"

"Hmmm?" I refocused on her and found her facing me, one hand on a hip, mug of coffee in the other.

"You were staring at me."

"Was I?"

She set down the mug in front of me, and I caught a hint of the scent of berries.

"Do I need to change? You were frowning."

"You don't need to change. I was just thinking about how your bruises are clearing up."

Her gaze dropped away from mine. I stretched out my hand and tipped her head up.

"It's interesting, you know. Most women in your position have been beaten down to the point of fearing every shadow. For you, it brought out the fighter instinct. You're wary, but you're not scared. You should be proud of that."

26

Eden

"Have you always lived in Glenville?" I twisted on the car seat so I could look at the man beside me. "It seems an odd place for a hitman and a ... a ... what do you call yourself?"

His shoulders shook with his quiet laugh. "A fixer, I guess. I don't really call myself anything other than Bishop. But to answer your question, no. I moved here a couple of years ago. Rook joined me a short while later."

"What about your other brother ... Knight?"

"He lives out of town. I'll take you to meet him next week."

"Why did you pick here to live?"

He glanced over at me before returning his attention to the road. "It's quiet, out of the way. No commuter traffic. Perfect location for people who don't want to be noticed."

"Where are you from?"

"Not Glenville." That dry note entered his voice again. One that I was beginning to think was something he did when he wanted to see how I'd react.

I rolled my eyes. "Fine. Don't tell me."

The corner of his mouth curled up. "Montana."

"Could you be more specific?"

"I could."

"But you won't."

"I don't think it's relevant. I haven't lived there for a long time."

"You don't sound like you're from Montana."

One eyebrow shot up. "And how does someone from Montana sound?"

"Not like you."

"Maybe I've worked on my accent to hide my roots."

I tipped my head against the headrest and closed my eyes. "That would make sense. Is that what you did?"

He chuckled. "No, it was simply a natural byproduct of not going back there for twenty years."

"Do your parents sound like they're from Montana?"

"They're not from Montana. They just lived there when we were kids."

"You're not very forthcoming, you know." I opened my eyes and speared him with a glare. He wasn't looking in my direction so didn't notice.

"I'm not usually on the receiving end of questions. It's my job to do that so I can build you the perfect new life."

"But you've barely asked me anything."

"I wouldn't complain too much. Once I get started, you'll feel like you're in an interrogation with no means of escape. I thought we'd get through the weekend first, so you don't behave like you want to kill me every time I open my mouth."

"Is it that bad?"

"The last person I worked for threatened to cut out my tongue if I asked her another question. And that was *after* I delivered her to her handler."

"Handler?"

"Everyone has a contact, a handler who helps them adjust to the new life we've created. They stay involved in your life for the first twelve months, at least. But they're available beyond that if you need anything."

"What did you mean by delivered her?"

"Once my part is over, I hand you off to one of my associates and that's the last time we see each other. It's safer for both of us that way."

"I see." I drew breath to ask another question, only to be cut off.

"We're here." He brought the car to a stop outside a sprawling one-story house.

The door to the house opened as I climbed out of the car, and Magdalena walked down the steps to meet us. Her smile was wide and bright.

"I'm so glad you came. I wondered if you'd change your mind."

"I wouldn't have allowed it." Bishop passed us both and

walked inside.

She waved her hands, putting on a gruff voice. "Just like his brother. Do this. Do that. I won't allow this. Me man, you woman!" I wasn't sure which of the two men she was impersonating, but her attempt made me laugh, all the same. "Sometimes I swear I'll wake up and find myself barefoot and naked in a cave somewhere."

"Sounds fun. I could start looking to see if there are any caves for sale." Rook strolled through the door, hands shoved deep into the pockets of his trousers.

Magdalena turned red.

"I quite like the idea of you being naked all the time."

"Rook!"

He came to a stop in front of her and dipped his head to press a kiss to her lips. "You're the one throwing out ideas, Dall. I'm just working out how to make them happen."

Her hand slid up his chest to hook around his neck. I turned away to give them a moment of privacy, and my eyes locked with Bishop's, where he stood at the top of the steps, near the door. He crooked a finger at me, and I was halfway toward him before I realized I'd moved. The half-smile on his face told me he hadn't missed my immediate reaction to his unspoken command.

"Rook is going to take you both into town. I'm going back to the house. If you need anything, call me. When you're ready to come home, drop me a text or call. Give me half an hour to get there." One hand lifted, and he pressed a finger beneath my chin to tilt my head up. "I need you to hear this, Eden, so focus. If I didn't think you were safe here, I wouldn't let you go off alone, but hear me. If you feel unsafe, or *anything* feels off at any point, *call me*. Listen to your gut. Your ex is a police officer, and they have a long reach. Don't convince yourself that a bad feeling is just paranoia. Play it safe. If something feels suspicious, *treat* it as suspicious. Understand?"

I nodded.

"I need to hear you say it." There was a new tone to his voice. Firm, uncompromising, *forceful*.

"If something feels wrong, I'll call you."

His hand dropped and he inclined his head. "Good girl."

27

Bishop

Back at my house, I made coffee then headed into my study. I had to make a couple of calls. Opening the drawer of my desk, I took out a cell phone and switched it on. While that booted up, I logged into the laptop, and used my thumbprint to sign into an encrypted partition. My email software—custom designed by Knight—opened and emails downloaded. I wasn't sure how the system worked, but Knight had explained that every email sent to the address went via an encryption system, which could only be unlocked by my thumbprint. It made reading emails long and tedious, but it was better than someone gaining access to them. Thankfully, I didn't receive much correspondence through it.

Another click of the mouse opened the address book—also encrypted and accessible via my thumbprint—and I scrolled through until I found the contact details I wanted, then tapped them into the cell.

The call was answered on the third ring.

"What?" It was more a growl than a word.

"When are you going to answer a call like a normal human being?"

"When those normal human beings are less annoying."

I laughed quietly. "Are you busy?"

"That depends on how interesting what you're going to say next is."

I rolled my eyes at the typical Deacon response. "Rook said you helped him out with Magdalena's situation a few months ago. If you're not doing anything, I could do with your help."

"Oh?" Interest brightened his tone. "Tell me more."

"A new job I've taken. The girl is being stalked by her ex-boyfriend. He's a detective in New York."

"And you want me to warn him off?"

"No. I want to know his movements."

"Ohhh, you want me to stalk the stalker?"

"Is that interesting enough for you?"

"Yeah. I'll take Gemma. She could do with practicing her stalking skills. Do you want this under the radar or as part of the Disperser Security contract you have with us?"

"Let's keep it between us for now."

"You got it, Brother. Send me the information and I'll get us on a flight to New York."

"Thanks."

He ended the call before I could. Deacon was worse for small talk than I was, so I didn't take it personally.

With that organized, I turned my attention to my emails. Two of them were annual check-ins from existing clients, confirming that their identities were still safe, and they hadn't needed to send out a distress call. Not that they needed to tell me that, I'd have known the second any call was sent out, but it gave them a sense of security to be able to reach out.

The third email was from Knight, with a file attached.

I know I said we'd talk next week, but you need to see this. DO NOT CALL ME. Email me back after you've read it, and we'll discuss the next steps.

I clicked on the attachment. A window popped up asking for my thumbprint. I sighed, but pressed my thumb against the reader, waited for it to turn green, and then the file opened.

The first page was a short biography of Detective Chester Dulvaney. Two photographs were at the top—one of him in his uniform prior to being made detective, the second in civilian clothes, his badge hooked to the waistband of his pants.

I scanned through the bio.

Age: 36
Height: 6'1
Weight: 216 pounds
Eyes: Brown
Hair: Brown

`Distinguishing marks: Tattoo of the name`
`Eden, left arm. Small panther on left bicep.`
`Bullet wound scar, right shoulder.`

Both his parents were still alive and lived in New York. No siblings. No blemishes on his police record.

Nothing that hinted toward any kind of domestic abuse. I drummed my fingers against the desktop and scrolled down to the next page.

There were three photographs on this page. All women. One of whom I recognized.

`Three ex-girlfriends, Knight had written.`
`I'm assuming the last one is your girl.`

Beneath the photographs were three names, addresses and cell phone numbers. I dismissed Eden's information and looked at the other two.

Jessica Cantrell, aged 29, and Claudette Rafferty, aged 34. One relationship lasted less than two years, the other approximately ten. And it seemed that both women had moved out of New York shortly after the breakup.

I reached for my cell again and tapped in the first number.

"Hello?" A soft feminine voice answered.

"Ms. Cantrell?"

"Who is this?"

"I'm calling about Detective Chester Dulvaney. Do you have a moment to—"

She hung up.

28

Eden

"I didn't expect the mall to be this big."

Magdalena laughed. "Because it's on the outskirts of town, it's a prime location for people who are driving to the city. Close enough to town for us to visit, far enough away for commuters not to want to detour into Glenville." She linked her arm through mine and led me through the entrance doors.

"The mall is over three floors. The top floor is mostly food courts and restaurants. There are some great second-hand stores tucked away if you like that kind of thing."

"Do *you*?"

"I love digging through them. You never know what kind of hidden gem you might find. I thought we could start with clothes. Bishop demanded I make sure you have some casual wear ... And you might need a swimsuit for the weekend. Rook says Crosby has an indoor pool."

I shook my head. "I don't think I'll have time for swimming."

"Maybe, maybe not. It's best to be prepared." She nodded toward a clothing store directly ahead. "Why don't we go and take a look in there first. I want some new jeans."

And that started a shopping expedition that I hadn't really expected to enjoy but did. We embraced the 'shop 'til you drop' experience, and eventually collapsed, exhausted, at the nearest table when lunch time arrived, surrounded by bags. Most of them were Magdalena's, but she'd convinced me to pick up a purchase or two of my own.

"I'm starved!" Magdalena announced and waved the menu at me. "What do you want to eat?"

I scanned over the menu. We'd stopped at a well-known fast-food chain. "Burger and fries. It can be nothing else."

She laughed. "Agreed. And shakes. No adult drinks for us today. You stay here, I'll go place the order. Protect our bags with your life!"

I was still laughing when she came back a few minutes later.

"They'll bring it over." She dropped back onto her seat. "My legs are killing me. I don't think I've walked so much in months. Rook won't usually let me out alone."

I must have made some noise or expression of concern because she smiled. "Oh, nothing concerning." She waved a hand. "He worries, that's all. And when we *do* come shopping, he scares everyone with his growls and glares." She didn't sound upset by that. "But it's nice to get out now and then with another woman."

I couldn't argue with that. Shopping with her was a slice of normality I'd been missing for a long time. I let out a soft sigh and leaned forward to rest my elbows on the table and propped my chin on my hand.

"I've enjoyed today," I told her.

Her smile was bright. "Me too. I don't have many girlfriends. Actually, I don't have *any*. I used to have a roommate, but ..." her lips twisted. "I don't know. Things just went weird, and it's hard to trust people these days. But you're with Bishop, and he's not going to be with someone he can't trust."

"It's that simple?"

"Once you've been with him for a while, you'll understand what I mean. They ... all three of them ... are very protective of their family, their privacy, and everyone's safety. They don't bring people into their circle without very careful consideration of everyone else."

I bit my lip. It would be so easy to tell her the truth, but Bishop had insisted we behave as though our marriage wasn't a lie to his brother and his girlfriend.

"Thank you!" Magdalena sent a smile to the server who placed our food down between us and popped a fry into her mouth. "When Rook told me Bishop had got married, I must admit it surprised me. I've been with Rook for six months and Bishop has *never* introduced a girlfriend. I know he's not been celibate in the time I've known him. A man like him ..." She laughed. "Anyway, here you are! Not his girlfriend but his *wife*.

I'm not ashamed to admit that I'm dying of curiosity about how that happened."

I took my burger and fries off the tray and pushed a straw into the shake. "I'm not really sure myself," I said slowly. "I guess he just … swept me off my feet. He's very hard to say no to."

"That's the truth. Rook is like a freight train when he sets his mind on something. There's no convincing him otherwise. The only time the word *no* enters their vocabulary is when they're the one saying it."

I nodded. "That's exactly it. Bishop said we're getting married and that was that. There was no changing his mind."

"He must have fallen really hard for you." She paused for a mouthful of milkshake. "Rook wondered if it was part of a job at first, but after seeing you both together. It's obvious he has feelings for you. Rook said he's never seen his brother focus on a woman the way he did with you at dinner last night."

"He spent most of it talking to Rook. I don't think he was that focused on me." I laughed off her words.

She didn't.

"You weren't paying attention. Every time you moved or spoke, he looked at you. When you dropped your napkin and leaned down to pick it up, his hand covered the corner of the table to stop you hitting your head, without a single break in his conversation with Rook. A man who isn't interested doesn't watch for things like that, Eden." She ate another fry. "But I don't need to tell you that. You *married* him, so you must be just as obsessed with him."

"I—" I broke off when one of the roaming security guards stopped near our table.

My stomach flipped.

Was he looking at me? Did he recognize me?

My fingers inched toward the cell in my pocket, but his eyes swept over us both and moved on. My exhale was shaky.

"Are you okay? You've gone white."

I blinked and refocused on the woman opposite me. "I'm fine. I think all the walking this morning has caught up with me. Let's eat and recharge."

29

Bishop

The call to pick up Eden and Magdalena came earlier than I expected. I didn't expect to hear from either of them until closing time at the mall, but Eden texted around two to ask me to collect them.

They were standing outside the mall, bags stacked around their legs, when I pulled up. I popped open the trunk, then climbed out.

"Do you know whose is whose?" I asked as I placed the bags inside.

"We do," Eden replied. "Most of them are the shopaholic's over there."

Magdalena laughed. "You did your own fair share. Don't let her convince you otherwise. I'm beat. I'm going home to take a long soak in the tub, and then see if I can convince Rook to order takeout for dinner."

"I doubt you'll need to try very hard." Rook didn't like to cook, so it would be takeout or go to a restaurant, if Magdalena didn't want to cook.

"Probably not, but it's fun when he pretends to need convincing."

"I don't need that visual in my head, thank you."

She pulled open the door to the back seat and climbed in. Eden took the front passenger seat. I slammed the trunk closed and walked back around to the driver's side. "What about you? Do you want to order takeout tonight?"

In the middle of clipping her seatbelt into place, she looked at me. "We can do that if you like. Unless you want to go shopping to fill the refrigerator up, and I can cook something."

"Let's drop Magdalena off and decide then." I started the engine and pulled out into traffic.

The two women talked the entire way back to Rook's place, and I didn't really pay much attention to their conversation until Eden mentioned how she saw the same security guard three or four times in different stores. I turned my head.

"Did he say anything to you?"

"No." There was a hint of concern to her tone. Not strong enough for the other woman to pick up on, but I did. "He just walked by a few times. I think he was watching for shoplifters."

"Hmmm." I couldn't push for more details with Magdalena in the car, otherwise she'd want to know why I was so interested, so I filed it away to revisit once we were alone.

Rook was standing on the steps leading to his front door

when we pulled up, and he walked down to meet us and help Magdalena with her shopping.

"Did you buy the entire mall?" he asked, and she laughed. "You don't buy this much when I'm with you."

"I don't like dragging you around all the shops." She leaned against his side, sliding an arm around his waist. "I had fun today. It was a nice change."

"Me, too." Eden smiled. "We should do it again. But not for at least a week. I need to recover from today!"

The other woman laughed. "I have your number now, so we'll work something out." She turned to me. "I like her, Bishop. Don't mess it up."

"No, ma'am." I looked at Rook. "I'll see you at Crosby's on Saturday."

***

We opted to stop at the grocery store on the way back to my house. Eden didn't want to eat out and offered to cook. I was going to argue, until she told me that she'd spent the last year mostly living off fast food because she was never sure how long she could stay in one place.

Back at the house, I sent her to unpack her bags and took the groceries into the kitchen. I had no idea what she was planning to cook, but she had taken such obvious delight in walking around the grocery store and selecting various ingredients that I hadn't even thought to ask. I assumed it was going to be a pasta-based dish since she'd picked up a large bag of the stuff. I wasn't a fussy eater, so it didn't matter too much to me what she decided to prepare. I emptied the bags, put the groceries away and opened a bottle of wine.

She came through the door just as I poured the second glass. I slid it across the counter toward her.

"You look like you need this." I waved a hand toward the door she'd just come through. "Why don't we go and sit down in the other room and talk."

"Talk?"

I walked across the kitchen and rested my hand against the small of her back to urge her into movement. "You were worried about the security guard."

"I was just being overly cautious."

"What did I say to you?" I opened the door leading into the living room and guided her inside. "Take a seat."

Clutching her wine glass, she perched on the edge of the couch. "I know. But I honestly don't think he was doing anything other than his job."

"What did your gut tell you?"

She didn't answer me, burying her face into her glass.

"Eden."

Her shoulders moved as she sighed. "I caught him looking at me at least four times. But it didn't mean he was really watching me. We were laughing and being noisy. That would make anyone look." Her protest was weak.

I sat down on the coffee table in front of her. "Describe

him to me."

"Bishop—"

"Did you or did you not tell me that no matter where you went, your ex always managed to find you? Do you think it's only the police force he has contacts in?"

"But we're not even in the same state as New York! He can't have people all over the country."

"You'd be surprised at the lengths some people will go to in order to get what they want."

"So, what am I supposed to do? Will changing my name even make any difference? Do I need to get facial reconstruction surgery to escape him? Shave my head? Where will it end?"

From the mild hysteria in her voice, I decided it wouldn't be wise to tell her that many of my clients did just that. It was something I was planning to discuss with her closer to the time. I wasn't sure why I was putting it off, other than not liking the thought of her altering her appearance so drastically that she would never be recognized as the woman I'd found in the trunk of a car again.

"That's what you think I should do, isn't it?" Her question warned me I'd stayed silent for a beat too long.

"I didn't say that."

"You don't say a lot!" she snapped. "Is that why your fees are so high? Why you *laughed* when I told you I had fifty thousand and told me it wouldn't cover your costs? Do you have plastic surgery in the fine details as part of the fee?"

"For some people, yes," I admitted. "Those who are in real fear for their lives will take whatever step necessary to ensure their safety."

"*Real* fear?" She leapt on the words I used. "You think I'm not scared? That I think this is all some joke?"

"That's not what I meant." It wasn't like me to speak out of turn. "I *know* you're scared, otherwise you wouldn't be sitting here right now with my ring on your finger."

30

Eden

I stared at him. He sighed.

"This wasn't how I envisioned this conversation going." Reaching out, he took my wine glass out of my fingers, and set it down beside his. "I know you've been running for a long time, looking over your shoulder waiting for him to catch up to you. And it's natural at this point for you to question your instincts whenever anyone glances in your direction. But, from experience, if your gut says there's a problem ..." He canted his head. "Well, then there's usually a problem. Don't discount the instincts you've honed over the time you've been hiding from him. You have developed a heightened sense of awareness of everything around you."

"Then why did I end up in the trunk of a car?" The words burst out of me before I even considered them.

"I have my suspicions, but I need to speak to Knight first."

"You're not going to tell me what they are?"

"I think you've had enough stress for one day, don't you?"

"I'm not a child. I deserve to know what you know."

"Even if I don't have any proof?" He quirked an eyebrow. "Eden, you trusted me enough to sign a contract and marry me. Trust me on this as well. You've hired me to change your life. I can't do that if you don't do the things I need you to do."

"It was just a mall security guard."

"You're sure?"

"Yes." Or as sure as I could be.

He stared at me for a moment longer, holding my gaze, and then he nodded. "Okay. It's too early to eat unless you're hungry now?" I shook my head. "Why don't you follow Magdalena's plan? Go take a soak in the tub, relax for a while. Watch a movie, read a book, whatever you want to do."

"What are you going to do?"

"I have a few more calls to make. If you still wish to make dinner tonight, how about we aim for seven? If not, we can still order in."

There was nothing unreasonable about his suggestion and I found myself nodding along with his words. A soak did sound good. My arms and legs were aching from all the walking around. And I'd picked up some luxury bubble bath, at Magdalena's insistence. It would be silly to buy it and not use it.

He rose to his feet and caught my hand. When I stood, he handed me my wine glass. "Go and relax."

***

As much as I didn't want to admit it, taking a bath *did* relax me, and I almost floated back downstairs on a cloud of passionfruit, wearing the new pajamas I'd picked up. In the kitchen, I found an apron, looped it over my head and tied it around my waist. Next, I found the tomatoes, onions, and peppers, then rummaged through the drawers until I found a cutting board. I selected a knife from the block and got to work preparing dinner.

The open wine bottle was on the counter, so I topped up my glass, balanced the cell Bishop had given me against the side of it and put on some music. I was singing along to 'Gold and Bones' by Friday Pilot's Club and dancing on the spot when a voice intruded and made me scream.

"It's not every day I get to walk into my kitchen and find a redhead shaking her ass while wielding a knife so professionally."

The knife in question clattered to the cutting board and I spun around, one hand pressed against my chest. My heart was racing, and there was a hot burn in my cheeks.

"How long have you been standing there?"

Bishop pushed away from the doorframe and sauntered deeper into the room. "Long enough to wonder whether you've ever taken professional singing lessons."

The heat in my cheeks burned hotter. "No."

"I'm surprised. You have amazing range."

I narrowed my eyes. "Are you mocking me?"

He paused in the middle of pouring the last of the wine into his glass. "Not at all. You have an incredible voice."

"Oh … umm …" I turned back to the cutting board and focused on the peppers I'd been cutting.

The music cut off abruptly and a tanned hand moved into my line of sight to take the knife from me.

"Let me guess, Dulvaney criticized your singing. Told you to stop, that you were terrible, and …" His hands curved over my shoulders and turned me to face him. "Maybe he said you were scaring small children or making his ears bleed. And eventually you stopped. Stopped singing, stopped talking, stopped being heard. Because it was easier, *safer*."

I reached back to grip the countertop and lifted my head to meet his watchful gaze. "Is this part of your new life adjustment plan?" I cleared my voice, hating the way it trembled.

"Maybe. Or I'm just trying to figure you out." He placed the knife beside the half-cut pepper. "You're a mess of contradictions, Eden. In all the ways I expect you to be broken, you're not. The damage he did to you was far more subtle than visible bruises and broken bones. You hide it well. So well, I almost missed it." He lifted a hand and curled a lock of my hair around one finger. "But I see it now."

"I don't … I don't know what you're talking about." Nerves dried my lips, and I licked them.

"You don't?" His gaze slid from mine to the hair wrapped around his finger. "Then allow me to explain it to you." He frowned, released the curl, and dropped his hand. "The abuse didn't start when he first hit you. It'd been going on from the day you started dating him. You just didn't realize it. It was verbal and mental. Subtle and ongoing. A criticism here, a comment there. Until he had molded you into behaving in a certain way. You told me that over time you lost contact with friends. Why do you think that was? Did they start falling away before the first time he raised a hand to you? Do you remember?"

L. ANN

31

Bishop

She didn't reply. Just stood there staring at me out of huge green eyes. I took a step back.

"I spoke to an ex-girlfriend of Dulvaney's earlier. She had some interesting things to say."

"Interesting how?"

I moved across the kitchen and took another bottle of wine out of the wine cooler. "Would you like another drink?"

"Interesting *how*?" she repeated.

I took the corkscrew out of the drawer and twisted it into the cork. "Claudette Rafferty was his childhood sweetheart. They dated throughout school and got engaged shortly after they graduated." The cork came free with a soft pop, and I filled both glasses. "She ended the relationship after ten years because she discovered he was cheating on her with other women. When she finished it, he refused to leave her alone. Turned up at her workplace, sent her flowers, begged for another chance, and promised never to do it again. The usual. She was fortunate in that she had her family surrounding her, and they closed ranks and cut him off. For quite a while, there seems to be no relationship details for him with anyone else. Then he met Jessica Cantrell." I took a sip of wine. "Ask me how they met."

She frowned at me, then turned back to the peppers she'd been chopping when I walked in. "Where are you going with this?"

"Humor me."

She savagely chopped the pepper for a minute or two. "Fine. How did they meet?"

"Her car broke down and he just happened to be nearby to give a helping hand." I leaned against the countertop. "Now ask me what happened to her car."

"What happened to her car?"

"She blew a tire." The chopping stopped abruptly. "And who showed up just in time? Detective Dulvaney. He stayed with her until a tow-truck arrived, then asked her to dinner. Is any of this sounding familiar?"

"You know it is."

"She was moved into his place within three months, because his apartment was closer to her work, and it made sense since she was there more often than not."

Eden's face drained of color.

"I doubt she's the only one. She's just the one I know about. I'm sure if I dig deeper, a pattern will form, but I don't think I need to. Knowing that both of you have the same story already tells me the pattern is there."

Movements stiff, she crossed the kitchen and poured pasta into a pot of boiling water. The chopped onions and garlic were dropped into another, and she stood over it while they cooked.

"That's not everything. What else did you find out?"

Clever girl. She was paying attention.

"Jessica left him after he broke her wrist. He repeated the same things that he'd already tried with Claudette. Pleaded for a second chance, told her it was because he loved her and wanted the best for her. That she'd made him so angry because she couldn't see what he saw, and it frustrated him. She changed jobs twice and moved four times. Then he suddenly stopped, and she didn't hear from him again. Care to take a guess when that happened?"

A plate of diced chicken, and the peppers and tomatoes joined the onions and garlic.

"Eden?"

Her head turned toward me. "When he met me."

"That's right. And the cycle started again. But even that isn't the most disturbing part." I pulled out the printout of the information Knight had sent me. Specifically, the photographs of Eden and the other two women. I unfolded it and held it out. "Take a look."

She took the sheet from me slowly and lowered her eyes. She frowned.

"Is this a joke?"

"No."

"He clearly has a type."

"This is beyond a type." She screwed the sheet up into a ball and launched it across the room. "What kind of psychopath is he?"

"One who never got over his childhood sweetheart, it seems. And is desperately trying to recreate her in the women who came after. Jessica and then you. And when you didn't meet the requirements, he grew angry and lashed out."

"That's insane."

I nodded. "Borderline at the very least."

She turned off the pasta and drained the water. The pasta was mixed with the other ingredients and then she turned down the heat.

When she next looked at me, her eyes shone with tears.

"Eden?" I took a step toward her.

She shook her head. "I'm okay. I just … I should feel guilty for that other woman. I *should*. But all I feel is relief at knowing that it wasn't my fault. I wasn't to blame."

32

Eden

I blinked, trying to stop the tears from falling. I didn't even know why I wanted to cry. I hadn't cried for so long.

"Eden, feeling relieved is understandable. Thinking you were to blame is something he instilled in you. But it was *never* the truth. The blame has always been his."

I found myself wrapped in warmth and lowered my head to the solid chest in front of me. Sucking in a deep breath, I inhaled the woodsy scent of his cologne and let the thud of his heart slow my racing thoughts. When I was certain I had myself under control, I lifted my head.

"Thank you."

"You're welcome." His voice was grave.

"I think we should eat." I sniffed and stepped away. "Before it burns."

"We can do that." I was thankful for the way he accepted my

need to stop talking about Chester and do something practical. He didn't question me, just opened the cabinet containing plates and put them on the counter beside the stove. "I'll set the table."

I nodded. "Okay, good. Thank you."

I portioned the food out onto the plates, then carried them across to the table. Bishop topped up our wine glasses and we sat down to eat.

"Who else will be at your friend's tomorrow?" I ate a mouthful of pasta.

"I'm not sure who's arriving tomorrow. Us, obviously. Crosby and Dana. Rook and Magdalena are arriving on Saturday."

"Will everyone be staying with them?"

"I doubt it. A lot of their friends live close by and will go home after the party."

"What about Susannah?"

He chewed and swallowed, then took a sip of wine. "Susannah and her husband will be staying at the house."

"Does Crosby know about … well, you know."

"No. I'd like to keep it that way if I can. David is a client of Crosby's, and I don't want my error in judgment to cause problems for him."

"Is she likely to say anything?"

He shook his head. "Not if she has any sense. Her husband is not known for forgiving people who betray him. And his wife sleeping in a bed other than his would be the ultimate betrayal."

"What would he do to you?"

"Kill me."

I choked on my wine. "Even though you had no idea she was married?"

"It's how it looks. Another man touched his wife. He won't be able to let that go."

I twirled my fork through the pasta. "So, we really need to convince both of them that there's no way you'd stray from me."

His lips twitched. "Something like that."

"We need a cover story for how we met."

"And for the bruises on your face."

My smile faded. "And those."

"Don't let it spoil the fun you can have this weekend." Something sparkled in his eyes, and the difference in the man opposite me from the one who had threatened to shoot me was immense. He was more relaxed, more willing to smile, to laugh.

Had it only been a few short days? It felt like I'd already known him a lifetime.

"How did we meet, Mr. Chambers?" I summoned back my smile and pointed my fork at him.

"Well …" He leaned back on his chair. "It was a dark and stormy night in Dallas."

"I'm pretty sure it was neither dark nor stormy."

"We could go with the truth instead if you like. I found you in the trunk of the car, hogtied and desperate. Nothing like a good kidnapping to heat the blood … and here we are."

I laughed. "We can't tell people that!"

"Why not? I'm fairly confident that Stockholm Syndrome is why so many people stay locked in unhappy marriages. They convince themselves they're in love, but really, they've just been conditioned to think what they're feeling is love."

"That's quite a cynical outlook on marriage. Are your parents divorced?"

"No, they're very happily married. Keyword being *happily* there. What about yours?"

"I grew up in the system. I don't know anything about my parents."

"Which would have made it even easier for Chester to separate you from people. The more I hear about him, the more obvious it becomes that he's a predator and uses his position of authority to make hunting his prey easier."

33

Bishop

She fell silent, eyelashes dropping to veil her expression while she ate. I didn't push her to talk. She'd heard a lot of information over the past few hours and needed time to process it. I needed her to be in a clear headspace to sell the story that we were happily married over the weekend, so I focused on my own food and let her process.

When she pushed her plate away and reached for her wine, I placed my silverware down and straightened in my seat.

"How about we met in Dallas? A chance meeting which resulted in you offering me a seat on your friend's plane back to New York. We hit it off during the flight and made plans to see each other again. And things progressed from there."

I considered it. "Enough of the truth with a vagueness that will be easy to expand on." I nodded. "That works."

"Okay, good." She toyed with the stem of her wine glass.

"Ask me."

Her gaze lifted and met mine. "Ask you what?"

"Whatever has you fidgeting and nervous."

Her tongue came out to sweep over her lips. "Your friend is expecting you to bring someone. A girlfriend. Someone you're intimate with."

"I did inform him I'd have someone with me, yes."

"He'll expect us to share a room."

"I imagine so."

She took a swallow of wine. "And a bed."

Ahh, that's the problem.

"You have nothing to worry about. I am in perfect control of my actions and won't leap on you."

Her cheeks turned red. "I wasn't trying to—"

"I know. It's a valid concern, but I assure you, you'll be as safe as you would be with a wall between us. There's no way I can ask for separate rooms without raising suspicion. But you have my word, the only time we need to present as a married couple is when people are watching. I doubt even that will be necessary. The mere fact I've brought someone with me should be enough to tell people it's serious."

"Because you don't introduce your girlfriends to your inner circle of friends and family. I remember." She tilted her wine glass, looking down at the red liquid inside. "Don't you think that might make it more interesting to people? They'll be watching to see how you behave with someone you're intimate with because they've never seen you in that situation before."

"Maybe. But they're hardly going to expect us to be fucking on the dining room table or anything." I purposely chose that phrase to see her reaction.

It didn't disappoint.

Her face turned as red as her hair and her jaw dropped, lips parting on a startled gasp.

"There we go. If people start to question the validity of our relationship, all I need to do is whisper something crude in your ear. That reaction should change everyone's minds."

"You wouldn't!"

"I might. I'm not ruling anything out. I need to send a message, but it also needs to be subtle and unoffensive." I reached for the wine bottle. "Would you like some more?"

She shook her head. "Not if you want me to wake up and be pleasant to people tomorrow." She stood. "In fact, I'll clear up and then I think I'll go to bed. I get the feeling tomorrow is going to be a long day."

"Leave it. You did the cooking, the least I can do is clean up."

She hesitated, hand hovering over her plate.

"Eden, leave it."

"Are you sure?"

"I'm more than capable of cleaning up after a meal. Go and get some sleep. Like you said, tomorrow is going to be busy, and you're going to need your wits about you."

***

I was in the kitchen drinking coffee when Eden wandered in, still in her pajamas. She tossed me a sleepy smile on her way to the coffee machine, and I watched her over the rim of my mug as she moved around making a drink, putting bread into the toaster, and taking out a plate, butter knife and spread.

She finally settled onto a chair, one leg bent with her knee leaning against the table, while she nibbled on the toast.

"How did you sleep?"

"Good, thanks. I set an alarm, so you didn't have to come and wake me." She sipped her coffee. "Do you have an overnight bag or something I can use to pack clothes for the weekend? I looked in the closet but couldn't see anything."

"I do. I'll get it out for you."

"Thank you." The wedding band on her finger caught my eye as she lifted her mug.

"We should add an engagement ring."

She blinked. "What?"

I nodded toward her hand. "A man in love would have bought you an engagement ring before the wedding ring. We'll fix that on our way to Crosby's."

"You don't need to. We could just say I left it here."

I shook my head. "That won't work. No. We'll leave a little earlier than I planned, and detour to a jeweler I know."

"Do you really think it's necessary?"

"I do. Susannah will be looking for any hint at all that things aren't what they seem. We don't want to give her any cause for suspicion."

Her sigh was soft. "Okay. It just seems like a waste of money."

I shrugged. "Call it a necessary expenditure." I drained my coffee and stood. "I need to shower and change. We'll leave at eleven. I'll put the overnight bag on your bed."

34

Eden

I looked down at the six-thousand-dollar ring adorning my finger, then over at the man driving the car. Bishop was focused on the road ahead, one hand resting loosely on the steering wheel. His other arm was propped against the window opening on the door.

"You're staring." His focus didn't change.

"You just paid six thousand dollars for a ring like it was a plastic toy from the Dollar Store."

"Appearances are important. Can't introduce you as my wife to Crosby with a cheap reproduction on your finger."

"Yes, but *six thousand dollars*, Bishop. There were cheaper rings."

"I didn't like the cheaper ones."

"Does it matter? It's not like I'll be wearing it for long, anyway."

"It matters." He turned his head toward me briefly, brows dipping into a frown. "Don't you like it?"

"What? No. Of course I like it. It's beautiful. That's not the point."

"What *is* the point?"

How could he not see the problem?

His gaze returned to the road when I didn't reply. "If you don't like it, we can swap it out for something else on the way back."

"I *do* like it. I just don't understand why it was necessary. There were so many cheaper options."

"I told you. I didn't *like* the cheaper options."

"Is that your reason for replacing the wedding band as well?" My eyes dipped back down to the gorgeous blue stone surrounded by diamonds set on a platinum band. He'd taken the cheap wedding ring he'd bought in Vegas off and replaced it with a new one that matched the engagement ring.

"They needed to match." He glanced over at me again. "Anyway, these suit your coloring more."

I gaped at him.

"Suit my coloring?" I managed to squeak out eventually.

His hand left the steering wheel briefly to wave toward me. "The aquamarine of the stone goes with your hair, and the platinum band suits your skin tone."

"Did the jeweler tell you that? You know he was just trying to get you to spend more money, don't you?"

"No, I told *him* that. I haven't gotten to where I am in life by being unaware of the things around me, Eden."

How could he be so casual about a wedding ring set that cost more than I'd earned in six months?

"You can always sell it once we're done. It'll give you a nice little extra in your savings."

"What savings?"

"The savings you'll have when our contract is done and it's time for you to move on."

I stared at him, then shook my head. He made it all sound so simple.

"How do you know what colors suit red hair and my skin tone, anyway?"

One corner of his mouth curled up. "I have eyes."

The car turned into a long circular drive which led up to a large two-story house. Bishop parked in front of a fountain and cut off the engine.

"Time to get into character, Eden. Are you ready?"

I took one last look at the rings on my finger, the weight of them felt unnatural. I ran my thumb over the bands.

"They're never going to believe us."

"Of course, they will. Stay there." He climbed out of the car and walked around to open my door. Holding out a hand, he helped me out. "What you have to remember is that people see what they expect to see."

"You really believe that?"

"Shall I prove it to you?"

Instead of backing away to let me pass, he moved closer, crowding me against the side of the car, then dipped his head to my ear. His hand lifted and he trailed his fingers along my jaw.

"All anyone looking our way right now sees is a man taking a moment to adore his woman after a long car journey."

His lips brushed against my ear, and I shivered.

"It really is that easy to convince people." He pressed a finger beneath my chin and tipped my head up. "All you need to do is look at me as though I'm your entire world, and I'll behave like I will burn down the world if that's what it takes to make you smile."

His mouth hovered over mine. "What do you think, Songbird? Do you think you can do that?"

I couldn't move my eyes from his. There was a gleam in the darkness of his gaze, and I felt like I was tumbling, *drowning*, with no way to stop my fall. My stomach was doing backflips, my lungs were tight with the need to suck in oxygen. Every nerve ending beneath my skin had activated and my entire being was focused on the thumb brushing over my lip, back and forth in a hypnotic rhythm.

"Put the girl down, Bishop!" A new male voice broke the spell he was weaving around me, and I jumped.

Bishop's head tilted slightly, and his eyes tracked over my face, his expression shifting into something new and then he laughed softly and turned to meet the man coming toward us.

"Crosby!"

I remained where I was, leaning against the car, and willed my heartbeat to slow down. My vision wavered in and out as I sucked in one shaky breath after another.

What had just happened? What was that?

35

Bishop

I moved to meet Crosby, leaving Eden behind me. I needed to put some distance between us because … *what the fuck had just happened?*

"You're late." Crosby's voice snapped me out of my thoughts, and I took the hand he was holding out and shook it.

"Traffic." The lie came easy.

"Typical. Ma held off lunch because she couldn't let her beloved Bishop go hungry until dinner."

I snorted. Crosby's mom had become like a second parent during my teen years, and I'd spent a lot of time at their house. Crosby often joked that she loved me more than him.

"I better go in and say hi to her then." I started to walk past him, then stopped and turned. "This is Eden."

At her name, her head jerked up and she pushed away from the car to join us.

"Hi."

Crosby's eyes swept over her, pausing at the way she was twisting the rings around her finger.

"Bish? Do you have something you'd like to tell me?"

I reached out my hand and drew Eden closer, linking my fingers with hers. "I'm officially off the market."

My friend frowned at me, then turned his attention to Eden. "Pleasure to meet you, Eden." His eyes darted back to me. "I feel like there's a story here, and you're going to tell me the whole thing after lunch."

"There's nothing much to tell."

"She's wearing a wedding ring. I think there's a pretty big story to tell."

"I met her. I married her. The end."

"Just like that?"

"Just like that."

His lips pursed. "I see. You know my mom isn't going to be satisfied with such a short retelling, don't you?"

I released Eden's hand and draped my arm across her shoulders. "And I'll be happy to tell her all about it. *After* we've unpacked and eaten. Or are you going to make us stand out here all day?"

My friend frowned at me for a second longer then smiled. "Where are my manners? Let's go inside. Welcome to Frogsmore, Eden. I'll get one of the staff to come and pick up your cases to take to your room. Come and meet the family."

Fingers lifted to find mine where they rested on her shoulder. I gave them a small squeeze. This was it. The moment we would discover if we could pull off the lie. If we couldn't convince Crosby's family that our marriage was real, there was no way Susannah would swallow it.

We followed Crosby inside and along the hallway to a spacious room where three other people were seated at various spots. An older woman was seated on an armchair, knitting needles on her lap and a ball of wool beside her. She tossed it to one side when we walked in and jumped up.

"Bishop! There you are." Her arms opened. "Come here and give me a hug."

I dropped my arm away from Eden and stepped into the woman's waiting arms. "Tallulah." My voice was warm, and I pressed a kiss to her cheek. "You look as gorgeous as ever."

"Stop flirting with my mom," Crosby grumbled from behind me. "Mom, Bishop brought a date."

"*What?*" Tallulah gave me a gentle push. "Where? Bishop, introduce me to the girl!"

Laughing, I turned and crooked a finger at Eden. "Tallulah, this is Eden."

"Let me look at you, girl." Crosby's mom stepped in front of me. "Oh my gosh, look at you!" She threw her arms around the unsuspecting redhead.

Eden's eyes were wide as she looked at me over the other woman's shoulder, and clumsily hugged her back. "Hi."

"You must be important if Bishop brought you here."

"They're not just dating, Mom." Crosby drawled. "Check out the rock on her finger."

"You'll pay for that," I mouthed to my friend, who smirked at me.

Tallulah released Eden and grabbed her hand. "Married? When?" She spun to face me. "Bishop, you got married and didn't tell anyone?"

"It was a spur of the moment thing." I shrugged.

"When?"

"Couple of days ago. We didn't want to take away from Crosby's weekend."

Tallulah waved a hand. "That's tomorrow. Today we celebrate you and your new bride. Come, my dear, we need to plan a small party for tonight."

"What? No, really—" Eden finally found her voice.

"Yes, really!"

I accepted the glass of bourbon Crosby handed to me. "You knew exactly what you were doing," I murmured.

"She's been driving Dana crazy. Now she can focus on your girl and give mine a break for a couple of hours." He slapped my shoulder. "I can't wait to hear how she stole your heart."

"It was unexpected." I ignored Eden's look of panic and lifted my glass toward her as Tallulah dragged her out of the room.

"I hope you're not expecting to see her for the rest of the day, son." Crosby's dad boomed out from across the room.

"She'll be fine. I wouldn't have brought her if I didn't think she could handle you all." I took a sip from the glass. "Where's Dana?"

"Her agent called. She went into the study to argue with her. They're trying to get her to fly to France for a photoshoot the week before the wedding."

"She doesn't want to do it?"

"Fuck, no. She told them weeks ago that the entire month was off-limits. Doesn't stop them from trying though. I'm not worried. She'll get her own way. She's too sought after for them not to work around her." He slung an arm over my shoulders. "Come on. I'll show you to your room, and then we'll go rescue your wife." He chuckled. "That's going to take some getting used to. Do Rook and Knight know?"

"They know. Rook has already met her. I haven't seen Knight yet. I'm taking Eden to meet him next week."

36

Eden

I was dragged out of the room and tugged along the hallway. The woman—Tallulah—had my hand in a firm grip and wasn't listening to my protests that I should stay with Bishop. I had a moment of panic when I lost sight of him, but then a tall blonde woman stepped out of a side door and the woman holding onto me stopped.

"T, what are you doing?" Her blue eyes shifted to me. "I don't think we've met before."

"No, I—"

"This is Eden. She's with Bishop," Tallulah spoke over me. "Dana, *Bishop* got married!"

The blonde's lips parted, but she recovered quickly, and her gaze returned to me. "*Bishop?*"

"Why does everyone say it like that?" I couldn't help but burst out. Magdalena had reacted in a similar way.

"Because Bishop can barely tolerate people. I'm not even sure he's human. Maybe a robot." She held out a hand. "I'm Dana."

"Crosby's fiancée."

She smiled, and I took her hand in mine in a quick handshake. "That's right." She glanced at Tallulah. "Where are you dragging her to?"

"They didn't have any kind of celebration after they got married. I thought we could throw together a small gathering this evening, before your main event tomorrow."

Dana turned to me. "Are you okay with that?"

"I don't ... I mean ... If Bishop wants to ... I just ..." I didn't want to offend either woman, and I wasn't sure how to get across how I felt without upsetting them. My babbling trailed off.

Dana sighed. "Tallulah, you didn't even ask her, did you?" She gave me a smile. "My soon-to-be mother-in-law loves celebrating everything for her boys, of which Bishop is one. She gets carried away."

"I never thought Bishop would ever settle down," Tallulah said.

"That's because he's not human, like I told you. Did you find a magic key to turn on his emotions?"

I wasn't really sure how to respond to that, so I said nothing.

"I'm sorry, that was rude of me. I like Bishop. It's just a surprise to have him not only bring a date, but a *wife*." She touched my arm. "I bet you haven't even been here long. Did Tallulah drag you away before you had a chance to unpack?"

The older woman's cheeks turned pink. "You must think

I'm awful. I was just so excited about Bishop finally meeting someone. That boy deserves to be happy."

Dana laughed. "Bishop is no more a boy than Crosby is."

Tallulah tutted. "They'll both always be boys to me."

"And that's why we all love you so much." Dana reached out to kiss her cheek, then hooked her arms through both of ours. "Come along. We'll show Eden to her room, then find the boys and have lunch."

Voices reached us when we stepped onto the upstairs landing.

"Crosby must have brought Bishop up," Dana said.

She moved ahead, leading the way to a door on the right. The two men stood just inside. When Dana walked in, they stopped talking.

"Darling." Crosby wrapped his arm around Dana's waist and pulled her close so he could kiss her. "I see you found Bishop's surprise."

"Hardly a surprise. I told you I was bringing a plus one." Bishop's voice was dry.

"A plus one, Bishop. Not a wife."

"What difference does it make?"

"Apparently none to *you.*"

"Boys, stop bickering," Tallulah cut in. "Bishop, we'll be serving lunch on the terrace in thirty minutes. Eden, we'll chat about a small get together this evening for a small celebration over lunch, okay?"

I wanted to beg Bishop for help, but he had turned away and

was looking out of the window. Instead, I nodded.

"Okay." What else could I say? I was pretty sure Crosby's mom was a force of nature and nothing was going to stop her from doing what she wanted, anyway.

Dana patted my arm. "Trust me, it's easier not to argue. Why do you think we're having a party tomorrow night when we've been engaged for a month and have already set a wedding date?"

"Don't pretend you're not looking forward to the party." There was nothing but affection in Tallulah's voice.

"Of course, I am. I love parties. It's why you're the perfect mother-in-law, and I'm going to make the perfect daughter." Dana laughed. "Anyway, let's leave them to get settled. I'm starving. If you don't let me eat food soon, I'm not going to be responsible for my tantrum."

"Heaven forbid." Crosby gave a mock shudder. "We'll see you downstairs, Bishop."

Bishop lifted a hand but didn't turn. Less than thirty seconds later, the door to the bedroom closed and we were alone.

"Your bag is on the bed."

My eyes jerked to the bed. I'd been avoiding looking at it, but at his words I couldn't look anywhere else. It was large, taking up the center of the room, and made from dark wood. A dozen or so pillows of different sizes covered the top end of the mattress. The overnight bag with my clothes in was at the opposite end.

I unzipped it and flipped it open. "Is it worth unpacking or ..."

"No point in living out of the case. Take whatever space you need. There's a bathroom through that door." He turned and jerked his chin to the wall on the left. His gaze swept over me. "You look a little shell shocked."

I straightened and took a breath. "You didn't warn me they'd be so ... so ..." I shrugged.

"I didn't want to scare you. You were already panicking about whether we could pull this off. Telling you what the family is like would have made it worse. This way your surprise at Tallulah's behavior was natural."

"It could have gone horribly wrong."

His lips curved up. "Wasn't going to happen. You're everything Tallulah would want in a woman for me."

"What does that mean?"

"Don't worry about it. I'm going to take a quick shower and change before lunch." He shrugged out of his jacket and tossed it onto the bed. "You might want to do the same. Lunch can last a few hours, and usually comes with an abundance of alcohol."

And with that, he left me and walked into the bathroom, closing the door behind him.

37

Bishop

I made sure the door was locked—not that I thought Eden was going to break in while I was showering—and stripped out of my clothes. It was only when I was under the hot spray of water that I realized I'd forgotten to bring a change of clothes into the bathroom with me.

Fuck. Where was my head at?

Forgetting something so basic was not what I did.

Nor was marrying a girl because she couldn't afford your fees. Or taking her to your best friend's house to meet his family.

I tipped my head back and let the water wash over my face.

Did you really need a wife to prove to Susannah that it was over? Be honest, Bishop.

No, I didn't *need* one, but it was definitely going to make the situation easier.

Not coming to the engagement party would have made the situation easier. Crosby didn't expect you to show up anyway. So why did you?

I reached for the shower gel and squeezed some into my palm.

Of course, I was going to accept the invitation to his engagement party. Crosby is my friend. He'd do the same for me.

You'd told him you were going to be out of town, working.

Plans changed.

Yeah, they did. Your plan changed from taking the next job, to marrying a redheaded girl on the run from a detective ex-boyfriend. And what the fuck is that all about, anyway? What happened to avoiding anything that brought you into a possible face-off with law enforcement that you hadn't orchestrated?

I shook my head, spraying water everywhere.

It's just business.

When did you last buy a client a six-thousand-dollar ring, a new wardrobe, give her your name and a promise to protect her at cost to yourself?

I'm entitled to one good deed during my lifetime.

This isn't a good deed. This is a midlife crisis. You've seen Rook settle down with Magdalena and you're scared you've left it too late for yourself. You're worried that you're going to die alone, with only your brothers to mourn your passing.

I scrubbed a hand down my face.

What the actual fuck? I loved my life. I hated people invading my space. I worked hard to get to where I was. Why would I regret anything?

Who said you regretted anything?

The question whispered through my mind.

"I *don't* regret anything." I said the words out loud.

The voice didn't reply, and I finished washing without any more disquieting thoughts. Cutting off the water, I stepped out. A pile of towels was on a shelf to one side. I dried off, wrapped one around my waist, and rubbed my hair with another as I walked across the tiled floor to the door.

"Oh!" The startled gasp brought my head up, and my eyes connected with wide green ones.

"Sorry. I forgot to take a change of clothes with me. Just came out to grab them." I rounded the bed and opened the case I'd left on a chair next to the dresser. Taking out a clean pair of pants, white shirt, and underwear, I tucked the bundle under my arm and turned back to the bathroom door.

Eden's eyes were on me the entire time as I made my way back inside. Even with the door shut between us, I could *feel* her gaze. Heavy, hot, burning between my shoulder blades.

I should have warned her before I walked out. She'd been surprised, shocked even. It was no wonder she'd stared at me.

I pulled on the clothes, folded the towels, and threw open the door.

"All yours."

"What?" She blinked at me.

"The bathroom."

"Oh!" Cheeks scarlet, she almost leapt from the bed and ran past me into the bathroom, only to reappear seconds later.

"Clothes!" She snatched up a neat pile of clothes she'd obviously picked out while I was inside the bathroom and disappeared again.

When she came out ten minutes later, she was pink-cheeked, fully clothed and her hair had been tamed into a thick braid. Makeup free, the bruise on one cheek was visible, but the split in her lip had almost healed.

"I need to put on some makeup," she said, clearly seeing the direction of my gaze.

"You don't need it."

"I'd rather people didn't stare or jump to the wrong conclusions."

"No one will think I did it. But you're right, they'll probably ask what happened."

"And we have no story to tell. Somehow, I don't think telling people the truth will make them believe this whole marriage thing."

"They would if I was Knight. He can be a bleeding heart at times."

"Not you, though." She rummaged through her case and pulled out a makeup bag. "Dana said you might be a robot posing as a human."

She passed me and walked back into the bathroom. I followed her.

"A robot?"

She smiled at me through the mirror as she applied her makeup, hiding the bruise on her cheek. "I guess you're not very emotional. From our own interactions, you're very ... logical, I guess. You don't let emotion rule your decisions."

"I can be emotional."

"When was the last time you cried?"

"Cried? I don't remember. Probably when I was a kid."

"Maybe that was a bad example. When were you last in love?"

I frowned.

"The fact you can't answer the question tells me everything I need to know." She turned to face me.

"Look what being in love did to you." I touched her cheek with one finger. "It brought you nothing but pain."

"Is that what happened to you?"

38

Eden

His frown deepened and his hand dropped away. "Of course not."

"Have you ever been in love?"

"My job doesn't really allow for personal attachments." He turned away and moved toward the door. "Are you ready to go down?"

"Were you in love with Susannah? Is that why you need to show her you've moved on?"

His shoulders tensed and he stopped.

"Bishop?"

He swung around. "You know this isn't a real marriage, and we're alone right now? You don't need to behave like you're jealous of any past relationships."

"That's not what I'm doing. But I think I need to know. If she was ...*is* in love with you, then who knows how she's going to react to my presence. I think it's only fair to give me the chance to be ready for anything she might throw at me."

He stared at me, and I thought he was going to leave without answering, but then he nodded.

"Okay, that's fair. No, I wasn't in love with her. I'm *not* in love with her now. Could that have changed? Maybe … if I hadn't found out she'd been lying to me for months."

"What about her?"

"I doubt it was more than scratching an itch for her, either."

"I don't believe that. If it was, then you wouldn't need me to play the part of your wife."

"I told you why."

"Because of who her husband is, I know. But if you really thought she had no feelings for you, then surely, she wouldn't care about the break-up, and you wouldn't need to have a wife."

"Interesting theory."

"You don't agree?" I stepped around him and walked back into the bedroom.

"I don't think it matters whether I agree or not, you appear to have it all worked out in your head."

I picked up a pair of flats and sat on the edge of the bed to put them on. "You never did answer my question, though."

In the middle of putting on his jacket, he paused. "What question?"

"Whether you've ever been in love."

"I'm pretty sure I did answer that."

"No, you just said your job doesn't really allow for personal relationships. That's not a no."

"I've never been hit by the urge to confess my love to a woman, other than my mother. How's that?"

I straightened, then stood. "Good enough."

He didn't move from where he stood, staring at me, brow furrowed.

"What?"

"You seem different today. Less unsure, more confident."

His words hit me … *hard*. I *felt* different. I hadn't really noticed, but once he mentioned it, it was obvious. I felt like the person I'd been before I met Chester. Before everything happened. Before I had to leave my entire life behind and run from a man who wouldn't leave me alone.

It was a feeling that had been building slowly over the past couple of days. Ever since Bishop took me to his home in Glenville.

I felt … *safe*. I didn't have to look over my shoulder in case Chester or someone he knew was watching me. I didn't have to go to sleep wondering if I'd wake up and find him in my room.

For the first time in months, I felt almost relaxed.

I smiled. "Maybe I'm just embracing my role. From the way everyone reacted to your announcement, you wouldn't marry a woman who was scared of her own shadow."

"No, I wouldn't." He held out his arm. "Ready to convince everyone we're destined to be together?"

I curled my fingers into his sleeve. "I do believe I am, Mr.

Chambers."

***

There were four new faces sitting on the terrace when Bishop led me outside. Two women and two men. Crosby stood when we arrived.

"I was wondering whether we'd need to send a search party. Grab a seat. Everyone, this is Bishop and Eden. Kennedy and Saul Hauptman. Kennedy is a friend of Dana's. David and Susannah Fletcher. David and I go way back." His eyes met Bishop's. "I look after his money the same way I do yours."

Bishop's arm flexed beneath my hand, but to his credit, that was his only reaction to hearing Susannah's name. David Fletcher unfolded himself from his seat—a big broad-shouldered man with a beard that covered half of his face—and I held my breath as he came toward us. He stopped and thrust out a hand.

"I've heard a lot about you, Bishop." His voice was a deep rumble. "Your line of work is interesting; I'd like to chat with you about it sometime."

"Sure." Bishop's voice was relaxed as he shook the other man's hand.

"Help yourself to food." Crosby jerked his chin toward a line of tables where an array of finger foods had been spread out. "The bar is also open." His hand waved to another part of the terrace where an actual bar was set up. Dana and Tallulah were standing beside it.

"Eden, honey, come over here!" Tallulah called.

I let my hand drop from Bishop's arm. "Nice to meet you," I said to David. "If you'll excuse me, I'll go and get us both a drink. What would you like, *darling?*"

Bishop didn't miss a beat. "Bourbon, neat. Thanks, sweetheart."

I nodded at David and walked over to where Dana and Tallulah waited. Dana handed me a drink.

"What is it?"

"Mimosa. You're going to need it, and more. I'd half-hoped Susannah wouldn't come but—"

"But?"

Her lips twisted. "I shouldn't speak ill of Crosby's friends, but that one is trouble."

"Can you really call David a friend?" Tallulah murmured, her back to the men. "I'd call it more of a mutually beneficial acquaintanceship. He's a man Crosby couldn't afford to insult by *not* inviting him. I'd hoped he would come tomorrow and not stay, though."

I glanced between them. "You don't like them?"

Dana sipped her drink. "Susannah tried to sleep with Crosby. Not liking her doesn't even come close to how I feel."

"Oh."

"Keep an eye on her, Eden. She'll come after Bishop."

"I don't think I have anything to worry about." She clearly had no idea that Bishop had already been in a relationship with Susannah, and I wasn't about to tell her.

"No, but it won't stop her from trying. It's a game to her. I'm not convinced David isn't aware of it, either. They're a strange couple."

L. ANN

39

Bishop

My jaw clenched when Susannah's laugh reached me. We'd been on the terrace for an hour. The food and drinks were flowing, while everyone chatted. Eden was still standing at the bar with Dana and Tallulah, and every so often I would see her smile in response to what the other two women were saying. I couldn't deny I was curious about their conversation, but they didn't look in my direction at all, so I couldn't attract her attention and find out.

Susannah laughed again, loud and abrasive to my ears. She was drunk. It was obvious from the slur in her voice as she talked to Kennedy and Saul. I kept my gaze firmly away from her and focused on the conversation between Crosby and David.

"—so, when I found out, I fired him. An employee flirting with my wife is completely unacceptable."

"Is 'fired him' code for something else?" Crosby lifted his

glass to his lips and took a sip.

David's smile didn't reach his eyes. "Let's just say it's unlikely anyone will hire him again."

I knew his type. Like I'd told Eden, his preferred method of removing someone was to kill them. I didn't doubt for a second that the employee he was talking about was dead.

"Do you have a high employee turnover?" I asked, and three sets of eyes turned to me. "If you fire everyone who looks sideways at your wife, I imagine you do."

"I *don't* fire everyone, just the ones who cross the line."

"And what *is* that line?"

"You seem very interested."

I shrugged. "I'd prefer not to get a bullet to the head if I say hello or pass her the salt over dinner."

He stared at me for a long second, then threw back his head and laughed. "I like him, Crosby. You were right. He is very dry."

Crosby sent me a curious look. "He is. And secretive."

"Secretive?" David's sharp gaze turned to me.

"My friend here told me he was bringing a plus one. That alone would be a first for Bishop. But it wasn't just a date he brought." Crosby shook his head. "No, Bishop here turns up with a *wife*."

"I didn't realize I had to inform you of every decision I made."

"You don't. But as your *friend*, I thought I'd at least get an invite to your wedding."

"It was spur of the moment. We didn't invite anyone."

"You're not a *spur of the moment* kind of person, Bishop, so you'll forgive me if that makes me extremely curious about your relationship."

My gaze shifted to Eden, drifting over the thick red braid hanging down her back. "She's rare. Seeing her smile makes me ..." I frowned and switched my gaze back to Crosby. "It makes me happy."

Silence greeted my words, then Crosby cleared his throat. "That's how it is for me with Dana." He patted my shoulder. "I don't blame you for locking that down fast. I should have done it a lot sooner myself." He turned to look at where the two women stood with his mother. "They seem to be getting along well."

"They do. It's a quality I've noticed about Eden. She seems able to connect to people. Like I said ... she's rare."

"Spoken like a man in love." David chuckled. "Make the most of it, boys."

"And, on that note, I think I'll go and remind my fiancée that I exist." Crosby lifted his glass to us both in a silent toast and walked across the terrace to the women.

"I think I might do the same," I said into the silence. "Eden never did bring me that drink she promised. If you'll excuse me ..." I inclined my head toward David and followed Crosby.

When I reached Eden, I tweaked her braid. "Did you forget about me?"

She twisted around at my voice. "No, of course not."

"Then what happened to my drink?"

She turned pink. "Oh! Maybe I *did* forget about you ... just for a minute."

"Sixty of them. You've been over here for an hour." I accepted the drink Crosby handed to me and tipped it toward her. "I could have died of thirst."

The pink in her cheeks deepened. "I doubt that would have happened."

"Maybe that was the plan." I eyed her over the rim of the glass. "Let me die. Become a widow. Steal all my ill-gotten gains."

She gave a startled laugh. "It *wasn't*, but now it's definitely an option."

"Better watch my back."

"That's okay, I'm happy to watch it for you." Her eyes widened and she bit her lip.

I tilted my head to one side. "Been watching my back, Songbird?"

"Hard to miss it when you come out of the shower half naked." She buried her face into the glass she was clutching.

I wasn't sure if I was meant to hear her muttered words or not, but I couldn't resist responding. "Maybe you should have joined me."

She choked on the mouthful of drink she'd taken. Everyone around us laughed. Tears streaming from her eyes as she spluttered, she pointed at me.

"You shouldn't have said that."

"And miss out on your reaction? I have to disagree." Teasing her was apparently an unforeseen bonus to our pretend marriage.

"Don't torment the poor girl," Tallulah chided, but she was

smiling as she looked at us both.

"I apologize. I'm very sorry." There was no hint of contrition in my voice.

"No, you're not," Eden said.

"No." I reached out and stroked a finger over her lips. "I'm really not."

40

Eden

Bishop flirting hit me in a way I didn't expect. He'd warned me that we needed to behave like a newly married couple who were in love, but I hadn't really believed he could pull it off. He was cool and detached and logical. But here he was ... *flirting* with me ... and I liked it.

I didn't think for a second he meant it. It was part of the lie. A requirement listed in the contract I signed, but it didn't matter. It felt nice. It felt *good* not to be on the receiving end of criticism for what I was wearing, how I spoke, what I'd chosen to eat or drink. It didn't matter that he was probably carefully considering each phrase and every move he made to have the most impact on the people around us. It just felt good not to be on high alert or need to second guess everything I did, and that fact alone relaxed me more than all his assurances over the past couple of days had.

I don't know why I trusted him, but I did. Actually, that

wasn't true. I trusted him because every promise he'd made so far, he'd kept. Was I foolish for thinking that would continue? Maybe. But although Chester had taken a lot of things from me, I refused to allow him to take away my belief that people could be *good*.

"What about you, Eden?"

I blinked, my name bringing my attention to the people surrounding me. "I'm sorry, I didn't hear you."

Bishop's laugh was soft beside me, and I glanced up at him. "Dana wanted to know if you would like to join her, Kennedy, and Susannah tomorrow. They're having a spa day."

"Oh, I … I'm not sure. I wouldn't like to impose."

"You wouldn't be!" Dana said. "If Magdalena is here before we go, we'll drag her along as well."

"I could text Rook and make sure they're here on time," Bishop offered.

Dana clapped her hands. "Do that!" She turned to me. "You're such a good influence on him. Maybe it is possible to housebreak him, after all."

Bishop snorted and pulled out his cell. His fingers moved rapidly across the screen, and it chimed a few seconds later. "Done. They'll be here in time for breakfast."

"Fantastic. We're leaving at eleven."

"I don't think—" I tried again.

"Nonsense! I made a block booking weeks ago, and said I wasn't sure what the final number would be. We've hired the entire place out, so we'll have it to ourselves for the day. We can be pampered ready for the party."

Bishop's arm slid around my waist, and he squeezed my hip. "You'll enjoy it. It's only a five-minute drive from here, on private property."

I had the impression that he was trying to tell me it would be safe without coming out and saying so. I nodded.

"Thank you, then. I'd love to go."

Dana gave a delighted laugh. "That's settled then! We should probably go and join the rest of our guests. We've ignored them for long enough, and Kennedy looks like she's in desperate need of rescuing."

**

As the afternoon wore on, everyone settled onto chairs and loungers on the terrace, and the conversations between the men turned to their various businesses, while Dana and Kennedy entertained with stories of the various photoshoots they'd done and the people they worked with.

The sun set, music played softly through hidden speakers, and no one showed any signs of moving. Drinks were topped up, and all the food from lunch had been removed and replaced with fresh platters by silent staff.

Bishop had discarded his jacket at some point, tossing it over the back of his chair. He sat forward, sleeves rolled up to his elbows, and he was deep in conversation with Saul. I was curled up on a seat beside him, feet tucked under my legs, half-listening to Dana and Kennedy, but mostly just enjoying the opportunity to relax without worrying that Chester might show up. When this was over, and I moved on to, hopefully, a new life, no matter how it turned out, I knew I'd look back on these days with appreciation.

"Tell me," Susannah's voice cut through the low murmurs around me. "How exactly did you two go from dating to marriage so quickly?"

I lifted my head and sought out the other woman. She was sitting directly opposite, eyes pinned to me.

"I guess when you know, you know."

"And you *knew* he was the one that quickly, did you?" Her voice was sharp.

I forced a laugh. "Goodness, no. I thought it was insane to get married. But … when Bishop decides on a course of action … Well, there's no swaying him from it." That wasn't a lie *at all*.

"How did he propose?"

"You don't want to hear about that." My protest was soft.

"Of course, we do." The other women joined in with Susannah, not realizing her reasons for asking. At least, I assumed they didn't know.

I risked a glance at Bishop. He was still sitting forward, forearms resting on his knees as he looked at me. When our eyes met, he smiled but didn't speak.

"Do you want to tell them?" I asked him.

His eyes glinted. I was certain he was laughing at me. His

next words confirmed it.

"Have at it, sweetheart. I know how much you like telling the story."

Apparently, Bishop had a penchant for causing trouble beneath that cool exterior.

41

Bishop

I fought to keep my features blank while I watched various expressions cross her face. The way it went from confusion to shock to annoyance. Her eyes narrowed, and I found myself looking forward to hearing whatever tale she spun to explain our marriage.

"I don't know how well you know Bishop," she began, and I smothered a laugh.

She knew *exactly* how well Susannah knew me, and the way the blonde's jaw tensed, I would have hazarded a guess that she was questioning how much Eden knew about my past. About *her*.

"But he's a very decisive person." Her eyes held mine. "And when he sets his mind on something, there's very little that can dissuade him from it. So, I doubt it'll come as a surprise to those of you who know him well when I say Bishop never asked me to marry him. He *told* me. He announced it on the flight from

Dallas to New York. We were getting married. He'd arranged everything. All I had to do was pick an outfit and show up." She gave me a sidelong look. "And when a man who buys you a ring because it compliments your hair and skin tone wants to marry you … you don't say no, do you?"

Three of the women sighed happily. Susannah stared at Eden's hand.

"Can I see your ring?"

"Of course." Eden held out her hand. The gemstone caught the light, sparkling on her finger.

"Very pretty. Unusual." Her voice was clipped.

"Just like Eden," I said and stood. "Unique, beautiful …" I stooped and scooped the unsuspecting woman up into my arms, then sank back down onto my chair, settling her onto my lap. "And mine." My arm tightened around her waist when she struggled to put space between us.

Her eyes flew up to meet mine, tongue sweeping over her bottom lip. She laughed, the sound a little shaky. I stroked along her cheek with my free hand.

"From the second I laid eyes on her, I knew she was mine. I knew I had to move fast otherwise she'd get away, so I didn't give her the chance to say no."

"I always said that when you finally fell, you'd fall hard." Tallulah said dreamily. "I'm so happy for you both."

"Thank you."

"I would never let a man dictate to me whether we should

get married or not. David had to ask me three times before I said yes." Susannah's voice was strident.

Eden tensed on my lap. I lifted my hand and ran my fingers down her arm lightly.

"Relax," I murmured close to her ear.

"And she didn't like the ring I bought her. She's had three different ones since we got married," David said.

Eden's hand rose and she looked at the ring. "I love my ring and wouldn't change it for the world. I know how much thought Bishop put into choosing it, and it shows how much he cares. I never felt like I had no choice. He might have told me we were going to get married, but he would never have forced me if it wasn't what I wanted." There was a fierce note to her voice.

I dipped my head and hid my smile against her shoulder. When my lips brushed against her skin, she shivered.

"Cold?"

"A little." But she was lying. It was there in her eyes. The shiver was because I touched her. I just couldn't tell if it was out of fear or something else.

"I think we're going to call it a night. It's been a long day, and it's going to be even busier tomorrow." I lifted Eden off my lap and stood, taking her hand. "Goodnight, everyone."

She didn't argue and let me guide her back indoors without comment. When we reached the bedroom and I closed the door, she turned on me.

"I don't like her." The ferociousness was still in her voice.

"What on earth did you see in her?"

I quirked a brow. "Do you really want me to answer that?"

She scowled. "You're not that shallow."

"How do you know that?"

"Because … you're just *not!*" She spun away, pulling out the tie holding her braid in place. Threading her fingers through her hair, she stalked across the room. "You pride yourself on being able to read people. Yet you didn't see how awful she is. Was it the sex? It can't have been *that* good, surely?"

I barked a surprised laugh at her words. "I admit, we didn't do a lot of talking when we were together."

The look she angled at me over her shoulder sent a sharp, unexpected, stab of guilt through me.

Why the fuck should I feel guilty for a relationship I had before I even knew Eden existed?

Why the fuck did I want to apologize for it?

And why the actual fuck did her disappointment in my actions bother me?

42

Eden

I took my pajamas out of the drawer, grabbed my toiletries bag, and crossed to the bathroom.

I had no idea why the thought of Bishop with Susannah annoyed me so much. It wasn't like he hadn't told me about her. The relationship was the *entire* reason I was married to him in the first place. It was the *only* reason he'd agreed to help with my problem.

So why was I furious with him?

Because he gave the impression of being someone who wasn't swayed by someone offering him sex. And that was the only reason I could think of for why he'd been with Susannah.

I slammed my toiletries bag onto the countertop.

It certainly wasn't for her personality. The woman was as horrible as her husband.

"Eden."

My eyes snapped up and met his through the reflection of

the mirror.

"I don't want to talk to you."

He propped a shoulder against the doorframe and folded his arms. "I can see that."

"Then why are you still in here?"

"When I met Susannah, I was on my way back from another job. It had been … taxing. The woman I'd been relocating was the daughter of a mafia boss, and there had been threats made against her life. I was almost killed twice. Once was an attempt by the woman herself. I was tired and giving serious consideration to retiring. I met Susannah in the bar of a hotel. She was funny and easy to be around. She made no demands on my time, caused no drama, and it worked for me."

"Why are you telling me this?"

"Because I don't want you to think my head was turned by a beautiful woman and the promise of sex. It was a no-strings relationship … until it wasn't. The last time we met up in a hotel in Nevada, she forgot to remove her wedding ring. I ended it. She caused a scene. Screaming at me for wasting her time … and I realized that the woman she'd been when we were together wasn't who she really was. It was an act. I'm not sure what her end game was, but I don't think it was marriage and babies."

"Is that what you were imagining?"

He snorted. "Absolutely not. Like I said, it was a no-strings thing. But I do wonder if she wanted something. I don't believe for a second she had any intention of leaving her husband, but I did begin to question whether the timing of our meeting wasn't as accidental as it appeared."

"Dana and Tallulah know she has affairs. They think her husband knows about them."

"I don't think he knows about me. I'm pretty good at reading people and—"

I laughed at that. "Not as good as you think, otherwise you wouldn't have ended up in this situation, would you?"

He inclined his head. "Point taken. In normal circumstances, I can read people then. Maybe I just didn't *want* to see the truth."

I continued to clean the makeup off my face, eyeing him through the mirror.

"You told me that you were coming to this party and that's why you wanted a wife. But Crosby said he hadn't expected you and you didn't confirm until you said you were coming with a plus one."

He remained silent.

"You lied to me."

Still nothing.

"When did you really tell him you were coming?"

"After the wedding."

"You arranged everything once you knew you had someone who you could use to put between you and Susannah." My voice was flat.

"I saw an opportunity that benefitted both of us."

I spun to face him. *"You lied to me."*

And that's when it dawned on me *that* him lying was the reason I was so angry with him. Not for falling for a woman like Susannah, but because he'd *lied* to me.

And it was a *stupid* lie. One that didn't even matter or change the circumstances around us. But it was a lie. And I'd heard enough lies to last a lifetime.

He pushed away from the doorframe and moved deeper into the bathroom. "I did, and I'm sorry." His apology, unlike the last one, sounded sincere.

"How many other lies have you told me? Can I trust the contract you had me sign?"

"You can trust it."

He didn't ask why I was making such a big deal out of a tiny white lie—because that's all it really was. He didn't accuse me of being dramatic or try to turn it around on me. He stood there and let me yell at him, even though I had no right. We weren't really married. I wasn't a jealous wife, and he hadn't cheated on me or lied about anything big.

I turned back, found my toothbrush and I squeezed toothpaste onto it.

"Promise me that during the rest of the time we're married you won't lie to me again. No matter how small or stupid it is."

He didn't even hesitate. "I promise."

43

Bishop

After giving her my word, I retreated and closed the door, leaving her in privacy to finish getting ready for bed. When she finally came out, hair loose around her shoulders and dressed in pajamas, I took her place in the bathroom, stripping out of my clothes and pulling on a pair of black pajama bottoms, so that Eden didn't freak out any more than necessary over sharing a bed.

She was under the sheets when I came out. I left my clothes in a neat, folded pile on a chair, flicked off the light and climbed into the opposite side of the bed. I settled onto my back, one hand tucked beneath my head and stared up into the darkness. The mattress bounced as Eden shifted beside me, bounced again, then a third time. I turned my head, squinting until I could make out her shape and watched as she twisted to face me, then away from me.

When she showed no signs of settling after five minutes,

I took matters into my own hands. Rolling onto my side, I stretched out an arm, wrapped it around her waist and pulled her back against my chest.

She froze.

"Stop fidgeting and go to sleep."

"What are you doing?" Her voice was a croaky whisper.

"Ensuring I don't get tossed onto the floor due to your desire to use the bed as a trampoline."

"I'm not—"

"Yes, you are. Relax and go to sleep."

She lay stiff and silent, and I could feel her heart hammering a rapid beat beneath my palm. I propped my head up on my hand and looked down at her.

"Eden—"

"I'm sorry for yelling at you." The words were a soft whisper in the darkness. "I just ... it bothered me more than I realized."

"I noticed that." My voice was dry.

Her body shook with a quiet laugh, and she relaxed against me. "I overreacted."

"No. Given the circumstances, I don't think you did." My thumb stroked a small circle on her stomach. "How about this? I give you blanket permission to call me out any time you think I might be lying to you."

She twisted to face me. "You promised you wouldn't lie."

"And I won't, but if you *think* I might be, then I want you to say so." I tweaked a lock of her hair. "Just so I can tell you you're wrong."

She laughed again. "You're funnier than I thought you'd be."

I pressed a finger to her lips. "Don't tell anyone. If you let that slip, then people might want to spend time with me. And we can't have that."

She turned away again and burrowed down beneath the sheets. "Goodnight, Bishop."

"Goodnight, Eden."

**

I woke up to a warm weight pressed against me. Eden had changed positions during the night, and closer investigation told me she had one leg thrown across mine and an arm wrapped around my waist. Her head was resting on my shoulder, and I could feel her steady breaths against my throat.

It was early. My alarm was set for seven and it hadn't gone off yet. I carefully reached out with one hand and groped around for my cell. Lifting it, I checked the time.

Four fifty-six.

I was wide awake. There was absolutely no chance of me going back to sleep, so I eased out from beneath the sleeping woman, and rose to my feet. I'd take a walk down to the kitchen and grab a drink. Maybe check my emails. That way I wouldn't disturb her.

I grabbed a t-shirt on my way past and pulled it over my head as I walked out of the door. The house was silent as I made my way down the stairs, along the hallway and into the kitchen. I'd spent enough time here over the years to know where everything was kept, and I had the coffee machine working within a few minutes.

While that brewed, I sat at the table and flicked through emails on my cell. There was nothing of note and it felt strange not to be working on *something*. When was the last time I took a vacation? I couldn't remember. I enjoyed working and keeping busy.

The coffee machine beeped to say it had reached temperature and I stood and made a drink.

I liked this time of day, especially if I was somewhere surrounded by people. I enjoyed my own company, the silence of early morning. It gave me a chance to prepare for the day ahead and think about things that might come up.

I laughed quietly to myself.

Not that I could have predicted Eden crashing into my orbit.

I built up a picture of her in my head—of the way she'd looked last night, eyes spitting fire at me—and compared it with the woman I'd met in Dallas.

Just a few short days together and she was already showing an inner strength that she must have been hiding for a long time. I liked that she felt safe enough to show who she really was, but a part of me questioned whether it would last once I set up her new identity or would she go back to constantly looking over her shoulder and waiting for someone to find her.

The scrape of shoe against tile distracted me from my thoughts, and I turned my head.

"Hello, Bishop." Susannah entered the room and took the seat opposite me. "I knew you'd be up early. Can we talk?"

44

Eden

I woke up alone. Bishop's side of the bed was cold, which suggested he'd been up for a while. Not necessarily a bad thing. I wasn't sure how I would feel waking up with him still in the bed. Last night had felt weirdly intimate and I was sure at one point I'd woken up cuddled close to him.

I rolled onto my back. Light was shining through the curtains, but it didn't feel late. It still felt early. That peacefulness that comes when most of a household is still asleep. Groping for the cell Bishop had given me, I checked the time.

Six-thirty.

Ugh ... *too early*.

But I was awake. And I was thirsty. So, I rolled out of bed, threw on the jeans and t-shirt I'd worn yesterday and crept downstairs. I'd shower and change before we were due to go out. Until then, if anyone else was up, they'd have to make do with my scruffy morning self. Hopefully, I'd find Bishop in the kitchen already so I wouldn't feel too awkward about helping myself to a drink of some kind.

Voices drifted along the hallway as I stepped off the bottom stair, and I tilted my head listening. One female, the other definitely male. But both were too low to make out the words. It was only when I reached the kitchen door that I recognized the male one as Bishop's. He sounded irritated—which wasn't unusual. I was sure irritation was his default setting.

I pushed open the door and stepped inside … and stopped.

A familiar blonde was seated facing the door, one hand resting on Bishop's arm as she leaned forward. The top of her robe was gaping open, and I had a direct line of sight down it to her more-than-ample cleavage. Her eyes lifted and met mine, and a slow smile curved her lips up.

The random thought that her makeup was perfectly in place flitted through my mind, followed closely by a sharp stab of anger at the way her red painted fingernails were stroking a circle over Bishop's arm.

I shoved it away and pasted a smile on my face. There was *no way* I was going to let her get a reaction from me.

I switched my gaze from her to Bishop, who had his back to me.

"Good morning." My voice was bright.

Bishop didn't react. He didn't jump, didn't pull away, just turned his head, and smiled.

"You're awake early." Nothing in his tone suggested he was

surprised or upset by my appearance.

He held out his hand, took mine when I was near and tugged me close enough to wrap his arm around my waist and pull me onto his lap. I followed his lead, looping my arms around his neck and pressed a kiss to his cheek.

"I woke up and you were gone. I guessed you came down to make coffee." Susannah could take *that* however she pleased.

"You guessed correctly."

I glanced over at Susannah, who made a show of removing her hand from Bishop's arm. I didn't comment on it. Instead, I let my head drop against Bishop's shoulder.

"I'm surprised I woke up. You wore me out last night."

He didn't miss a beat, dipping to kiss the top of my head. "I wear you out most nights."

Susannah's eyes narrowed. "Well, it was nice to catch up. I better go before David wakes and wonders where I am."

"We wouldn't want that." I kept my voice bland.

Her gaze jumped to me. "Yes … well …" She pushed to her feet. "I'll speak to you later, Bishop."

Bishop didn't respond. Instead, he lifted me off his lap and stood. "I'll make you a coffee. Do you want breakfast?"

I shook my head. "Too early for food." I took the seat Susannah had vacated and watched as Bishop moved around the kitchen.

When he set down a mug of coffee in front of me and retook his seat, I stood and crossed the room to close the door.

"I can't keep her away from you if you're having early

morning meetings with her." I refused to ask why they were in the kitchen together. If he wanted me to know, he'd tell me.

"It wasn't through choice, believe me. She came in shortly after me."

"You looked very cozy."

"If, by cozy, you mean I was trying to keep her quiet and not wake everyone in the house by losing her shit and screaming at me … then, sure." He took a mouthful of coffee. "She said that she understood why I brought someone with me, but that she would never let her husband know about us."

I snorted into my mug.

"She also told me that she believes I married you on the rebound and that she forgives me."

"Forgives you for what?"

"Ending things between us."

"And now she wants you back because she's the only one who understands you, right?"

One side of his mouth tipped up. "Exactly."

"And now I have to spend the day with her," I muttered.

"I have faith that you will handle it." He reached out, took my mug away and placed it on the table, then pressed a finger beneath my chin and tipped my head up.

I frowned at him. He leaned forward, and before I could register what was happening, he kissed me. It was just a brush of lips, his against mine, over before it really began. But even after he drew back, his thumb running over my jaw, I could still feel the pressure of his mouth, a tingling sensation that had me wanting to lick my lips. Instead, I cleared my throat and summoned a frown.

"What was that for?"

He smiled and shrugged. "It seemed like the right thing to do."

L. ANN

45

Bishop

The look of confusion on her face mirrored the one I was feeling.

Why did I kiss her?

There was no one here to see us pretend. There was no reason to behave like I had any right to kiss her.

So why?

The answer wasn't as straightforward as it should have been.

I'd been relieved when she arrived in the kitchen. Susannah had been building toward a tantrum. No matter how many times I told her I hadn't changed my mind, we weren't going to get back together, and my marriage to Eden wasn't a lie, she wouldn't listen. All she kept repeating was that it was a clever idea to keep David from discovering our affair, and how she was glad I'd thought of it.

When Eden stepped through the door, Susannah had just

caught my arm to stop me from leaving, pleading with me to stay and listen to her. I'd seen the flash of anger in her eyes when Eden didn't react to her touching me. She wanted to make a scene, cause a confrontation. Instead, Eden had behaved as though she had no reason at all for jealousy—which she didn't. I had absolutely no interest in reigniting anything with Susannah. That was the whole point of marrying Eden in the first place.

Something I'd forgotten when she curled around me, pressed her lips to my cheek and settled onto my lap like she had every right to be there.

From that moment, the only thing in my head was the desire to kiss her. And not the chaste, brief touch of lips I'd given her. No, I wanted more than that. But the logical voice in my head had stopped me, cautioned me against it, forced me to curb the desire to part her lips and possess her mouth.

But now the thought was there, it had taken root, and I knew it was only a matter of time before I let myself fall into temptation.

And that was a problem.

I didn't let emotion lead me. I didn't get involved with my clients. I certainly didn't *kiss* them. It led to too many problems, too many complications. That wasn't me. I wasn't that person.

So *why the fuck did I kiss her?*

I could almost hear Rook laughing at me … the same way I'd laughed at him over agreeing to a pretend date with Magdalena.

"Bishop?" Her voice snapped me out of my thoughts.

Her features came into focus. I was still leaning forward, still stroking along her jaw with my thumb. Her skin was so fucking soft, so warm.

Fuck it.

I slid my hand down her throat, wrapped my fingers around the back of her neck, pulled her closer and kissed her again.

Her soft gasp parted her lips, and I'm not ashamed to admit I took advantage. My fingers moved up, tangled into her hair and I tugged her head back, and thrust my tongue into her mouth to slide along hers.

She tensed and, for half a second I wondered if she'd bite it off, but then her hands came up to cup my face, palms pressing against my cheeks as her lips moved beneath mine.

When we parted seconds, minutes, hours later, her eyes were wide, green irises almost swallowed by her pupils as she stared at me. I ran my thumb over her bottom lip and licked mine.

"You still taste like trouble." I pressed another kiss to her lips and stood. "Finish your coffee. Rook and Magdalena should be here soon."

I walked out, leaving her sitting at the kitchen table staring after me.

***

Standing under the shower, I replayed the kiss in my head.

What happened to not getting involved?

I'm not involved.

How many other clients have you kissed lately?

This is different. I didn't spend that much time with any of my clients, especially not in an intimate situation like this one. It wouldn't be a problem. It just made our lie look more realistic.

Who are you trying to convince?

I shook my head. Three more weeks. By then, I'd have everything in place for her to move on, and my life would return to normal.

Eden was in the bedroom when I finally exited the shower. She was sitting cross-legged on the bed brushing her hair. She didn't say anything as I moved past her to dump my worn clothes into the suitcase. I straightened and turned to face her.

"While the spa Dana has hired is on private ground and has been block-booked for her and her guests for the day, the same rules apply as when you went shopping with Magdalena. Keep your wits about you. If something feels off, treat it like it is. Anything suspicious, contact me."

She paused mid brush stroke and lifted her head to look at me. "Maybe it would be better if I didn't go."

"Absolutely not. Go, enjoy yourself. You'll be surrounded by people. I have no doubt it'll be safe."

"What do you plan to do?"

"I'm going to try and get some work done."

46

Eden

My lips still tingled from his kiss, but I followed his lead and didn't mention it. Maybe he'd heard someone and thought they were coming into the kitchen and that's why he kissed me. As far as everyone was concerned, I was his wife, and we were still in the honeymoon phase. It would be natural and expected that if no one was around we'd want to touch and kiss each other. That's what I signed in the contract, and in return he was going to reinvent my life.

So why had it felt real?

Why had heat zipped through my veins when his fingers curled around the back of my neck?

Why had my stomach flipped and twisted with anticipation and not fear?

Why did I want him to do it again?

He paused, one hand on the door, and looked back at me.

"Everyone will meet in the kitchen at eight-thirty for breakfast. I'll leave you to shower and get ready for your day ahead." He pulled open the door.

"Bishop?"

"Eden?"

"Why did you kiss me?" Apparently, I wasn't following his lead, after all.

He stepped out into the hallway, and I thought he wasn't going to answer me, but as the door swung closed, his voice drifted back.

"Why did you let me?"

I threw myself off the bed and darted across the room. Opening the door, I looked outside, but he was gone.

"Eden? Is everything okay?" Dana came out of a room down the hall.

"Hi. Yes, everything's fine. Bishop just headed downstairs. I hoped to catch him, but I was too late."

"I'm going down now. Did you want me to send him back up?"

I shook my head. "No. No. It's okay. It wasn't anything important." I retreated into the bedroom, closed the door and leaned against it.

What did he mean?

I didn't *let* him do anything. *He* kissed *me*. I hadn't been expecting it. He caught me by surprise!

Hurrying across the room, I snatched up the clothes I'd laid out and went into the bathroom. I didn't linger long in the shower. I wanted to speak to Bishop before I had to leave with Dana and her friends for the spa. I wanted to know why he kissed me.

I washed, did my makeup, threw on my clothes as fast as I could, and almost jogged down the stairs and along the hallway.

"Eden!" Magdalena jumped up from her chair at the kitchen table when I entered the room.

I gave her a distracted smile and looked around, but there was no sign of Bishop. In fact, only women were in the room, Susannah included.

"Where's—"

"Rook and Bishop are down at the stables with Crosby and the others," Dana said before I could finish speaking.

"Stables?"

"Horses, dear," Susannah said.

"I know what stables are for," I couldn't stop myself from snapping.

Dana looked between us. "One of the mares had a foal a couple of days ago. Crosby wanted to show her off." She sipped her juice. "Does anyone want breakfast, or shall we get moving? We could get there early and take a trip to the shopping mall afterwards."

"I thought you booked for a certain time?" I wasn't sure about going anywhere other than the spa. The more time I spent outside, the more risk there was of someone seeing me and contacting Chester, but I couldn't tell Dana that without getting into everything else.

Dana laughed. "Oh, honey, that doesn't mean *anything*. I

hired the place out for the entire day. That means no one will be there until we arrive."

"I'll organize a car," Kennedy said, when no one protested.

"I'm going to call Rook and let him know." Magdalena stood and moved to the door. "He doesn't like it if I disappear and don't tell him where I'm going."

"You know, that's a terrible red flag," Susannah said.

"It really isn't," Magdalena said. "If you'll excuse me …" She lifted the cell phone to her ear.

***

"What is Susannah's problem with you?" Magdalena leaned close so she could talk to me in a low voice.

We were seated side by side in the nail salon, getting mani-pedis. Susannah, Kennedy, and Dana were on the opposite side of the room, safely out of hearing range. Not that they were paying much attention to us. It was obvious that the three women had a history and were talking about people they knew. I don't know if Magdalena felt the same way, but I was ready to get out of here and go back to the house. The more the women talked, the less I felt I had in common with them.

Dana was lovely, making every attempt to involve the two of us in their conversations, but Susannah ensured it revolved around things neither of us could contribute to. I was sure she was doing it on purpose.

"I don't think it's a problem with *me*, exactly." I didn't want to lie to Magdalena. I liked her, and although once my contract with

Bishop was over, I'd never see her again, I didn't want to spoil the tentative friendship that was building between us.

"Bishop?"

I sighed. "She likes him … a lot."

"Isn't she married?"

"Yep."

"Somehow, I can't see Bishop being interested in her. She doesn't seem his type."

Oh, you have no idea.

I smiled but didn't answer her.

The mani-pedi was followed by lunch, during which Dana, Kennedy and Susannah discussed clothes.

"We definitely should hit the mall. There's the most divine store that sells one-off dresses there," Susannah said.

My stomach plummeted. I'd hoped that plan had been shelved. I didn't want to go shopping. Logically, I knew the chances were low of anyone connected to Chester seeing me. We were thousands of miles away from New York. But there was always that *one* chance in a million.

How could I get out of it without raising too many questions?

47

Bishop

I was in the middle of a friendly poker game with Crosby, Rook, David, and Saul when Rook's cell chimed. He placed his cards face down and picked it up.

"The girls have gone to the mall."

"Does that woman of yours tell you every move she makes?" David asked.

"She does if it's a change from what she planned. In our line of work, even retired, one can't be too careful with the lives of the people we love. I need to know where she is just in case something happens."

"Susannah would have my head if I demanded that level of detail."

Rook snorted. "Like you don't have a tracker on her cell. You know where she is every second of every day. At least I'm open about my need to know Dally's whereabouts."

The fine hairs rose on the back of my neck.

"I thought she might be planning to divorce me." David shrugged and leaned back on his seat. "I didn't want to be taken by surprise. She's had flings before, but this last one ..." His gaze shifted to me. "It was different."

"Different how?" Crosby leaned across the table to top up everyone's drinks.

"Usually, her dalliances only lasted for a date or two. This last guy ... she saw him regularly for at least six months. I thought she was preparing to ask me for a divorce, but then everything changed, and she's been very ... focused on our marriage lately."

"When did you put the tracker on her cell?"

"Too late to find out who she'd been seeing, unfortunately. I don't care who she fucks, but the rule has always been no more than a couple of times with the same person. If it hadn't already ended, I'd have searched him out to make that clear." He smiled at me.

"Did Magdalena say what mall they'd gone to?" I turned to my brother, who shook his head.

I pulled my cell out of my pocket.

ME: Are you okay?

Three little dots immediately popped up, but when no reply came through for almost a minute, I sent another message.

ME: Don't lie to me. Are you okay?

The response was a photograph of a pile of clothes.

ME: What's that?

EDEN: I'm hiding in a changing room with six pairs of jeans, seven t-shirts and three dresses that I have no intention of buying.

ME: And why are you doing that?

EDEN: Because everywhere is so open and I feel like I'm being watched.

ME: Do you want me to come and get you?

Those little dots bounced across the screen again.

ME: I'm coming to get you. What mall are you at?

EDEN: I'm not sure. Fern something?

ME: Fern Glen. I know it. I'll text you when I'm there. Stay put.

I pocketed my cell and stood. "Sorry, I have to go. Eden is sick and needs me to bring her back to the house."

Rook frowned at me. "Sick?"

"All the flying through time zones we've done over the past week is probably catching up with her."

Rook's expression didn't change, but I could still tell he knew I was lying. "I'll text Dally and get her to wait with Eden."

I nodded, grabbed my jacket from the back of the chair and walked out of the room. Rook followed me. Once we were out of hearing of everyone else, he caught my arm.

"What's really going on?"

I gave him half of the truth. "Stalker ex. She's feeling a little too out in the open and unprotected."

"Makes sense." His eyes tracked over my face. "I'll speak to Dally. Bring her back with you."

**

ME: I'm outside. Do you need me to come and fetch you?

EDEN: No. I'm with Magdalena. Where are you parked?

ME: I'll wait by the entrance and walk you back to the car.

I cut off the engine, climbed out and locked the car, then walked over to the entrance. It wasn't a huge mall, and there was only one way in or out. I could see why Eden felt trapped. If Chester or one of his friends had been there, she wouldn't have been able to get out without them seeing her. I thought it was unlikely that there would be anyone who recognized her inside, but I'd also been around long enough to know that anything was possible.

Leaning against the wall beside the entrance, I watched as people moved in and out, milled around outside, caught up with friends or said their goodbyes. After a couple of minutes, two familiar figures stepped through the doors. I straightened and walked over to them.

"I'm parked over here."

I took a position slightly behind them both and guided them to where I'd parked the car. From where I walked, I could see if anyone looked in our direction. Nobody did, and we reached the car without incident. Popping the trunk, the girls put their purchases inside.

Eden caught me looking at the bags, and flushed pink.

"Let me guess. Six pairs of jeans, seven t-shirts and three dresses?"

Her cheeks darkened further. I knew what had happened. She'd grabbed clothes to justify spending a long time in the changing room, and then when she came out felt obliged to buy them.

I said nothing, closing the trunk, then opened both passenger side doors for them. Magdalena climbed into the back while Eden took the front. I rounded the car and settled behind the steering wheel.

As we pulled out of the parking lot, Magdalena leaned forward between the seats.

"You know the thing I hate the most about Rook's former job is the people he has to associate with. I *really* don't like Susannah."

48

Eden

"I'll pay you back."

Bishop straightened from putting the bags on the floor near the dresser. "For what?"

"The clothes."

"Don't be ridiculous."

"I spent over five hundred dollars." Just saying the amount made my stomach tighten.

"That's why I gave you the credit card."

"Yes, but—"

He turned to face me. "You can never have too many pairs of jeans." There was absolutely no tone to his voice, but I swear he was laughing at me.

"It's not funny."

"It's a little bit funny." He walked over to where I was perched on the edge of the bed. "Did you at least pick up the correct sizes?"

"Yes, of course I did."

"Then don't give it another thought."

"I'll pay you back." I repeated the words firmly.

Instead of arguing, he sat beside me. "Do you want to tell me what happened today?"

"It was stupid."

"Tell me."

"Everything was going fine. There was no one other than us and the staff in the spa. The restaurant Dana picked was secluded and we were seated away from any windows. She'd mentioned a couple of times about wanting to go shopping, and I told myself it'd be fine. What were the chances of Chester being here right now? But then we got there ... and there were so many people. It wasn't like the mall near Glenville. That was busy, too, but it was different somehow." My fingers twisted together on my lap. "I concentrated on picking up clothes. I wasn't going to buy anything; it was just to keep my attention on that and not on all the people around us. But all I could think about was how it would only take one person, one security guard, one police officer to see me and recognize me."

I kept my gaze down, focused on my hands. "And then I guess I panicked. I grabbed clothes as I walked, told the others I was going to try them on and found the first empty changing room. I couldn't get the thought that Chester was there, that he was already watching me, that it would only be minutes before he turned up, out of my head."

"Take a breath, Eden." A warm hand covered mine, and I discovered I was almost gasping, panting, as I rushed the words out.

"You must think I'm an idiot." I dashed at my eyes angrily with one hand.

"I don't think you're an idiot."

"Well, you should. *I* do!"

He laughed at that, the sound warm and low. It did something to my insides, twisting them up into tighter knots, and horror washed over me when I finally connected the dots. This was a business arrangement. He was being kind to me because it was what he'd agreed to do.

I *could not* be attracted to him.

Oh my god.

I was attracted to him!

Movements jerky, I lurched to my feet.

"Where are you going?" His question froze me to the spot. Mild curiosity coated the words.

He had no idea. *No* idea about how he was affecting me. A slightly hysterical laugh bubbled up and escaped past my lips.

I couldn't be attracted to him. It was simply because we'd spent so many days together. I was starved for human contact that didn't require me to be on guard. That was all.

I wasn't attracted to him.

He stood, frowning. "You've turned white. Maybe you should lie down." I stumbled backward, evading his fingers as he reached out to touch my cheek.

"I'm fine. I just … I …" I looked around wildly. "I need to use the bathroom." I bolted across the room, and slammed the bathroom door shut behind me, twisting the lock, and spinning to press my back against it.

"Oh my god," I whispered, sliding down the door to the floor and drawing my knees up to my chin. "What is wrong with you?"

"Eden?" Bishop's voice just beyond the door made me jump. "Are you okay in there?"

I scrambled to my feet. "I'm fine." I hurried across to the sink and splashed water onto my face. Gripping the edge of the marble countertop, I glared at my reflection. "You are not attracted to him."

An image of him as he walked out of the bathroom wrapped in nothing but a towel around his hips swam in front of my eyes. The surprising tattoo sleeve covering one arm from wrist to shoulder, a colorful mass of images that my eyes hadn't been able to decipher in the few seconds it took me to realize I was staring and look away. The scar along his right side, which disappeared beneath the towel. The intricate back piece as he walked back into the bathroom with his clothes tucked beneath one arm. What had that been? I hadn't dared to look for long enough to make out the image.

I squeezed my eyes closed.

"Stop it!" I hissed. "Why do you even remember? You didn't look at him for *that* long!"

"Eden?" My name was joined by a rapping at the door.

I pushed away from the counter, sucked in a deep breath,

then turned back to the door.

He was standing, one hand raised, when I pulled it open. His head canted slightly, dark eyes sweeping over me.

"Are you okay?"

I nodded. "Emotion overload. I'm sorry. I'm okay now." I kept my voice brisk and walked past him. "What time is the party? Is there anything I can do to help set it up?"

He laughed. "We just have to turn up at seven. Tallulah hired caterers and music." He checked the watch on his wrist. "I was considering a nap, to be honest."

"A nap?"

"Something wrong with that?"

"No, but I didn't see you as the napping type."

"And you base that on what?" He sank onto the bed, stretched out onto his back, and tucked one hand beneath his head. He turned his face to the side and stared at me.

I shrugged. "The fact you're a self-confessed workaholic, I guess."

"I'm on vacation." A smile tipped one side of his mouth up. "You look dead on your feet. Tonight is going to be chaotic. I think a nap would do you good as well." He patted the mattress. "I'll set an alarm for an hour. Come and take a nap with me."

49

Bishop

What exactly do you think you're doing?

That voice—my conscience, maybe—whispered.

She had a major panic attack. I'm trying to settle her back down.

Sure, that's what you're doing.

I ignored it and patted the space beside me again.

"Stop looking at me like I'm about to murder you." She was standing at the end of the bed, eyes wide as she stared at me.

"Aren't you?"

"It's not on my immediate to-do list, no."

She took a step toward the bed. "What *is*?"

"Is what?"

"On your to-do list?"

"Right now? A nap. Socializing with friends this evening. Bed, breakfast, and then back home to work on your new identity. A visit with my youngest brother on Tuesday to wrap up some final details, and then start thinking about the best place for you to relocate."

She gaped at me. "You really do have a to-do list."

"Did you think I was joking?" A third pat of my hand on the mattress changed the direction of her gaze. "Have you stopped trusting me?"

"No, of course not."

"Then why are you still over there?"

"I don't think I could sleep. It's too light."

"Close the curtains and turn off the light."

She skirted around the bed and walked over to the window. Two silken ties held the curtains open. She pulled them loose and let the thick material fall closed, then changed direction and found the light switch. The room was plunged into darkness. I counted to five in my head. On four, the mattress dipped beside me.

I smiled in the dark and waited for my eyes to adjust to the change.

The only sound in the room for the next five minutes was her quiet breathing. I didn't try to make conversation. I wanted her to relax, to find her way back to the comfortable headspace she'd been in for the past two days.

"How could I have forgotten so quickly?" Her voice was little more than a whisper.

"Forgotten what?" I had a good idea what she meant, but I didn't want to voice it just in case I was wrong. This woman had surprised me several times already and I was hesitant to assume I knew where her mind was going.

"When we were in the mall, I had this overwhelming sense of fear ... No, *terror*. It was too open. I felt like one wrong move, and I'd be discovered. How could I have forgotten that feeling? When I went shopping with Magdalena, other than a few moments where I thought the security guard was looking at me, I was fine. Why was today different?"

"That's how trauma works. Maybe there was something about today that brought everything closer to the surface. Something that your subconscious picked up on."

"I hid in the changing room like a scared little girl."

"Your fight or flight instinct engaged, that's all. It's not a bad thing. it's something that's helped to keep you alive all this time."

"Dana and the others must be wondering whether I'm crazy." She gave a little laugh, one that ended in what suspiciously sounded like a choked sob.

"You've just spent the better part of a day with them. Do you really think that's what they're going to be talking about? Magdalena told them you were feeling unwell and that she was going to accompany you back to the house. There's no reason to believe they'll think it's anything more than that." I rolled onto my side, facing her. "In fact, I would put money on your slight wobble today being due to a mix of tiredness from the travel, your brain suddenly catching up to the fact that you're no longer running, and your body deciding enough is enough."

"Slight wobble?"

"Slight wobble." I repeated the words firmly. "I'm surprised it hadn't happened already. I've been expecting it for a couple of days." I reached out and stroked a finger down one arm, following the line of it until I found her hand where it rested on her stomach. I squeezed her fingers. "My advice … take that nap. I promise, you'll feel better for it."

***

"You said an *hour*." Eden glared at me through the reflection of the bathroom mirror as she applied a coat of lipstick.

I shrugged. "It was an estimate. You needed to rest and wouldn't have agreed if I told you I wasn't going to wake you until it was time to get ready."

"But *four hours*, Bishop!" She snapped the lid back onto the lipstick and shoved it into her makeup bag.

"If you hadn't been tired, you wouldn't have slept that long. Now you're all refreshed and ready for the evening ahead."

"Refreshed," she muttered, and I hid a smile at her eye roll.

"You're going to need to be on point. Everyone's in a party mood. Drinking, dancing. You have a part to play and tonight you really need to sell it."

Because I was confident that David had his suspicions about me and Susannah, and I needed Eden to convince him we were madly in love and that I was no threat to his marriage.

She straightened, turned, and walked toward me. A smile softened her lips, her hands were outstretched toward me, and her hips swayed from side to side. My gaze slid over the form-fitting A-line black dress, noting the way it clung to every curve. With every step forward, the split gave a quick flash of bare leg.

When she reached me, she lifted one hand and curved it over my jaw, rested her other hand against my hip and leaned up. Her breasts brushed against the front of my shirt, and then her lips pressed a warm kiss to mine.

"I think I can convince them, don't you?" she whispered, drawing back to look at me through her lashes.

I held myself still, an unfamiliar tension zipping through my frame. The hand on my arm toyed with my sleeve and I had to squash the urge to wrap one hand into her hair and bring her back toward me for another kiss … one that wasn't quite … so … sweet.

Clearing my throat, I summoned a smile. "That should do it." I crooked my arm. "Ready to go?"

"I just need my shoes."

"You could go barefoot. I doubt anyone will complain." I looked down at the pink-tipped toes curling into the carpet.

"I think I need the height boost my shoes will give me."

She tightened her hold on my arm as she slipped first one foot, then the other, into black shoes. The heels gave her an added two, maybe three inches, to her height, bringing her up to the perfect level to kiss without having to lower my head too far.

The stray thought caught me by surprise.

Stop thinking about kissing her. She's a client. This is a job. In three weeks, you'll drop her off in a new location and never see her again.

50

Eden

Lights adorned the terrace area, casting a warm glow over everyone standing around. Music played through a sound system set up, and outdoor seating and tables had been placed at intervals on the grassed area at the bottom of the wooden steps.

In front of the sound system, a makeshift dance floor had been laid out, and there were already people swaying to the low music.

Servers dressed in white shirts and black pants or skirts moved amongst the guests, carrying trays of champagne and canapés. When one stopped beside me, Bishop reached out and took two glasses, handing one to me.

He lifted the glass to his lips and took a sip. "Not bad."

"Not bad?" I took a suspicious sip of my own, the bubbles tickling my nose.

"Tallulah is notorious for not wanting to overspend. Crosby

is a self-made millionaire. His mom spent many years holding down two or three jobs to make sure there was food on the table and clothes on her kids' backs. Some habits are hard to break. She doesn't see the point in spending a lot on expensive things without a good reason." He took another swallow of champagne. "This is her way of saying that celebrating her son getting engaged is a good reason. It's her silent blessing on his choice."

"That's really lovely."

"Crosby will be breathing a sigh of relief. It could have gone either way. Tallulah would never say anything to him if she didn't like Dana, but she wouldn't have paid out for decent champagne. If she didn't like Dana, we could easily have been drinking vinegar right now."

I laughed. "She wouldn't, surely?"

"Oh, she would. Don't be sucked in by that sweet smile of hers."

"Bishop, don't you be scaring Eden off, now!" The woman in question came up from behind us, shaking her head.

Bishop smiled and dipped his head to kiss Tallulah's cheek. "Just telling it how it is."

"I would never serve vinegar to all my unsuspecting guests." She patted Bishop's chest and winked at me. "I'd just make sure the people I didn't like were served it."

A shocked laugh escaped me. "Should I worry?"

"No, dear. But if Bishop doesn't behave, he should."

"I always behave." The words were delivered in a dry tone.

"You forget I knew you as a teenage boy. Behaving was

something you struggled with on a daily basis." She reached up to pat his cheek. "He was in trouble all the time for backtalking the teachers or fighting."

I found that hard to imagine. Bishop was far too in control of himself to say anything without considering all the likely repercussions first.

"I can see from your face that you don't believe me." Tallulah laughed. "The man you see before you right now is *not* the wild teenage boy who Crosby brought home one afternoon. There was a time when I thought he'd never be housebroken."

"He still isn't housebroken. You should see the mess he makes when he comes to my house. Clawing the furniture, chewing the table legs ..." Rook's words heralded his and Magdalena's arrival.

Tallulah threw Bishop's brother a look that needed no words. His eyebrow rose and she peered at him. I stifled a laugh.

"This from the boy who carved his name into my kitchen table and threatened to stab anyone who sat in your chosen seat?"

Rook shrugged. "I'm territorial."

"You *all* are. All these smart suits and smooth words are just masks that hide your true natures."

The two men laughed, unconcerned by her words. I wondered how true they were, though. I knew Rook had been a hitman, taking contracts to kill people. Bishop had access to a network of people who could wipe a person's existence from the world and replace it with a new one. People who were dangerous in their own right. Yet they both moved in those worlds with confidence, ease, and a distinct lack of fear. Standing here amongst movie stars, supermodels, and rock stars, it would be easy to believe they were CEOs or important executives. But the truth was vastly different and far more deadly.

"Anyway, my darlings, I need to go and hurry Dana and Crosby along. There's a difference between making a fashionably late entrance and missing your own party." She reached up to kiss Rook and Bishop's cheeks, hugged Magdalena and then I found myself engulfed in a hug of my own.

"Don't let Bishop's distance and cool nature put you off, my dear. There's a lot of passion hiding beneath that mask. All it'll take is a small spark to light it. But you married him, so I'm sure you already know that." She whispered the words in my ear, kissed my cheek, and was gone before I could respond.

"What did she say to you?"

I dragged my gaze away from the woman's retreating back to look at Bishop. "Just that beneath that cold exterior, you're a hothead."

"A hothead?"

I nodded.

"You know," Magdalena said, "I could see that."

Bishop's gaze turned to her. "You think I'm a hothead?"

"Not now. But when you were young, I could see that. It would explain why you're so in control of yourself now. Rook's the same."

Her boyfriend rolled his eyes. "You break one man's fingers and you're labeled as a hothead."

Magdalena laughed. "*That's* your claim? You killed a man two days after we met."

I gaped, then snapped my mouth closed. *Retired hitman*, I reminded myself. But Magdalena said it so matter-of-factly.

"He was going to kill you. I don't see the problem." He draped an arm over her shoulders. "And it was three by the end of the day, I believe."

He said it so casually, like killing people meant nothing. I don't know if I made a noise or pulled a face but the next thing I knew, Bishop had leaned close to me.

"I killed two people the night we met and left the third unconscious as a message for the person who'd dragged me out of my hotel room in the middle of the night," he whispered in my ear.

My head snapped around to find him mere inches from me, a smile playing about his lips. His eyes were gleaming as they met mine.

Time slowed to a stop.

I couldn't look away.

Why didn't his admission fill me with horror? I thought back to his suggestion to have Chester killed, and my horrified reaction to it. *What had changed? Why didn't the thought chill me as much as it did?*

On the outskirts of my attention, I heard Rook murmur to Magdalena that they should leave us alone. I couldn't turn my head, couldn't acknowledge them.

I was trapped in a dark-eyed gaze with no means of escape.

51

Bishop

I watched the play of emotions cross her face. From horror, to concern, to surprise and then to confusion. She thought she was good at hiding her thoughts, and maybe amongst people who didn't need to be able to read people in order to survive she might be right. But reading micro-expressions was integral to my ability to work a situation to my advantage.

These days I might spend more time organizing and fixing, but for a long time I was just as active as Rook in a far more deadly arena and the instincts honed over those years were still very much alive.

And right now, those instincts were telling me that things were shifting, changing, *evolving*. This was no longer a business deal, a means to an end. It was something else, something unexpected. For the first time in a lifetime of making split-second decisions, I wasn't sure what my next move should be.

Someone jostled Eden from behind, driving her forward a step. My hand curled around her elbow, steadying her. Her skin was warm beneath my palm, and I slid my hand up from her elbow to her shoulder.

A wry voice inside my head acknowledged my mistake.

I'd avoided touching her as much as possible because, somewhere deep inside, I'd known the second my skin touched hers I'd want more.

My fingers traced a path along her shoulder, up her throat, over her jaw until I could brush over her bottom lip with my thumb. Her lips parted, those green eyes wide and trained on me. I took another step closer and lowered my head … slow enough that she could turn away if she chose.

She didn't.

My mouth touched hers, her lips soft and sweet with the faintest flavor of the champagne she was clutching in one hand. My hand slid up the back of her neck, cupping her head, and my tongue slid between her lips.

With every second that passed, I waited for her to pull away, to demand I stop, but she didn't. Instead, she stepped closer, her hand smoothing up the silk of my shirt to loop around my neck. The move brought her flush against me, tipping her head back further and the kiss we shared deepened, grew hungrier, until it was me who dragged my mouth from hers.

Her eyes were closed, lips slightly parted, lipstick wiped clean away. I briefly wondered if it had transferred to my mouth, but I couldn't summon up the effort to care.

"Eden." My voice came out as a rough whisper.

Her lashes fluttered and slowly her lids lifted to reveal eyes slightly glazed. A blink or two and she focused on my face. Her tongue came out to lick over her lips, and I found myself copying the action.

"What—" She cleared her throat. "I …" She glanced around. "Did she leave?"

"Who?" I frowned.

"Susannah."

"Susannah isn't here."

"Then why …" Her brows pulled together into a small, tight frown.

I stroked the outline of her lips with one finger. "Why not?"

Her teeth sank into her bottom lip, but she didn't look away from me.

"Tell me now if I'm reading this wrong."

Her throat moved as she swallowed. "No, you're not reading it wrong." Her reply was soft.

I nodded and dropped my hand to take hers. "Dance with me."

She didn't resist as I drew her across the terrace and down the steps to where couples swayed together to the music. Turning, I slipped an arm around her waist and tugged her close to me. Her hands lifted to rest on my shoulders, and we moved around the dance floor.

"I never get involved with clients."

Her eyes jerked up to meet mine when I spoke.

"It's bad for business. Emotional entanglements can cause errors in judgment."

She didn't speak.

"A clinical approach to building a new identity for someone is paramount. Emotion has no place in my line of work."

"I understand."

I scowled. "*No*, you don't. I don't fool around with my work, Eden."

"Okay."

I tightened my hold on her waist and dropped my forehead to rest against hers. "That's just it. It's *not* okay." My confession came out as a raw whisper. "I want to kiss you again."

Her response to that was to find my lips with hers and wind her arms tighter around my neck.

"Fuck." The curse ripped out of me on a low growl when our mouths separated. "This wasn't part of the plan."

"Do you know what my biggest fear has been?" Her head dropped to rest against my shoulder, and she spoke in a voice low enough for only me to hear.

"I don't."

"That the last emotional interaction I'd have with someone would be the one when Chester found me. His hands around my throat while he told me what he was going to do to me for running away." Her lips brushed against the side of my neck as she spoke. "If I have to take on an entirely new identity, I'd like my last memories as Eden Marshall to be ones I can look back on fondly instead of with fear." Her fingers curled into the front of my shirt. "Would it really be so far outside of the contract we signed to give me that?"

52

Eden

I could barely hear anything above the sound of my heartbeat hammering a rapid rhythm in my ears. Bishop had gone still at my words, the hand on my back flexing briefly.

When he didn't reply, not even to refuse my less-than-subtle suggestion, I took that as his answer, and started to draw away. The hand on my spine flattened, refusing to let me move.

"You don't drop a proposition like that and then run away." There was no hint in his tone to what he thought.

"You do when the response is silence." My voice on the other hand was croaky and shaking. "I'm sorry. I was out of line. I should never have said it."

"My silence was not meant to be an answer. I was fighting the urge to find that fucking lowlife and teach him what real fear is." He dipped his head and rested his lips next to my ear. "Are you sure you don't want to change your original answer and have me kill him?" His voice was rich, and deep, and full of darkness.

My heart lurched in my chest. It would be so easy to say yes.

What has changed? Why are you willing to consider it without saying no outright? Why are things different now?

"Eden?" His lips moved over my cheek.

Before I could reply, another voice cut in.

"Well, don't you two look cozy. You don't mind if I cut in, do you?"

"I do, actually." Bishop didn't even look at Susannah.

She laughed, high pitched and shrill. "You don't mean that. Excuse me, Eden, I'd really like to talk to Bishop."

Her words woke something inside me. I turned to face her. "My husband said no. Maybe you should give *your* husband the same attention you seem to be giving all the other men in here. Now if *you* will excuse *us*, I was dancing with my husband. Please ... respectfully, get lost."

The blonde's jaw dropped and then she spun to Bishop. "Are you going to let her talk to me like that?"

"She was far more polite than I intended to be. Fuck off, Susannah."

Her face turned red, and she gaped at us both for a moment longer, then her eyes narrowed. "You'll regret this, Bishop."

"I already do." He took my hand and started to walk off the dance floor, then stopped and turned around. "Believe me, I've never fucking regretted anything more than the day I bought you that first fucking drink. Go back to your husband, Susannah, and stop fucking around."

He set off at a speed that had me trotting to keep up with him.

"Bishop, slow down!" I clutched at his arm with my free hand.

He stopped abruptly and I crashed into him.

"Were you serious?"

"About what?"

"Making another memory."

My cheeks flushed. "It was stupid."

"Is that a no? Because I'd be happy to change the terms if you want to add it to the contract."

"You're just angry with Susannah." Butterflies took off in my stomach.

He shook his head. "I'm angry with myself. I shouldn't have been so stupid. But that has nothing to do with *this*. She interrupted our conversation; I'm simply returning to it." Warm hands cupped my cheeks. "So, tell me, Eden, do you want to change our contract?"

***

Bishop's arm brushed against mine as he reached for his drink. I jumped, the contact sending bolts of nervous tension through my veins. The last couple of hours had been a new kind of hell.

After admitting that, *yes*, I did want to change the terms of our contract, he'd given me a smile that curled my toes and a kiss that left me gasping for breath, then led me over to Rook and Magdalena where he spent the rest of the evening behaving like we hadn't just decided to do … *something*.

What *had* we just agreed to? More kisses? Foreplay? *Sex?*

I wasn't sure, but there was *no way* I was going to ask him to clarify, which meant my senses leapt into high alert every time he moved, every time he spoke, and I found myself constantly sneaking glances at the time and wondering when it would be acceptable to leave the party.

Midnight came and went, and the party showed no signs of slowing down. Magdalena was curled up on Rook's lap, head resting against his shoulder with her eyes closed. When she yawned for the fourth time, he chuckled.

"I think that's our cue to leave." He lifted the sleepy woman off his lap. "Come on, darlin', let's get you to bed."

Magdalena sent me a smile. "You look beat. Maybe you should think about going to bed as well." She curled her fingers around Rook's and leaned against him. "We're leaving early, so if we don't see you, I'll call you during the week and we'll meet up."

I smiled at her. "I'd like that."

"Not Tuesday. We're going to see Knight," Bishop said. "Let me know if you want to come." He directed that at Rook, who nodded.

"I'll meet you there. Drop me a text with the time." He led Magdalena across the terrace and indoors, pausing to speak to Crosby and Dana on the way.

I covered a yawn with one hand and shifted on the seat. I was exhausted, which surprised me considering I had a four-hour nap, but I didn't want to say anything in case Bishop …

In case he what? Took it to mean you wanted to have sex?

Oh god ... my stomach flipped as I thought back to what I'd said to him.

I basically asked him to have sex with me so that Chester wasn't the last person I'd slept with as Eden Marshall.

"When you're finished having your panic attack, I think we should get out of here."

My eyes snapped to Bishop, who lounged in the seat beside me sipping a glass of whiskey.

"I'm not having a panic attack."

His lips curled. "I've spent enough time around you now to know when you're on the verge of panic. Relax, Eden. Nothing's going to happen that you don't want."

He unfolded himself from the chair, took the glass from my hand and set it down on the table, then reached down to pull me upright. With a hand pressed to the small of my back, he guided me across the terrace.

"Congratulations on your engagement." He stopped to shake Crosby's hand and kiss Dana's cheek. "We're getting out of here before it gets rowdy." He glanced over to where David and Susannah were clearly arguing.

"That your doing?" Crosby asked.

Bishop shrugged. "She doesn't understand the word no."

"Thought as much. I'll speak to David."

"I'd appreciate that." The hand on my spine moved, urging me forward.

By the time we reached our room, I was shivering. Bishop opened the door and stood back to let me enter first, then followed me inside. The click as the door closed was loud in the silence of the room.

The butterflies in my stomach were performing loop-de-loops, my heart was thrashing against my ribs so hard I was sure it was going to break free.

"I'm just going t-to freshen up." I stumbled over the words and turned toward the bathroom.

Bishop didn't stop me and once inside, with the door closed, I clutched the countertop, closed my eyes, and sucked in a breath. One that ended in a surprised yelp when warm lips pressed against my shoulder.

Eyes flying open, I watched Bishop kiss his way toward my throat through the mirror's reflection. His hands moved at my back and the bodice of my dress came loose as the sound of the zipper being drawn down broke the heavy silence. I pressed a hand against my breast to stop the dress from falling.

"Let it go," he murmured against my throat. "I've seen you naked before, but this time I want to pay closer attention."

Heat warmed my skin, a flush that started at my breasts and worked its way up to my face. Bishop's hands curved over my shoulders, and smoothed down my arms until they covered mine. He linked our fingers and then pulled my hand away from my chest.

The dress fell free, dropping in a whisper of silk to my waist.

Even if I wanted to cover myself, I couldn't. Bishop's grip on my fingers stopped me from moving, and he slowly drew my arms down to my sides. His warm breath brushed over my ear.

"Beautiful," he whispered.

53

Bishop

She was trembling, and the desire to cover herself and run was clear in her expression. I released her hands and brushed a finger across the fading bruise just above her right breast.

"Another couple of days and it'll be like it was never there."

"Only on the outside."

I met her gaze through the mirror. "On the inside, too."

I took a step back and dragged a finger down her spine. She shivered.

"Time to decide what you want."

"What do you mean?"

"I can walk out right now, and we stick with our initial plan. We're leaving tomorrow, so there's no need to keep pushing the pretense. Once we're back in Glenville, I'll continue to prepare everything you need to move on." I lowered my head and kissed a path up her throat.

"Or," I whispered against her ear, "we say fuck the initial plan and I wipe your ex-boyfriend out of your mind."

My arm slid around her waist, and I pulled her back against me.

"What do you say, Songbird? Want to sing for me?"

In reply, she turned in my arms and pulled my head down to hers.

"What would you like me to sing?" Her lips touched mine.

"My name while I make you come."

I lifted her off her feet and strode back into the bedroom. When I set her down and stepped away, the dress slipped the rest of the way down her legs to pool at her feet. She stepped out of it while I let my gaze roam over her. Most of the bruises I'd seen had faded, but the ones that remained stirred my anger.

No matter what she claimed about not wanting him to die, if I ever came face to face with Chester Dulvaney, I knew I'd come away with his blood on my hands—both literally and figuratively.

"Come here." I reached behind her, tugged her hair loose from its braid and threaded my fingers through it. "Your hair is like fire." I wound it around my hand and tugged her head back, arching her throat. "I find it incredibly distracting."

"I'm sorry."

"Don't be." I backed her toward the bed and followed her down when her legs hit the mattress and she tumbled backward.

With one hand braced beside her head, I leaned over her. "You've been a distraction from the moment I opened the trunk of the car and found you inside." I captured her lips with mine and untangled my fingers from her hair.

She moved beneath me, one leg lifting to hook around mine. Her fingers found the buttons on my shirt and popped them open, one by one. When it was hanging open, she ran her palms over my chest, and then gave me a gentle push.

I complied, rolling onto my back, and she climbed across me, straddling my hips, bracing her hands against my shoulders. I ran my fingers over her hip, following the lacy edge of her panties.

"Looks like you have me trapped," I said.

"Looks that way." She bent and pressed her lips to my chest. "Tallulah said something earlier tonight." Her tongue flicked out and licked across my nipple.

I hissed, and my hand flexed on her hip.

"She said that the suits just hide who you really are."

"Did she?"

"It makes me wonder …" Her head lifted.

"Wonder what?"

"What you become once the suit is off."

I cocked an eyebrow. "Do you really want to know the answer to that?"

She bit her lip and nodded.

I rolled, tumbling her onto her back and caught her hands, pinning them above her head and kissed her. Holding her wrists in one of my hands, I ran the other down her body, over the curve of her breast, her stomach, and down until my fingertips touched lace.

"If we do this, if I touch you like this," I told her, "there's no going back. You understand that, don't you? It will change everything."

"I know." Her voice was barely more than a whisper.

Her hips arched, and my fingers slipped beneath the lace.

"Take off your suit, Bishop. Show me what lies beneath the mask."

54

Eden

For all my brave words, my entire body locked up the second his fingers found my clit. I wrenched an arm free from his grip and grabbed his wrist.

"No. Stop." The words came out as a strangled cry.

I couldn't breathe. My heart hurled itself against my ribs in an attempt to escape, and my stomach churned. The hand withdrew, moving to curve over my hip and roll me onto my side.

"Eden."

My name. One word. In a voice that *wasn't* Chester's. My eyes snapped open and met his.

"I'm sorry. I'm sorry."

He didn't reply. Instead, the hand on my hip slid around to my back and he pulled me against his chest.

"Just breathe."

And that's what I did. I pressed my face against his chest and sucked in breath after breath, and slowly my heartbeat returned to a normal pace and the tightness in my chest eased. His hand smoothed up and down my spine and eventually my body relaxed. Releasing a shaky breath, I eased back a little and lifted my head.

"I'm sorry, I didn't think—"

"You need to stop apologizing for things outside of your control." He palmed my cheek, tilting my head up, and kissed my forehead, the tip of my nose, then the corner of my mouth, before lifting himself up on one arm.

I clutched at his shirt. "Where are you going?"

"I was just going to dim the lights."

"You're not leaving?" I didn't know why the idea caused panic to take hold again.

"I'm not leaving." He untangled himself from my grip and rose from the bed.

I didn't take my eyes off him, watching as he crossed the room, shrugging out of his shirt as he went, and fiddled with the lights until they dimmed from a bright glare to a softer glow. When he turned back to face me, his expression was serious … *more* serious than it usually was.

I pushed up onto my elbows. "What?"

His eyes dipped to my breasts before rising back to my face. One corner of his mouth lifted, breaking the stern look he wore.

"You look like you're torn between diving off the bed to block my escape and opening the door to throw me out."

His hands moved to his waist. The sound of his belt

unbuckling sent tension through me.

"Interesting."

My gaze jerked up to his. "What is?"

"The things you react to."

He pulled the belt from his waist and tossed it to the floor. My eyes followed it and stayed there.

"Eden, look at me."

When my attention returned to Bishop, he was naked and standing at the end of the bed.

"You still want to—" I bit my lip.

"Just waiting for you to give me the green light." His hand moved, and my gaze dropped, lips parting at the sight of his fingers wrapped around his erection. "Say yes, Songbird."

I licked my lips, my heart rate picking up again but this time for a different reason. "Yes ... please."

***

I was slick with sweat, my fingers gripping the sheets, while the man stretched out beside me played with my body like it was his favorite instrument. Twice he'd had to cover my mouth to muffle my whimpers and moans, while his fingers thrust in and out of me and his thumb stroked over my clit. The roughness of his fingertips caused a delicious friction, sending bolts of electricity through every nerve ending.

I couldn't catch my breath. My heart was racing. Someone was moaning, crying, pleading, begging for mercy.

"Sing for me." The words were a husky whisper, and I forced

my eyes open, searching out the man who was drawing sounds from me that I'd never heard before.

"Bishop."

He smiled. "Again."

"Bishop." His name was a sigh, a moan, a plea.

"Good girl. Once more."

His fingers pushed deep inside me, angled, and hit a spot that made me cry out. My back arched and my eyes closed as pleasure crashed through me in a tsunami that I couldn't control.

His name was a chant, falling from my lips over and over.

"Perfect." His lips found my breast, closed over my nipple and he sucked and flicked at the sensitive peak.

When he withdrew his fingers, I couldn't stop a whimper of protest. He chuckled, the sound vibrating over my nipple, then moved. His weight settled above me, and he reached across the bed. A second later, there was a rustle of paper, followed by a tearing sound, and I forced my eyes open to see him rolling on a condom. My eyes widened at the glint of silver between his fingers. He caught me looking and smiled.

"Yes, you're not imagining things."

"You have a piercing *there?*"

"You'll like it." He fisted his dick, ran his thumb over the barbell piercing the head, then rubbed the tip over my clit. "Ready?"

I nodded, then moaned. *Nothing*—not his fingers or his mouth—could have prepared me for the sensation of him pushing inside me. It was incredible, like nothing I'd ever felt before. My hands found his ass, and I dug my nails in, urging him closer, deeper.

He laughed, the sound a little ragged, and nipped a path along my jaw as he thrust into me. His tongue licked over my ear.

"Feel good?"

"So good," I breathed.

His laughter was warm, sending a thrill through me. And then there were no more words, no more thoughts. Just sensation and pleasure. I swore I could *feel* that piercing inside me, stimulating my nerve endings into a frenzy, until all I could do was hold on tight and hope I didn't fall apart under the orgasm tearing through me.

When I finally floated back down, Bishop's lips covered mine in a fierce kiss, tongue thrusting in and out of my mouth in time with his dick. His teeth sank into my bottom lip, the nip leaving a sharp sting of pain behind which he soothed with a long, slow lick. Then he rolled, taking me with him, until he was on his back, and I was above him.

His hands gripped my hips, and he pulled me down, driving his dick deeper inside my body. The new angle sent new waves of pleasure through me. He lifted one hand to my breast, teasing my nipple between his fingers, twisting and tugging, until I was writhing and sobbing, grinding down onto him in my quest for release.

And when it finally hit, I was certain that the intensity of it made me pass out for a second. When I surfaced from the crescendo, I was on my back again, my legs wrapped around his waist, as he slammed into me, movements uncoordinated as he found his own release.

The utter loss of control as he came thickened his voice into a feral growl, sending a new thrill through me, and then he collapsed, spent, on top of me. "Fuck."

55

Bishop

I lay on my back, Eden curled against my side. In what seemed to be her signature move, she had one leg thrown across mine, and a hand resting on my stomach. Her breathing was warm and steady close to my ear. She'd fallen asleep a while ago, but while my body was tired, exhausted even, my mind wasn't ready to switch off.

Her unspoken reactions in response to certain things I'd said and done played in a loop in my head. From her initial panic when I touched her to the way she followed my belt when I removed it. I wasn't stupid, I knew what they meant. That wasn't what kept me awake.

No, it was the burning need to confront the man who had instilled such a deep-seated fear into the woman beside me.

Confront him.

Torture him.

Kill him.

All it would take would be a call to the station he worked at, set up a meeting, entice him with the thought he could be involved in an arrest that would make his career.

It would be so easy.

"What would?" Eden's sleepy voice broke the silence.

"What would ... what?"

"What would be easy?" She burrowed closer.

"Nothing. I was just thinking out loud. Go back to sleep."

"You woke me up with your growling." Her lips touched the side of my neck in a series of kisses.

"I wasn't growling."

She bit the lobe of my ear. "You were definitely growling."

I moved, flipping her onto her back.

"I wasn't growling, I was muttering. *This* is growling." I took a breath and let out a low growl against her throat.

"Oh." The sound was a soft exhalation and went straight to my dick.

I rubbed my cheek against hers. "You like that?"

I pushed my thigh between her legs, and the wetness there gave me my answer. She pressed against me, rocking against my thigh. I covered her breast, her nipple hardening against my palm as I plumped and squeezed. With my other hand, I reached down to fist my dick. Precum coated the tip, so I swept my thumb over it then pressed it against her lips.

"Lick."

Her tongue swept over the pad, and she made a contented sound that hardened me more.

"I don't have any more condoms with me, so why don't you give me a taste of your pussy instead?"

A shiver rocked her, her lips parting at my words. I didn't give her time to protest, sliding down her body until I could hook my hands over thighs and pull her legs apart. Her pussy was bare, shaved, and I could see the gleam of wetness coating her skin. Lowering my head, I ran my tongue up one thigh and down the other. Her hips jerked.

"Tell me what you want."

Fingers landed in my hair. "Bishop."

"Tell me." I used my thumbs to spread her open. "Do you want me to lick you?" I touched the tip of my tongue to her clit.

She gasped.

"Say it."

"Please."

"Say it," I repeated.

"Please, lick me." The fingers in my hair clenched.

"Where?"

"Anywhere!"

I tutted and blew gently against her clit. "That's not an answer. Be specific."

She squirmed.

"Do you want me to taste you, Eden? Do you want my tongue on your clit? Do you want my fingers inside you?" With each word, my lips brushed against her pussy. "Tell me what you want."

"Yes, all of that."

I dragged my tongue over her pussy, around her clit, then drew away.

"In detail."

She groaned, and tightened her fingers, dragging my face against her wet, fevered flesh.

"I want you to make me come with your mouth. I want your tongue and your teeth. I want you to make me beg."

I flicked my tongue over her clit. "Tell me more."

"Oh god." Her hips jerked up. "I want you to fill me up with your fingers while you suck and bite me."

I pushed a finger inside her. "Like that?"

"More!"

A second finger joined the first. "Enough?"

"No!"

A third finger stretched her, and she cried out.

"What else?"

"Your mouth … please."

"Are you asking me or telling me?" I gave a leisurely thrust of my fingers and nipped at her inner thigh.

Her nails raked over my scalp. "Fuck me with your fingers. Play with my clit. Make me come."

"Good girl." I sealed my lips around her clit and sucked, flicking at it with my tongue, until she was whimpering and writhing.

When she tried to wriggle away, I pressed a hand down on

her stomach, pinning her in place and continued my assault on her clit, while my fingers pumped in and out in a steady rhythm until she cried out, her ass lifting from the bed. I didn't let up, my tongue and fingers driving her orgasm higher and higher until she tried to push my head away.

"I can't … please … ohmygod … ohmygod!"

Her thighs were trembling, her fingers flexing in my hair. I lifted my head, reached up to capture one nipple between my fingers, and pinched gently.

"That was perfect."

56

Eden

I waved one last time at Tallulah and Dana through the car window as Bishop drove away, then settled into the seat and tipped my head back, closing my eyes.

"We'll stop somewhere on the way and grab lunch."

I opened my eyes and peered at Bishop.

"You didn't eat breakfast."

"How do you know? You were with Crosby and Rook."

"Am I wrong?" He kept his eyes on the road ahead.

I sighed. "Tallulah told you, didn't she?"

"How I got the information isn't important. You need to eat breakfast, Eden."

I narrowed my eyes at him, not that he was paying me any attention. "Did *you* eat breakfast?"

His head turned, gaze sweeping over my body from head to toe and up again, pausing to hover on my thighs. His lips tilted.

My cheeks heated.

Don't say it.

"I ate earlier this morning."

My eyes closed so I couldn't see the amusement on his face.

"Your cheeks are on fire. Whatever are you thinking? Crosby, Rook, and I had breakfast before you woke up."

I turned my head toward the window. "You think you're so funny."

Fingers touched my jaw, turning me back to face him. "I'm a little bit funny."

"Your sense of humor is not normal."

He chuckled. "Maybe not, but we're still stopping for food."

"You're also very bossy," I muttered.

"You like it."

There wasn't much I could say to that without embarrassing myself further, so I ignored him and refocused my attention on the scenery speeding past.

The truth of it was I *did* like it. It made me feel secure, like I knew where I was with him. He was clear and concise. There was no having to guess what he was thinking. That made me comfortable.

Not that *he* meant it that way. He was referring to the night we'd just spent together.

He hadn't been there when I woke up, so I didn't need to go through the morning after awkwardness, but that had left me with a confused jumble of emotions and was why I hadn't eaten breakfast. I didn't think my stomach would have been able to handle food, not when I wasn't sure how Bishop was going to behave once we were alone.

I should have known better, though. Bishop was .... *Bishop.* No different from how he'd been before he'd feasted on me like I was his own personal banquet.

Oh god, don't think about it!!

I shifted on the seat, heat flooding me as images of the night before flashed in front my eyes. Of Bishop's head between my legs, of the way his mouth felt on my body, and the way he'd spoken.

I stabbed at the button on the door to lower the window, praying that the cool air would reduce the heat in my cheeks.

"Do you want to talk about it?"

No, I want the ground to open up and swallow me.

"Absolutely not."

He laughed, and the sound skittered over my skin like a caress.

"Well, if you change your mind, I'm open to a discussion."

"I just bet you are." I slapped my hand over my mouth.

I had to stop talking. What the hell was wrong with me?

The car swerved and the next I knew, Bishop had parked at the side of the road, unclipped his seatbelt and turned to face me.

"We can do this one of two ways. We treat last night as a one-off. It was in a neutral location, away from home, and we never refer to it again, and continue forward with the original plan."

Butterflies took off in my stomach. I licked my lips. "Or?"

Bishop's gaze tracked the movement of my tongue. "Or we don't do any of that, and we see where this takes us. Three weeks remain on the contract we signed. We use that time to … get to know each other."

"What happens at the end of the three weeks?" I could barely hear my voice above the sound of my heartbeat hammering like a bass drum in my ears.

"We revisit the situation. See where we're at, and if necessary, renegotiate the terms."

"What about Chester?"

"I'll deal with it."

57

Bishop

I counted down from five in my head and reached three before she spoke.

"How will you deal with it?"

"That's not something you need to worry about."

"But now you've said it, that's all I'm going to think about." She twisted on her seat. "Bishop, *how* will you deal with it? He's a police detective."

"That's not as big a deal as you think it is." I put my foot on the gas and took the car back onto the road. "But since we're talking about it, does that mean you've made a decision?"

"On what?"

"On which option you want to pursue."

I could feel her eyes on me as I drove along the highway, but I stayed silent and waited for her to answer me.

"If I choose option two, I have some conditions."

Interesting. "What are they?"

"You can't treat me like a client."

I glanced over at her. "I don't sleep with my clients. I told you that."

"I know, but I don't want to be just there for when you want to … to …" The color in her cheeks deepened. "You know what I mean."

"You want to be more than a bed warmer." I took the turnoff for Glenville, and we were almost at the town limits before I carried on talking. "For the record, you're a bed hog. If I wanted a bed warmer, I'd buy a hot water bottle. It'd take up less space than you do."

I hid a smile at her sharp intake of breath, and continued to speak before she could protest. "But I understand. I can't promise you an in-depth involvement in my life. Not this quickly. My job is complicated, occasionally dangerous. If we decide to part ways in three weeks, I'd rather do so without you having inside details that could get one or both of us killed. So, I will offer a compromise. Until the three weeks are up, I will treat you like you are my wife in every sense of the word, apart from anything related to my work."

"That's acceptable." Her attempt to sound professional was ruined by the slight quiver in her voice, but I didn't comment on it.

"What are your other conditions?"

"There's just one."

"And that is …"

"I want to know what you plan to do about Chester."

"That comes under work." I took a left turn and pulled into a parking space outside the town's best diner.

"But it affects me."

"It only affects you if he finds you." I cut off the engine and threw open the door. "He can't find you if he's dead."

She was out of the car and waiting for me by the time I rounded it. "You can't *kill* him," she whispered, eyes darting left and right.

"Of course, I can." I pressed a hand against her back and urged her forward toward the diner's entrance.

The doors glided open, and I guided her into a secluded booth near the back. She took one of the bench seats and I slid onto the one opposite her and handed her a menu.

"What would you like to eat?"

She slapped it down onto the tabletop. "Bishop, you can't seriously be thinking about—" she cast another look around.

"It was how I suggested you deal with it when we first met, if you recall."

"Yes, but I said no."

"You did, that's true, but now you've set down conditions, Eden. And if you want me to follow those conditions then I see no other option."

"What? I don't understand. I never made *that* a condition."

"No, but you want me to treat you like my wife." I leaned

across the table, let the easy smile drop from my face and nailed her with a look that had been known to put the fear of God into Mafia Dons. "And since you're my wife, it's my duty to fucking kill *anyone* who has hurt you."

Her jaw dropped.

She still hadn't recovered when the server came over and asked what we'd like to order.

"Coffee. Eden, what would you like to eat?"

She glanced down at the menu. "Grilled cheese, please."

"Make that two. Thank you."

The server nodded and hurried away, only to return a moment later with two mugs of coffee. "Would either of you like cream or sweetener?"

Eden nodded.

"I'll bring it over for you."

"Thanks." As soon as the server had gone, she nailed me with a glare. "You're making use of a loophole."

"Tell me you wouldn't be happier if you knew for sure there was never any chance of him ever showing back up." I leaned back on my seat and took a mouthful of coffee. "If you can convince me that you're not going to spend the next fuck knows how many years looking over your shoulder waiting for him to show up, then I'll reconsider."

58

Eden

I glared at him. He sipped his coffee and waited. He was right, and we both knew it.

I *would* rest easier knowing Chester was never going to appear again, but that didn't mean I would ever be comfortable with the idea of someone killing him for me.

"Think about what he put you through."

"It doesn't matter."

"Of course, it matters."

"If you can't respect my decision on this, then I want to change my choice."

His jaw clenched. I held his gaze, fighting the urge to look away.

"Fine." His mug hit the table, sloshing coffee over the side. "I won't go looking for him, but if he turns up, I'll deal with him however I see fit."

"What does *that* mean?"

"It means I'll use whatever means necessary to remove him from your life for good. Do you agree, or do we need to negotiate the terms further?"

"Does everything need to be a negotiation?"

"Having the terms laid out in advance removes any risk of misunderstanding later."

"Don't you ever do something without thinking through all the possible outcomes first?"

"I let you out of the trunk of a car and took you to New York with me."

"You weren't going to. You were going to leave me there."

The server returned with our grilled cheese, forestalling any response Bishop might have given. She set down the plates and silverware, then smiled.

"Enjoy your food." Her voice was bright and cheerful as she walked away.

"Spontaneity doesn't really work in my life. It can get you killed," Bishop said once she was out of hearing.

"You can't plan *everything* in advance."

He took a bite out of his grilled cheese, chewed slowly, and swallowed. "No, but you can make sure you have prepared for all eventualities. That way, there's always an option."

I stared at him. "That's not living, Bishop. When do you get to just *enjoy* something?"

One eyebrow rose. "Around three this morning. I got to enjoy something just fine then."

I choked on the mouthful of food I'd taken, groped for my coffee, and took a huge swallow, gasping at the heat as it slid down my throat.

"Moral of *that* story. Don't ask questions you're not prepared to hear the answers for," he said when I stopped spluttering.

"You're really not funny."

"My mom thinks I'm hilarious." His voice was completely serious, but there was the faintest hint of a smile teasing his lips. "Eat your lunch."

***

"You might as well move your things into my room."

I spun at the sound of his voice and found Bishop leaning against the doorframe of the bedroom, watching while I unpacked.

"Your room?"

"If we're planning to play house for the next three weeks, it seems reasonable to assume you plan on sharing my bed." His head tilted. "Unless you want to negotiate specific days and times for conjugal visits?" He pushed away from the doorframe. "I assume you *do* want conjugal rights in our new contract?"

I was certain he was phrasing it that way just to tease me. I was quickly learning that his sense of humor leaned very much toward dark and dry, and not very obvious.

I refused to let his words embarrass me and turned back to the suitcase on the bed. Arms slipped around my waist from behind.

"I hereby give my agreement for Eden Chambers nee Marshall to have her wicked way with me whenever she deems fit, thus checking off the box for required spontaneity." His warm breath tickled the back of my neck as he whispered.

I shivered, heat pooling between my thighs and my nipples beading. Shoving away the surge of arousal, I gritted my teeth and turned in his arms, so I could tilt my head back and look at him.

"You are far more annoying than I thought you'd be." My voice didn't come out as firm as I'd wanted, instead it was husky and thick with desire.

A smile spread across his face, and he backed me toward the bed.

"Oh, I haven't even begun to annoy you yet."

59

Bishop

I tapped the pen against my lips, staring down at the two texts that had come in minutes apart. My gut said it wasn't a coincidence.

KNIGHT: You need to come over right now. I don't care what the fuck you're doing, get your ass to my place ASAP.

DEACON: Your boy is on the move. So am I. I'll be at your place by the end of the day.

We'd been back in Glenville for almost forty-eight hours. I was supposed to be going to see Knight on Tuesday. What had happened for him to bring it forward by a day?

If Deacon was coming here, then that meant Chester Dulvaney knew where Eden was and was also headed this way.

My mind calculated the various outcomes. If I told Eden he was coming, she'd panic. If I didn't tell her and she found out when Deacon arrived, she'd accuse me of keeping things from her.

I went over the agreement we'd made. The loophole was clear. I told her I'd treat her like my wife in all ways, *except* work. I could, with a clear conscience, not tell her about her ex-boyfriend's whereabouts.

Except ...

She also demanded that I didn't treat her as a client.

If we had come together in any other way, would it be a reasonable assumption that I would tell her if an ex-boyfriend was sniffing around? Logic said no, I wouldn't, yet my gut said that would be a mistake.

Tell her. Don't tell her. The two options spun around in my head. Maybe I should wait until I knew what Knight and Deacon had to tell me. That way I'd have all the information instead of just part of it. It would be a valid argument that I didn't want to cause undue stress when I didn't know for sure what he was doing and where he was.

Decision made, I dropped the pen and tapped out the same reply to both of them.

ME: Okay.

Pocketing my cell, I stood and walked across my study to throw open the door.

"Eden?" I shouted her name, and she appeared at the end of the hallway a minute later.

"We're going out."

"We are? Where?"

"To Knight's place. He wants to see me today instead of

tomorrow." I stepped out of the room and closed the door behind me. "Grab your coat …" My eyes dipped to her bare feet. "And shoes. We'll leave in ten minutes."

***

Knight's apartment was an hour's drive outside of Glenville, on a privately owned complex surrounded by walls, trees, and electric gates. A security guard was seated in the small hut to the right, and I slid down the window as the car rolled to a stop.

"Hi, Mr. Chambers. Your brother called down earlier to say he was expecting you. Go straight through."

"Thanks." I waited for the gates to open, then followed the road around to the four-story building Knight lived in. Residential parking bays lined the road and we pulled into the second one owned by Knight, next to his black SUV.

I climbed out, strode around to open the passenger door, and held out a hand to help Eden out, and we walked across along the path to the doors. A set of buzzers were to the side of the door, and I pushed the one with Knight's name beside it.

"What?" Knight's voice, distorted by the speaker, replied.

"It's me."

"Come up." The door unlocked and we walked inside.

"Knight owns the entire building. He lives on the top floor. He just bought the rest so he didn't have to deal with any neighbors," I explained as we waited for the elevator. "The only way to get into the top floor apartment is via elevator. He blocked off the stairs."

"That seems a little excessive."

A quiet ding heralded the arrival of the elevator a second before the doors slid open. We stepped inside and I hit the button for the top floor.

"Knight is not as sociable as me and Rook."

I quirked a brow at her quiet laugh.

"I wouldn't put sociable in the same sentence as you. I'm not sure about Rook. But you are *not* sociable."

"And yet I'm still more sociable than Knight."

The doors swished open. "Just along here." I led her to the left and rapped on the door at the end of the hallway.

There was a series of clicks, and then the door swung open. Knight stood beyond it. His eyes moved from me to Eden and then back again.

"Hmm. Wasn't expecting you to bring her with you."

I shrugged. "Safer than leaving her at home."

His smile was crooked. "Sure, that's the reason. Come in."

60

Eden

The interior of the apartment didn't match what I'd imagined. I'd expected something like the things you saw on television when people went into the homes of long-term hoarders, with a man dressed in scruffy old clothes.

The reality was very different.

The man himself was dressed in a pair of gray sweats and a plain white t-shirt. Tattoos covered both arms. His dark hair was longer than Bishop's, falling down into his eyes and looked like he'd run his fingers through it more than once. But his eyes were the same as his brother's—dark, knowing, and sharp.

The apartment was large, with clean white walls, a dark wood floor and minimal furniture. Two doors led off from one end of the main room, and a third door was on the opposite wall. A television took up almost the entire third wall, while the fourth was glass and I could see out onto a secluded balcony, with walls high enough to give anyone sitting out there privacy from the street below.

"Can I get you anything to drink?" Knight's voice pulled my attention away from the room and back to the two men.

"No, thank you."

He nodded. "Okay, well I need to talk to Bishop, so ..." He waved a hand toward the couch on the opposite side of the room. "The remote control is on the table. Help yourself to drinks from the refrigerator or there's a coffee machine on the side." He jerked his chin to the kitchen area which swept around to the right of the door we'd come through.

"Knight." Bishop sighed.

His brother shrugged. "You know the rules, Bish. I don't know her. She's not coming in."

"It's fine." I wasn't sure what he was talking about, but I didn't want to cause any arguments.

"See, it's fine," Knight said and walked over to the single door on the far side of the room.

Bishop shook his head and looked at me. "I'll be as quick as I can." While there was nothing in his tone or face to suggest it, I was sure Knight's behavior was irritating him.

"Bishop." Knight called his brother's name from beside the door, and Bishop's gaze shifted to him.

"Make yourself at home. Just don't open any doors. They'll be alarmed."

"I won't." I crossed to the couch and sat down, reaching

forward for the television remote.

I'm not sure how long I spent flicking through the channels. Longer than thirty minutes, less than an hour. I watched the last ten minutes of a well-known sitcom, caught the tail end of another show I'd watched before, and then jumped through the channels again.

Something familiar caught my eye as I channel-hopped, and I frowned.

That couldn't be right.

I flicked back, and my entire body locked up.

No way.

I grabbed the remote control and stabbed at the volume, turning it higher.

"—missing girlfriend of Detective Chester Dulvaney continues. The last confirmed sighting of Eden Marshall was a week ago in Dallas. The security camera footage from a nearby late-night store shows Ms. Marshall getting into a car with an unknown person. If you have any information on her whereabouts or the identity of the man with her, please call …" The presenter gave the number for a dedicated missing person's hotline.

I stared at the grainy photograph of myself on the screen. It showed a side profile view of Bishop as he marched me to his car. Thankfully, it hadn't caught the gun he was pointing at me or gave a clear image of his face.

Thankfully?

Laughter, shrill and slightly hysterical, bubbled up and I pressed my lips together firmly to stop it escaping.

Chester had reported me missing.

He'd organized a manhunt to track me down.

There was no longer anywhere to hide.

Chester was going to find me, no matter what I did.

And now I'd dragged Bishop into it with me.

Oh god. Bishop!

What would he say when he discovered we were both splashed across the news? He was going to kill me.

My eyes darted around the room, and for half a second I thought about leaving while he was occupied with his brother. I even stood and hurried to the door, but then I stopped.

What are you doing?

I sucked in a breath, trying to calm my racing heart, and let my hand drop from the door handle.

What had Bishop said to me? I thought back to the conversation we'd had in the diner.

... Since you're my wife, it's my duty to fucking kill anyone who has hurt you ...

... I won't go looking for him, but if he turns up, I'll deal with him however I see fit ...

My gaze returned to the tv screen.

Chester was going to turn up. Someone was going to recognize me and call in a sighting.

Bishop was right.

I was never going to be able to rest until he was removed for good.

61

Bishop

"That was rude."

Knight didn't respond. He closed the door and bolted it, then crossed the room to the desk which spanned one wall.

"Knight."

"I know, but I wanted you to hear about what I have found before she does. Then you can decide what you're going to do with the information. Trust me, you'll thank me for it." He tapped a couple of keys on the keyboard, and the screens on the wall came to life. "Let's start with Sandro Trebuni."

He pulled out a chair and sat down, fingers moving rapidly over the keyboard. "It took me a while to track him down."

An image of the man from the warehouse where I'd found Eden flashed up onto one of the screens.

"He works out of New York as an associate with the Ricci

family. Sandro Trebuni is not his real name, so the ID you found was fake. He uses quite a few other names, but once I had a clear photograph and some identifying tattoos, it made things easier."

A new photograph replaced the first. The same man, slightly younger. "Meet Ricardo Rossi, low-life drug dealer and regular informant for the NYPD."

A third photograph joined the two on the screen. Of Trebuni and another man.

"Rossi is Detective Dulvaney's CI."

"So, Dulvaney hired Rossi to track down Eden." That had been my hunch, so I wasn't particularly surprised by it.

Knight leaned back on his seat. "This is where it gets interesting. The screen name you gave me, *FreedomIsPainful.* Once I got through all the redirects, it finally pinged on a contract phone out of Baltimore." He spun the chair around to face me. "You'll never guess who owns it."

"Tell me."

"Guess."

"I'm not playing games, Knight. Just tell me."

"Susannah Fletcher."

People rarely shocked me. I could count on the one hand the number of times anyone's actions had rendered me speechless. For the most part, humans were creatures of habit, and once you knew them well, they became predictable.

This was *not* predictable.

"Susannah? Are you sure?"

"There's no doubt at all. I won't bore you with the technical details on how I tracked it down. All you need to know is the end result. And *that* is the fact that Susannah Fletcher is *FreedomIsPainful*."

It made sense, in a way. She knew my line of work—enough to give Eden details that would make me wonder who she had spoken to. If she'd been watching me, then she would have known my whereabouts.

The only question to be asked was *why?* Why had she sent Eden in my direction in the first place?

"Your relationship with Susannah was the worst kept secret ever," Knight said when I didn't speak. "I'm pretty sure her husband has been aware of it from the start. Because, when I said this is where things get interesting, I wasn't talking about Eden's contact being Susannah."

I frowned. "Then what did you mean?"

"You told me, Eden was sent to meet you. From what I've pieced together, Trebuni was sent by Dulvaney to take Eden back to New York. Somewhere along the way, he acquired a second job which paid better than the first."

"A *second* job?"

"You said there were three people at the warehouse. Trebuni and two others. You left one alive to take a message back to his employer."

"That's right."

"Those other two men weren't originally with Trebuni.

They were sent along by his new employer to help ensure his instructions were followed. Instead of being charged with taking Eden back to Dulvaney in New York, he was paid to have Eden lead them to you. Eden was just a means to an end at that point. They probably would have killed her once they had you secured. Only that went horribly wrong for them. The guy you left alive scurried back to his boss and passed on your message."

"And I assume you know who *that* is?"

Knight's lips stretched into a smile. "Come on, Bish. You know the answer to *that*. Just think about it for a second."

A recent conversation flashed through my mind.

... I don't care who she fucks, but the rule has always been no more than a couple of times with the same person. If it hadn't already ended, I'd have searched him out to make that clear ...

I scrubbed a hand down my face.

Trebuni must have seen an opportunity to work both angles.

On behalf of Dulvaney, he questioned me about Eden. Once he'd gotten all the answers he needed about my part in her planned disappearance, I had no doubt he would have then moved onto Fletcher's part of the job and the message he wanted to send, which I'm certain would have resulted in my death.

Would Eden have survived that night if I hadn't killed Trebuni? At this point, it didn't matter. I *did* kill him, and *she* survived.

"The good news is you're not dead, so I guess Fletcher was satisfied with what he saw at Crosby's over the weekend." Knight's voice broke my internal thought process.

"And the bad news?" Because there was *always* bad news.

"Dulvaney has issued a missing persons alert on Eden." He tapped the keyboard and brought up a news report. "If I was a betting man, I'd say he's on his way to Glenville to get back his property."

"Eden isn't his property."

Knight's lips tipped up. "I'm aware of that. Apparently, she's yours. But the point is, he'll be on his way, so you need to get ready to deal with him."

62

Eden

I was sitting down on the couch again by the time the door swung open, and Bishop and Knight walked back into the room. I jumped up when they appeared and threw out my hand toward the tv screen.

"We're both on the news. Chester reported me missing." The lack of reaction from either man told me they already knew. "When were you going to tell me?"

"I've only just found out myself," Bishop said.

"What do I do? People are looking for me! He might already know where I am. What if someone at the diner saw us and called their hotline?"

"They probably did. The only thing that's changed is instead of not knowing if or when Dulvaney would turn up, we now know he will and soon."

I stared at him. He was so calm, so unruffled, where I was

ready to bolt at the slightest sound. My stomach churned, the butterflies turning to hornets in my stomach, spinning and twisting. I felt like I was going to vomit.

"I need to use the bathroom."

"Door on the right," Bishop pointed toward one of the two on the opposite wall to the room he'd just come out of, and I dashed across the room.

"No, wait. Don't—" Knight's voice reached me as I threw open the door. "Fuck."

I stopped, and it took a moment or two for what I was seeing to register in my brain. I blinked, rubbed my eyes, blinked again, but the image didn't change.

Voices sounded behind me, followed by footsteps but I didn't take my eyes off the figure on the floor beside the radiator.

"Knight," Bishop said from close behind me. "Why is there a woman chained to the radiator in your bathroom?" His hand closed over my shoulder and drew me away so he could take my place.

Knight cleared his throat. "Funny story, really."

"You've kidnapped someone?" I whirled to face him. "What kind of man are you?"

Bishop's hand stretched out and wrapped around my arm, grip tight. "Settle down, Eden. Knight, explain."

"It's not really kidnapping when they break into your apartment." Knight shoved a hand through his hair, raking it back from his face. "It's more …." His head rocked back and forth. "Well, it's more a case of delaying their escape, isn't it?"

I twisted back to peer into the bathroom again. The girl on the floor lifted her head, her lips twisting into a sneer. "Fucking asshole." Her voice was raspy, low, and full of venom.

"You're the intruder here, not me." It sounded like it wasn't the first time he'd said that.

Bishop blew out a breath. "D'you know what? I don't want to know. Come on, Eden. We need to get back to the house."

"You're just going to leave her there?"

"It's none of our business."

"But—"

"Knight has it handled. If he needs help, he'll ask for it."

"I don't need help." He pulled the door closed, sealing the woman back inside. "I only locked her in there because you were coming over."

"Where have you been keeping her?"

"Radiator in here." He jerked his chin across the room.

"How long has she been here?" Bishop asked.

"Couple of days. Caught her trying to break through the balcony window. She hasn't said anything yet, so I don't know who paid her or what she's here to steal. But I'll wear her down."

"Okay, well if you need any help with that, let me know. We're going back to the house. Deacon is on his way. I've had him keeping an eye on Dulvaney." He released my arm and pressed his palm against my back. "Let's go."

I let him steer me toward the door and out into the hallway beyond.

"If anything else comes up, I'll call you," Knight said. "But I think I've uncovered everything you need already."

Bishop nodded, and less than a minute later we were in the elevator traveling down to the entrance hall.

"You weren't surprised by the girl in the bathroom, were you?" I said when the doors opened.

"I didn't expect him to have a girl handcuffed to the radiator, if that's what you mean. But him dealing with an intruder that way isn't a surprise, no. Knight guards his privacy and his computer systems ruthlessly. If she's been sent to steal something, he won't stop until he finds out what it is and who sent her."

"Will he hurt her?"

His head turned toward me, and his eyes tracked over my face. "In a normal world, it's easy to say a man should never hurt a woman. And I stand by that sentiment wholeheartedly. But the world we live in isn't black and white, Eden. And there are circumstances where it becomes difficult to distinguish between right and wrong."

"That didn't answer my question."

"Because I can't answer it. I don't know what he will do. Knight is the least violent amongst us, he prefers his computers and own company over spending time with people, but he *will* protect what's his by whatever means he deems necessary. If he needs to hurt her to stay safe, then I have no doubt he will do it. But he will do everything he can *not* to cross that line."

L. ANN

63

Bishop

I was wrapped up in my own thoughts most of the drive back to my house. Key information Knight had brought to light was making me view my initial meeting with Eden in a different way.

We were meant to cross paths, one way or another. But why? Why had Susannah gone to all the trouble of putting her on my radar. Had Eden just been a random pawn in whatever game Susannah was playing, or had she been chosen specifically.

The only way I could find out would be to speak to the woman herself, which made me wonder if *that* was the sole reason she'd done it in the first place. But then she had to believe that I'd find out she was behind it. And she'd gone to a lot of trouble to hide who she was.

And that didn't account for the fact her husband had somehow discovered what was happening and added his own agenda to the situation.

Four people—Susannah, David, Dulvaney and Eden. One outcome—me taking the job. A scenario that wouldn't have come about if I hadn't needed her to play a role for me.

"Who's that?" Eden's voice broke the silence, and I glanced over at her. "There's a man sitting on the steps." She pointed to the steps leading to the front door.

Dark haired, in jeans and a t-shirt, he had his forearms resting on his knees as he watched my car approach. When I parked, he rose to his feet and padded down to meet us.

"That's Deacon." I looked around when I climbed out. "Where's Gemma?"

"She's gone home. Cormac wanted her to do something for him. Dulvaney is holed up in a hotel in town."

"Already?"

"He's eager to get the girl back. He took a trip to the local hardware store and bought supplies."

I paused in the process of opening the passenger door and looked at him. "Supplies?"

Deacon shrugged. "The usual. Duct tape, rope. Nothing too suspicious."

"His plan is to grab her, then. That makes our next move easier."

"No." Deacon rested his hand against the door, stopping me from opening it. "He doesn't plan to grab her, Bishop. He plans to kill her." His voice was low. "This isn't some low-level stalking in the hopes of getting back together. This is, in Gemma's words, Misery-level shit. If he can't have her, no one can." He stepped back, and I opened the door for Eden. "Funny thing is, though, there was a woman waiting for him in town when he got here. She paid for his room and bought him dinner."

"A woman? Describe her." I took Eden's hand as she climbed out to steady her and looked at Deacon.

"Dominant, conniving, smelled rich and rotten."

I frowned. "That's not a helpful description."

He huffed out a breath. "Gemma said the same thing. She told me to take a photograph and show it to you." He pulled a cell phone out of his back pocket, tapped on the screen then turned it to face me.

A familiar blonde filled the screen.

"Wait. Isn't that Susannah?" Eden said.

"Susannah?" Deacon pocketed his cell.

"Married to David Fletcher. Gangster who works out of Baltimore," I explained.

"Now why would *she* be meeting with a low-level detective from New York?"

I tipped back my head and looked up at the sky. "It's a long and, apparently, complicated story, but the short answer is I have no fucking idea. Let's go inside and I'll fill you in."

***

"Why me?" Eden asked when I finished explaining everything I knew to both of them.

"We have to assume you were just a random choice. We had no connection prior to meeting. The real question is why was she looking to put someone in my path?"

Eden toyed with the sleeve of her top, plucking at a loose thread. "She told me you'd helped a friend of hers in a similar situation."

"I haven't. That was a lie to make her look more believable and convince you to contact me. She must have been looking for someone who was desperate enough to take the word of a stranger."

"And now you have a photograph of her meeting with Chester. When was that taken?"

"Earlier today," Deacon replied.

Eden paled. "They're both *here*?"

I reached out to cover her hand with mine. "I'm not going to let anything happen to you."

"You can't promise that."

I held her gaze. "You know that I can. That's why you sought me out in the first place, remember. That hasn't changed, Eden. No matter what happens between us over the next three weeks, I *will* still protect you from him."

Deacon's eyes shifted from me to her and back again. "You're just like your brother. He ended up involved with his client, and now you are."

"It's not the same."

Deacon snorted. "You keep telling yourself that." He stood and stretched. "I'm heading back into town. I'll take a look around your property before I leave, just to make sure there's no one sniffing around."

"I don't think he'll try anything tonight. He'll want to check the lay of the land first."

"I agree, but there is no harm in being cautious. I have a room at the same hotel as him, so I'll keep you updated on his movements."

We walked to the front door. "Thanks, Deacon."

He patted my shoulder. "Anytime, Brother."

When I returned to the kitchen, I found Eden on her feet, pacing the room. I moved into her path, blocking her way. She stopped in front of me, hands twisting together.

"He's never going to stop, is he?"

"No." There was no point in lying.

"I don't know what to do."

I looped my arms around her waist and tugged her against my chest. "You don't have to do anything. I'll deal with it."

And, for the first time since we met, she didn't argue with me.

64

Eden

"What if I called the police station and told them I'm not missing?"

Bishop looked up from where he was stretched out on the bed. "I was going to talk to you about that in the morning. We could call them, or we could take a trip into town, go to the station and let them see you're alive and well. My only concern is whether Dulvaney has been there already."

I sat on the edge of the bed. "What could he have said? If I speak to them, surely that proves I'm not missing."

"It proves that you're not dead and gives a confirmed location of where you are, yes. But it doesn't prove you're here willingly. I don't want to let you go alone, but on the other hand, if we insist on a call or them coming here, they might think I'm forcing you to tell them what I want you to say. Especially if Dulvaney has told them I grabbed you."

"Do you think he'd do that?"

"He's started a manhunt to search for you. At this point, I'd put nothing past him."

"So going in person is really the only option."

"If we want the news to stop reporting you as a missing person, I think it is."

I tried to ignore the fear churning in my stomach and nodded. "Will you come with me?"

"I have no intention of letting you go alone." His tone sent a chill down my spine.

I twisted on the bed to look at him. "What aren't you telling me?"

"I'm not lying to you."

"But you're keeping something back."

He lifted a hand to wrap a lock of my hair around one finger. Using it as an anchor, he tugged me forward until I was leaning above him, hands braced against his shoulders.

"He's a New York detective, so he has no jurisdiction here, but professional courtesy means the local officers might allow him to be there while they interview you."

I tensed.

"And *that's* the exact reason I didn't mention it."

"I can tell them I don't want to talk to him, can't I?"

"You can. But it doesn't mean he won't be nearby." He released my hair and stroked the back of his hand over my cheek. "I'll be there with you. Deacon will wait outside, so he can watch for any surprises Dulvaney may have organized."

"Surprises?"

"He wants you back in his control, Eden. That's what this is about. And he's using his position on the police force to do it. If he can't get you through legal means, by making everyone believe you're here under duress, he'll have something set up to grab you once we leave. I'm confident that he's purposely set this up to make sure you have no choice but to go to the station."

I swallowed, fear solidifying into a cold lump in my chest.

"Why is he doing this?"

"Partially because you left him. But his pursuit of you isn't consistent with his pattern."

"What do you mean?"

"The two women before you … he continued to pester them for a while after they split up, but he quickly moved on to the next. With you, that doesn't seem to be the case." A faint smile teased his lips. "I can't fault him for that, really. There is definitely something appealing about you."

"You find me appealing?" The knot of fear inside me eased a little at his words.

His hand slid around to the back of my neck and pulled me down, then rolled and pinned me beneath him.

"Appealing, and very, very distracting." His lips kissed a path along my jaw, while one hand found its way beneath the hem of my top and slid up over my ribs to palm my breast.

"You can be a little distracting yourself." I wound my arms

around his neck and let myself fall into the heat of his kiss, only to break away when someone pounded on the main door to the house. "What was that?"

Bishop's brows pulled together. "Stay here."

He rolled off the bed, pulled open the door at the bottom of his nightstand. My eyes widened when he took out a gun. With a practiced move, he released the magazine and checked how much ammunition was in it, then slammed it back into place.

"Do not leave this room," he warned me, and strode across the floor.

I leaned up, watching as he opened the door. "Bishop, what if it's Chester?"

He didn't reply.

"Bishop?" I called after him.

"Stay put." His voice was clipped. He pulled the door closed behind him and I was left alone in the room.

65

Bishop

Whoever was hammering on the door seemed determined to take it off its hinges. I flicked off the safety on my handgun as I approached, put my left hand on the handle, and leaned against the wood.

"Who is it?"

"Police. Open up."

I frowned. "What can I do for you, officers?"

"Open the door or we'll break it down. Step back and put your hands on your head."

I reset the safety, glanced around and slipped the gun into the pocket of Eden's jacket, then turned the lock on the door. Stepping back, I lowered to my knees and linked my fingers behind my head. I didn't want any trigger-happy officer blowing my brains out because he was scared of me.

"Door is unlocked," I called out.

The door swung open, and three handguns immediately pointed at me.

"May I ask why you're here?"

"Shut the fuck up." One of the officers stepped forward. "Bishop Chambers?"

"That's right."

"We're arresting you on suspicion of kidnapping. Anything you say…"

I tuned out the rest of the words while I studied the officers in front of me. I didn't resist when the officer talking pulled my hands down to handcuff me and haul me to my feet. But when he tried to force me out of the house, I stopped.

"You should probably let my wife know. She's upstairs. Please announce yourself before going into our room. I'd rather you didn't scare her needlessly. She'll be shaken enough over this idiocy."

"We're well aware of the woman you have trapped here, Chambers."

"You've been misinformed. The only woman here is my wife, and she is free to come and go as she chooses."

"You'll get your chance to tell us your side of things at the station. Now move."

I clenched my jaw, resisting the urge to snap back. It wouldn't do me any favors right now. Hopefully Eden would have the good sense to call Magdalena's number and tell Rook what was going on. If not, well I always had a phone call to look forward to.

The biggest problem was that with me out of the way, even

if it was only for long enough to clear up the misunderstanding, it left Eden alone and unprotected, and there wasn't a damn thing I could do about it.

As I walked down the steps to where the patrol car waited, a figure stepped out from beside a second car.

"Thanks, officers. I'll bring Ms. Marshall down to the station separately." Chester Dulvaney smiled in my direction. "I'm sure she'll be relieved to know she's finally safe from this madman."

"Officer, you need to make sure she's not alone with him." I resisted as he tried to force me into the car. "Listen to me!"

"In the car, Chambers, unless you want to add resisting arrest to the list of charges."

"Fucking listen to me!"

"Don't make me shoot you."

I ground my teeth in frustration. Dead, I was no use to her. I had to trust that she'd keep her cool when she saw Dulvaney and wouldn't go anywhere with him alone.

***

I drummed my fingers against the desk. Three hours I'd been sitting here, handcuffed and alone. No one had been in to talk to me since leaving me here, and I was getting annoyed.

I hated not knowing what was going on, but I also knew there was a strong chance that someone was watching me through the one-way glass.

I turned my head toward it.

"If you're not going to question or charge me, you should let

423

me go. You're just wasting my time and yours by keeping me here. Or, and I know this is a crazy suggestion, but maybe you should speak to Eden. She could clear this whole mess up in seconds."

Where was Eden? Surely, they'd have spoken to her by now. *What had Dulvaney said to her? Was she okay?*

The frustration at not having the answers was getting under my skin, which I'm sure was why I'd been left alone for so long.

I tipped my head back and glared at the ceiling. "I want my lawyer." Maybe that would bring someone into the room. I was confident I didn't need a lawyer. I just needed someone to come into the fucking room.

"What the fuck is going on?" I bellowed the words, anger finally overcoming my good sense.

The door swung open a second later, which surprised me, and I narrowed my eyes to glare at the plain-clothes detective who walked in.

"Finally. Would you like to tell me where my fucking wife is?"

"I'm sorry to keep you waiting, Mr. Chambers." The detective leaned close and unlocked the handcuffs and took them off my wrists. "We were trying to sort through the mess. I'm Detective Flannigan. Can I get you something to drink?"

"No, you can get me my wife." An expression settled onto his face that turned me cold. I leaned forward. "Where. Is. Eden?"

"We're not sure."

"What the fuck do you mean you're not sure? She was in the house when I left. When you left her with—" My hand slammed down onto the tabletop and I surged to my feet. "You fucking idiots," I roared. "You left her with him, didn't you?"

"Please sit down. We need you to tell us exactly what's happened over the past two weeks."

"And how do you think that's going to help? Where the fuck did he take her?"

He looked away, Adam's apple bobbing as he swallowed. "He was supposed to follow the patrol car back to the station. It seems that somewhere along the way, he ..." he licked his lips. "Well, neither of them arrived. We've had cars patrolling the route for the past two hours, searching for them."

"Am I free to go?" My voice was clipped.

"While you're not under arrest, I would appreciate your time while we piece together what has happened."

I stalked toward the door.

"Mr. Chambers—"

"Fuck you." I threw the door open and walked out.

66

Eden

"Ms. Marshall?" A uniformed female officer walked into the bedroom, after tapping on the door. "We're here to take you home. Is there anything we can do for you? Are you okay?"

"I'm fine. What do you mean take me home? I'm home already."

She wrapped a hand around my arm. "If you'll come with me, we have a car waiting for you."

"Wait. Where's Bishop?"

"Mr. Chambers will meet us at the station. Do you need to bring anything? Are you hurt at all?"

"What? No. I'm fine." I pulled my arm free. "We were going to come to the station tomorrow. Can't this wait until then?"

"It's okay, Eden. I can call you that, can't I? You're safe now."

I blinked at her. "What are you talking about?"

"I know it's confusing, but if you'll come with me, we can

get you settled somewhere comfortable and then we'll talk about everything. We have a doctor at the station waiting to check you over, if you're comfortable with that?"

Her soothing voice grated on my nerves. "I want to see Bishop."

"We'll arrange that, I promise, but first let's go down to the station, okay?" She drew me out of the room, pausing to scoop up a pair of shoes from near the door. "Are these yours?"

I nodded.

"Do you have a jacket anywhere?"

"Hanging near the door."

"Okay, good. Why don't you put that on, and we'll go out to the car?"

I found myself ushered down the stairs. Police lights flashed outside, and three uniformed officers were standing near the door. The female officer handed me my shoes and coat. I slipped both on.

"Can I ride with Bishop?"

"I'm afraid not. He's already left. You'll see him at the station."

I followed her outside.

"Here, this is your ride." She opened the back door of an unmarked police car. "We thought you'd prefer not to have attention drawn to you."

"I ... umm ... appreciate that." I climbed into the back of the car and settled onto the seat. She slammed the door, sealing me inside. "Wait ..." I reached across to the handle, my intention to open it, but nothing happened, and there was no way of lowering the window. "Damn it."

The driver's door opened, and someone climbed in and started the engine.

"Can I go back inside and get my phone? I need to call someone." I wanted to call Magdalena who could tell Rook what was going on, just in case.

I didn't get a response, the car rolling forward past the police cars. One lifted a hand to wave, and then we were sailing down the drive.

"Excuse me, officer? I need my cell. Can we go back please?" I leaned forward and tapped on the security bars separating me from the front of the car. "Officer?"

"Don't worry, Eden. You don't need your cell phone. I have everything you need right here."

My heart stopped beating.

"Chester?" The word came out as a whisper.

"Hello, darling." He glanced back at me. "You've been a very bad girl. We're going to need to have a long chat when we get home. I'm not impressed that I had to come all this way to get you. What were you thinking?"

67

Bishop

A familiar face was in the hallway near the entrance of the station when I walked out of the interview room.

"Mr. Chambers, wait!" The detective was hot on my heels.

I lifted a hand and turned to my brother. "Well?"

"Dulvaney left his hotel around nine and came down to the station. Deacon followed. He called me when a squad of uniforms set off to your place. He saw them take you and hung around. They put Eden into a car with the fuckwit stalking her. I came straight here, while he followed Dulvaney."

"You know where they are?"

Rook nodded. "My car is parked across the street; Dally is safe at home. I'm ready to go when you are."

"This is a police matter. The girl was registered missing. At the very least tell me what you know?" the detective demanded.

I swung to face him.

"What I *know* is that one of your own has lost his fucking mind. That girl, *my wife*, escaped from that fucking asshole and *you* handed her back to him. If she's hurt in any way, you can kiss your career goodbye." I turned back to Rook. "Show me." We set off along the sidewalk.

"Wait. I'll come with you. You can fill me in on the details on the way."

I stopped, and turned slowly, frowning. "Why aren't you demanding more information?"

His eyes shifted away from me. I advanced on him. "You knew. You *fucking* knew. You let him take her because you needed proof. This entire fucking thing. Announcing her as missing, turning up at my house, taking me to the station and leaving her with him … you used her as fucking bait."

"Bishop." Rook's hand touched my arm. I shook him off.

"We had nothing on him other than suspicions. We needed something concrete."

"Concrete?" My voice was soft. "How's this for fucking concrete?" I punched him.

He staggered backward. I'd have gone after him, only my brother grabbed hold of me again. "We don't have time for this." He forced me back around and shoved me forward. "Keep moving. Detective, if you really want to take this fucker down, you can follow along, but don't get in our way."

When we reached Rook's car, I stopped. "Where are they?"

432

"Deacon said he was holed up in a motel just outside of town. I told him to hold off going in until we got there unless he needed to."

Unless Dulvaney hurt Eden, he meant.

"Being a cop means we can't just go in and take the fucker out," Rook continued. "He'll be missed, and with Eden all over the news as a missing person, it would be too easy to link his death to you."

"That's why you invited Detective Flannigan along. To give us credibility when I blow his head off."

Rook unlocked his car and opened the door. "Something like that."

I nodded. "Let's go."

***

"There's Deacon." Rook nodded toward a dark shadow which peeled away from the wall when we turned into the parking lot.

I was out of the car before it rolled to a stop. "Update me."

"They went inside a couple of hours ago. I've heard shouting from him, but your girl hasn't said a word that I could hear."

"Any signs of violence?"

Deacon's head canted, brown eyes gleaming under the light of the motel sign. "If there had, you wouldn't have found me standing out here," he said softly.

The detective's car pulled into the space beside us. Deacon frowned as he climbed out.

"This is Detective Flannigan. Apparently, Dulvaney has been on their radar for a while. He hasn't shared what for." I slanted a look at the detective. "But he's going to tell us right now. *Aren't* you?"

"We have reason to believe that Chester Dulvaney has been using his position as a detective working out of New York to commit various crimes … mostly against women, including rape and murder."

I started toward him again.

"Bishop. What the fuck is wrong with you? Calm down." Rook stepped between us.

"When he put in a missing person report for Eden, we thought that she might already be dead, and it was his way of covering his tracks. But then a sighting of her was reported here in Glenville. The detective investigating the case in New York reached out to tell us Dulvaney was traveling here, and I was asked to keep an eye on him."

"And you thought that using an innocent girl, who's already been his victim in too many fucking ways to list, would be the way to catch him?" Anger simmered under my skin, an emotion I wasn't used to feeling. I flexed my fingers. "If she's hurt—"

"Okay, enough. We're not getting anywhere standing out here arguing." Rook, the voice of reason, cut in.

"If Eden Marshall is really your wife, then I understand why you're angry and upset."

"You have no fucking idea," I growled.

"But the fact of the matter is unless we have proof that he's kidnapped her, there's nothing we can do. For all we know, they're celebrating being reunited in there."

I lost the battle to control my temper.

68

Eden

on't panic.

I took a couple of deep breaths. "Where are we going?"

"I booked a room in a motel so we can talk."

"Talk?"

"I think it's important to have open communication, don't you?" His voice was calm.

My heart rate increased. I knew that tone. When he was calm, he was at his most dangerous. A single word could send him over the edge into violence.

"Eden, you didn't answer my question."

My mind blanked. *What had he asked?* I scrambled to think about the words he'd spoken instead of the tone he'd used.

Oh, that was it.

"Yes, communication is very important."

"I'm glad we agree."

A flashing motel sign came up on the left, and he turned the car into the attached parking lot.

"I'm going to open the door and let you out. Our room is directly ahead. Number seventeen. Walk straight to it. If you scream or try to bring attention to yourself, I won't be happy with you."

"I understand."

He turned off the engine and threw open the driver's side door. I took the opportunity to remove my wedding rings and slipped them into my jacket pocket. If he saw them, he'd kill me, I knew that as surely as I knew my name. My fingers touched something cold and solid.

When he opened the passenger door, I slid across the seat and climbed out. His hand gripped my forearm, and he pulled me across the parking lot. I went with him, without fighting.

I needed to stay calm, be patient, and find a way to escape. I'd done it before. I could do it again.

I waited quietly while he unlocked the door, and walked inside when he instructed me, taking a seat on a chair beside the small, stained table on the far side of the room. I avoided looking at the bed.

"Why are you sitting there?"

"I thought you wanted to talk." I kept my eyes focused firmly on the floor.

"I do. But you don't deserve to sit on a chair yet." His tone hardened, and every part of my body tensed. "Get on the floor, like the bitch you are."

I rose from the chair and lowered myself to the floor on my knees.

"Crawl to me."

I glanced up to mark his position and leaned forward until I was on my hands and knees and crossed the floor to where he stood. His fingers tangled in my hair and yanked my head back.

"You climbed out of the window and ran away, Eden. You made me search for you. And what do I find? You're with another man."

"Not through choice." *I'm sorry, Bishop.* "He killed the people you sent after me. I was scared he was going to kill me, too."

"Why would he kill you?"

"I don't know. He threatened to shoot me. He fired his gun at me when I ran."

Chester's eyes narrowed. "Are you lying to me?"

"No! He shot at my feet, and then forced me to get into his car. I was scared, Chester. But you worked it out. You found me, and you brought the local police to arrest him." I hoped reminding him that the police knew I was with him would make him pause.

The hand in my hair flexed, and then he shoved me backward. "Take a shower. You stink of him. Scrub yourself clean."

I scrambled across the floor and darted into the bathroom. Shooting the lock, I leaned against the door, my breathing shaky. Once I'd got my breathing under control, I scanned the room. He'd been careful this time. There were no windows, no way for me to escape from the bathroom.

A bang on the door made me jump.

"I don't hear the water running. Do I need to come in there?"

"No. No, I'm just taking my clothes off."

I crossed the small room, twisted the knob for the shower and pulled the shower curtain across. I had no intention of stripping or showering. But I could stall for at least thirty minutes while he *thought* I was showering.

Maybe if I kept reminding him that the police knew I was with him, it would keep him from doing anything else.

69

Bishop

Deacon held my arms, while Rook stood between me and Detective Flannigan.

"I guess you really like this female, huh?" Deacon said.

"I'd say he does, but he needs to get his emotions in check, or she might just be dead when we get to her." Rook glared at me.

"I'm fine." I shook Deacon off.

"You're clearly *not* fine. I don't remember the last time you lost your shit."

I ignored my brother and turned my focus on the detective who was dabbing at his lip with a tissue. "If you get in my way—"

"You can't kill him. I need to take him in. I'll turn a blind eye to everything else, but he has to be alive." He held my gaze.

My jaw clenched.

"Mr. Chambers … *Bishop*, right? I know who you and your brother are. I did my homework. I know what you can do, and

I'm willing to let you do whatever you feel is necessary *except* murder him."

"I don't murder people." My voice was cold.

"Maybe you don't call it murder, but that's how everyone else will view it. If we don't take him alive, we can't take him to court and bring all the shit he's done to light. If you kill him, I will have to arrest you. And I don't think that will go well for your brother this time around, do you? He'll be implicated by simply being here with you. So, you can go in there and subdue him, and I will arrest him. Deal?"

"What exactly will you arrest him for?"

"He's overplayed his hand. He was supposed to take Eden directly to the station, not bring her here. I'm sure she will testify that bringing her here was against her will and give a statement about everything else he's done."

I gave an abrupt nod. "Fine."

"How do you want to do this?" Rook turned to me.

"It's the wrong time for room service, but perfect for a drunk going back to their room and trying to open the wrong door."

Deacon chuckled. "Guess that's my cue." He rolled up the sleeves on his shirt, untucked it from his jeans, and ran his hands through his hair to mess it up. "I'll get him to open the door, be ready to go inside. I don't know if he's armed, so be prepared."

"I'll wait out here. It's best I don't witness what you do. I'll come in once you have him locked down. Give me a nod or something when you're ready for me." Flannigan walked back to his car and sat inside.

"Do you need a gun?" Rook asked.

I shook my head. "If I have a gun, I might accidentally squeeze the trigger."

Deacon snickered. "Okay, let's do this. The doors open inward to the right. If he's cautious, he'll put his head out and look around, which means he'll see both of you, so you need to move fast once the door is open. Ready?"

I nodded. "Let's do this."

70

Eden

I had no way of gauging how long I stayed in the bathroom, but it can't have been more than five minutes before he banged on the door again.

"What are you doing?"

"Making sure I'm clean, like you said."

"Then make some noise. Sing."

I paced the floor. If I picked the wrong song, he'd come in to punish me for it.

"What do you want me to sing?"

"Something I like."

I bit my lip. It was a statement designed to make me fail. I sang the opening lines to 'Feel Something' by Pink. When he didn't burst through the door, I continued, moving closer to the shower.

When I finished that song, I started another … and another … and another … He remained on the other side of the door, quiet.

I hoped that if I carried on singing, he'd stay right where he was.

It was around song nine or ten when he finally banged on the door again. "You should be done by now. Get your ass out here."

"Just a minute." I ducked my head beneath the spray to wet my hair, then twisted it into a knot on top of my head, tossed a towel into the tub, letting it get wet, then opened the door.

He glared at me.

"Why the fuck are you wearing those clothes again?"

"They're all I have."

"I never told you to get dressed." He dragged me out by my arm.

"I thought if any of the police officers who were with you at the house came to check, you wouldn't want me to be naked."

An expression flashed across his face, gone before I could decipher it, but he nodded. "Sit down."

I let out a quiet breath and sat on the edge of the chair.

"When we get back to New York, we're going to get married, and *you* are going to apologize to my parents for all the stress you've put them under. They were scared someone had murdered you." His lips twisted. "It would have been easier if that had happened, but no, you have to get yourself caught on camera with another man." He stalked around the room, waving his hands. "And now I have to come out here and get you."

"I'm sorry."

"Not yet, you're not. But you will be." He advanced on me.

"Shouldn't we go to the police station before they come searching for us?"

He stopped, head tilting then one corner of his mouth curled up. "I know what you're doing."

I stayed silent.

"You think they'll believe your lies about not wanting to be with me. But you're wrong. I've already explained how stupid you are, how you *need* me to keep you safe. Why do you think they let me come and get you, stupid girl? They think the idiot whose house you were hiding in is the one who's a danger to you. And that's exactly what you're going to tell them before we leave." He nodded. "Yes, that's what you'll do."

And that was the moment I realized that Chester wasn't just a man who liked to hurt women. He wasn't completely sane. Had he *ever* been sane?

"I will. I promise. But you need to tell me what I need to say, so they aren't confused."

Keep him talking. If he's talking, he won't do anything else. Someone would come searching. If Bishop was allowed to make a call, he'd speak to his brother or his friend, Deacon. Someone would eventually ask why we weren't at the police station. I just had to keep him talking until then.

I slipped one hand into my jacket pocket and let my fingers curl around the cold heavy weight of the gun Bishop must have put there. I couldn't let Chester know I had it. He was bigger and stronger and would take it from me. But its solid presence gave me hope.

Hope that Bishop would convince the police officers that he

had done nothing wrong.

Hope that they would release him.

Hope that he would find me.

***

What time was it?

I couldn't tell. Chester had the curtains firmly closed, which made it hard to keep track of time. But I knew it had been almost one am when the police came to the house, and at least a couple of hours must have passed.

Every time Chester stopped ranting and came toward me, I reminded him about the police and how they knew I was with him and were expecting us to go to the station. It had distracted him so far, but awareness that it was only a matter of time before it stopped working was a constant thought in my head.

I had to think of something else. My head ached, my eyes were gritty and tired, and my throat was sore from the constant talking.

My fingers gripped the gun in my pocket. A lifeline, a talisman. If I kept hold of it; If I didn't let it go, Bishop would come. He'd find me.

A heavy thud sounded against the door. My head jerked up just as Chester spun toward it.

"Fuck." A deep, slurred voice growled. "Fuckin' key. Where's my key?" Another thud.

Chester pointed a finger at me. "Don't say a fucking word. Don't move. Don't even fucking breathe."

I nodded. "I promise."

He strode to the door, made sure the safety chain was on, then opened it slightly.

"What do you want?"

There was a short silence. "Why the fuck are you in my room?"

"This isn't your room."

"Don't fuckin' lie to me." Another thud sounded, and the door jolted back, the chain snapping taut. "Get the fuck out. I paid for this room."

"You're drunk, asshole. Get the fuck out of here." Chester started to close the door.

"Yeah, no." The next hit to the door was so hard it snapped the chain. The force of it sent Chester back a step, and the door banged off the wall and started to swing closed. Before it did, a figure slipped through.

"Get the fuck out!" Chester surged forward.

"Sorry, I can't do that." The slur dropped from the newcomer's voice, and his head turned briefly toward me. "Hey, Eden."

My lips parted.

Deacon was here.

71

Bishop

eacon dropping the drunk act was the signal for both me and Rook to move. Rook blocked the door from closing, and I followed Deacon inside.

Deacon stepped to the side, leaving Chester in my direct path. I didn't even pause. My hand lifted and wrapped around his throat. I kept moving forward, shoving him along in front of me.

His fingers clawed at my wrist, trying to make me release him. I ignored his struggles until his back slammed against the wall. And I still kept moving until we were so close, I could see the pores in the skin covering his pasty white face.

"Did you really think I wouldn't come for her?" I squeezed, cutting off his airflow. "In what scenario, did you ever see yourself coming out on top and taking her back to New York with you?"

He whispered something. I leaned closer.

"I wasn't going to take her back with me." His lips curved into a twisted sneer. "I'd have dumped her body somewhere along the way covered in your DNA because the stupid bitch refused to wash you off her skin, and then made an anonymous tip-off."

I buried my fist in his stomach. When he doubled over, I released my grip on his throat and brought my knee up and rammed his face into it. He dropped to the floor, on his hands and knees, one palm cupped over his nose. I studied him for a second, then swung my foot into his ribs, and sent him onto his side.

Dismissing him from my attention, I turned scanning the room and came to a stop on the redhead standing at the far side of the room beside Deacon. Our eyes met and locked.

"Everyone, get out." I didn't recognize the sound of my own voice. It was low, rough, *angry*. "Take that lowlife with you."

"Bishop." That was Rook. I didn't look at him.

"Get. Out."

He sighed. "We'll be waiting outside."

Deacon patted my shoulder on his way past. I didn't move, didn't shift my gaze from Eden's. Somewhere behind me there was a grunt, followed by a thud and then the door clicked shut. Less than a second later, I staggered back when Eden crashed into me.

My arms circled her waist automatically and I lowered my head. "Are you okay? Did he hurt you?"

She shook her head against my chest, fingers clutching my shirt.

I untangled one arm and pressed two fingers under her chin to tip her head back. "Look at me."

She blinked, bottom lip caught between her teeth.

"Did he hurt you?"

"No. No, I kept him talking. I thought if I just kept him talking, you'd find me."

My thumb brushed over her lips. "There's a detective outside waiting to arrest Dulvaney. They're making a case against him for several—" I broke off. She didn't need to hear how she might have been trapped for the last couple of hours with a murderer and rapist. "We need to go to the station so you can make a statement. Are you feeling up to that?"

She nodded.

I tightened my hold on her waist. "Eden—"

"I'm okay."

"You're sure?"

"I am now."

I lowered my head but didn't kiss her. The knowledge that I *wanted* to kiss her made me pause, hesitate, and instead I brushed my lips over her forehead, then guided her to the door.

Outside the motel room, Deacon and Rook were handing Dulvaney over to Detective Flannigan. As the detective turned to open the back passenger door of his car, Dulvaney lunged forward, grabbed the gun from the detective's hip holster and spun, lifting it.

Someone shouted.

Shots rang out.

Multiple shots.

In quick succession.

Dulvaney laughed, then frowned, and looked down to where a red stain spread out across the front of his shirt.

"Rook?" I turned toward my brother where he stood next to his car.

"Wasn't me."

I looked to my left. Eden stood there, a gun clutched between both hands and still pointing at Dulvaney.

"Eden?" I reached out slowly and took the gun—*my* gun, the one that I'd hidden in the jacket she was wearing—from her unresisting fingers. "Did you have that with you the entire time?"

Her head turned, green eyes huge in her pale face. "It was in my jacket," she whispered. "I didn't realize until I took off my rings and hid them in a pocket. I didn't want to let him know I had it. I was scared he'd take it from me." Her eyes jerked back to the man lying face down on the ground.

I caught her jaw between my fingers and brought her face back to me. "Don't look over there. Look at me."

"Is he—"

"Bishop," Detective Flannigan cut in. "We're going to need to take her to the station."

"Later."

"I've called it in."

"You witnessed what happened. I'll bring her later. Once she's had a chance to rest. She's been through enough."

"Bishop—"

"I *said* later."

I walked Eden past him, careful to keep my body between her and Dulvaney, and got her settled into the back of Rook's car. Deacon took the front passenger seat, and Rook climbed into the driver's side.

Flannigan didn't stop us as we drove out of the parking lot.

72

Eden

"Shouldn't we go to the police station? Won't they want to arrest me?" I looked at Bishop, where he sat beside me.

"No. We're going back to the house. We'll head to the station later and you can give your statement."

"But I shot him." I bit my lip. "I think I killed him."

"I fucking hope you killed him," Bishop growled.

"Detective Flannigan witnessed everything. You acted in self-defense." Rook said from the front of the car.

"He didn't fire the gun."

"He did. The bullet clipped my arm." Deacon twisted on his seat, and grinned. "His aim wasn't anywhere near as good as yours."

"You're hurt?" Bishop leaned forward. "Show me."

"It's nothing. Gemma has drawn more of my blood than that bullet did." He faced forward again and tipped his head back against the seat. "I'll probably head home today. I don't think you need me here anymore."

I'm not sure if I dozed off or just tuned out, but it seemed like barely any time had passed before Bishop touched my arm.

"We're home."

I blinked, frowning, and peered through the window at the familiar building.

"What time is it?" The sky was light, but I couldn't see the sun.

"Almost five. Wait there." He opened the door and climbed out and a few seconds later, the door beside me swung open. "I'll call you later and let you know what's going on," he said to Rook. "Thanks for all your help, DJ."

The man in the passenger seat waved a hand. "Always happy to cause trouble, you know that."

"Let's get you inside." Before I could move, he scooped me up into his arms.

"I can walk," I protested.

"I'm aware." He used his foot to shut the door and turned to the house.

Tires crunched on gravel behind us as Rook drove away, while Bishop strode up the steps to the front door.

"Keys are in my right pocket. Can you reach them?"

I reached down and found the pocket on his jacket, hooked my fingers around the keys and took them out.

"Unlock the door."

Trusting him not to drop me, I leaned forward, pushed the

key into the lock and turned it. The door swung open. Bishop walked inside and kicked it shut behind him. Instead of going through to the kitchen or living room, he immediately headed upstairs, through his bedroom and into the bathroom, where he lowered me to my feet.

He slid the jacket off my shoulders and down my arms, then tossed it to one side. The pajama top I was wearing was next. When he hooked his hands into the waistband of my pants and drew them down my legs, I broke the silence.

"What are you doing?"

His fingers stroked over my cheek, then reached up to pull my hair free of the messy knot I'd left it in.

"Making sure you weren't hurt."

"He didn't touch me."

"You'll forgive me for needing to make sure of that myself." Taking my hand, he led me into the walk-in shower.

"I don't need to shower for that to happen."

"Agreed, but I can see how tense you are. The heat of the water will help you to relax." He leaned past me and hit a button. Water cascaded over us both.

"Your clothes are getting soaked."

"Doesn't matter. Face the wall."

The second his hands touched me, I sighed. There was nothing sexual about the way he was touching me, but the way his hands ran over my body as he checked for bruises and marks and his fingers kneaded the knots of tension out of my shoulders, loosened the fear still holding me in its grip.

I tipped my head back, letting the water flow over me, and closed my eyes.

When he turned me to face him, I didn't resist. His hands stilled their movement, resting on my hips, and I forced my eyes to open so I could focus on him.

He was staring down at me, dark eyes unreadable. His hair was wet, slicked back from his forehead, and beads of water trickled down his face. Not really thinking about it, I rose on my toes and licked away the drops from his jaw.

He hissed and drew back.

"Eden."

Lifting my arms, I looped them around his neck. "Bishop." My voice was soft.

His mouth crashed down on mine, the hands on my waist tightening as he pulled me closer to him. I went willingly, pressing against him, and frowned when my skin met wet silk. Dropping my hands, I worked at the buttons of his shirt, struggling to pop them through the wet material.

"It's not fair that I'm naked and you're not."

A smile tilted up one side of his mouth. He grasped the front of the shirt and pulled. Buttons came loose, flying across and hitting the shower screen. I dragged the now open shirt down his arms and off.

When his hands went to the belt at his waist, I froze. Warm fingers touched my face, lifting my chin until I met his watchful gaze.

"You do it," he said softly.

73

Bishop

The anger that coursed through me every time she reacted to something because of what the asshole had done to her was white hot. If I wasn't sure Dulvaney was already dead, I'd be walking out to finish the job myself. Instead, I held myself still while she chewed on her bottom lip and stared up at me.

When her hands dropped and set to work on my belt buckle, the surge of triumph that went through me surprised me. For the first time I acknowledged that I was lying every time I told myself it was just another job, just another client. My resolve to keep it purely business had collapsed into a burning mass of 'what the fuck are you doing?' long before the first time she gave herself to me. But I couldn't bring myself to regret crossing that line, not when her hands were slipping beneath my waistband to curl around my dick.

I kicked out of my pants. A stray thought that it was a good thing I wasn't wearing socks because they'd be a bitch to get off while wet flitted through my mind, and I laughed quietly.

"What's funny?" Eden's warm breath brushed against my hip.

"Absolutely nothing at all." I drew her to her feet and caught her mouth with mine, tongue delving between her lips to tangle with hers.

Her fingers stroked over me, dancing over my skin, dragging over the piercing through the head of my dick. I groaned.

"Did it hurt?"

"A lot."

She toyed with the bar. My jaw clenched as I gritted my teeth against the sensations it sent through me.

"Then why get it done."

"Misspent youth. It seemed like a good idea at the time."

"Do you still think that?"

"I still have it. What do you think?"

"I think I need to investigate further."

"Oh?" I cocked an eyebrow. "And how do you see that investigation going?"

Her lips curved up, and she slowly lowered herself to her knees. "By getting closer, of course."

I'd had blow jobs before. Of course, I had. But not one of them prepared me for when Eden's tongue licked over the tip of my dick, then wrapped her lips around it.

"Fuck." I couldn't stop the curse falling from my lips.

Her eyelashes lifted, green eyes gleaming as she tipped her

head back and took me deeper. Her cheeks hollowed as she sucked, and licked, and slid up and down the entire length of my dick. The visual of it disappearing into her mouth, the way the waterdrops from the shower hung from her eyelashes, the soft moans she made that vibrated over my skin unraveled my control. My fingers fisted her hair, and I battled against the need to control her movements, to fuck her mouth the way I wanted to. Instead, I let her dictate the depth she took me, and fought to stop myself from erupting like a teenager.

When her tongue flicked over my piercing, I used my grip on her hair to pull her off me and drag her to her feet.

"No more."

I spun her to face the wall, buried my face into the curve of her throat, and ran my palm down her stomach until I could reach between her legs. When my fingers made contact with her clit, she let out a soft moan and arched her throat. I nipped my way up to her ear, wrapped my free hand around her jaw and pulled her head around so I could kiss her.

Her arms rose, hooking around my neck, and the move arched her back and lifted her breasts. My hand dropped from her jaw, and I stroked a circle around one nipple, then the other, while the fingers of my other hand dipped past her clit to push inside her. Her stance shifted, legs parting.

"I want you inside me. I want to know how it feels with nothing between us." She moaned the words, hips jerking as she rode my fingers.

"You want me bare?" Why did that idea make me harder?

Her ass pushed back against me, dislodging my fingers. "Yes, please."

"Right here?" I ran my hand down her spine, and squeezed one ass cheek, then fisted my dick. "Put your hands against the wall."

She moved, placing her palms against the wet tiles.

"Spread your legs a little more," I whispered against her throat, and wrapped an arm around her waist to lift her onto her toes. I positioned my dick against her pussy and slowly pushed inside her.

We groaned in tandem. The feeling of her body around mine without any barrier between us was incredible. I didn't move. *Couldn't* move. Until she reached around to dig her fingers into my ass.

"Bishop." My name falling from her lips sent my hips surging forward, driving me deeper into her body.

When she didn't tell me to stop, I did it again ... and again ... until the only sounds that could be heard were our panting, groaning breaths as flesh pounded against slick, wet flesh. I teased her nipples, pinching, twisting, and tugging, until she was a whimpering, writhing mess, then dropped my hand to play with her clit as I slammed in and out of her body.

When she came, her entire body shuddered, her whimpers turned husky and her feet scrambled for purchase on the floor. I held her tight, stopped her from falling, and continued my assault on her senses with my fingers, my teeth, and my dick.

Maybe if I gave her enough pleasure, when our contract was up, she'd stick around. I used the thought to distract me from my own building need to come, chasing it around my head. Would she want to stay here after everything that had happened? There was no real need for me to build her a new life now. She could go back to New York and pick up her old life again.

"Bishop." Her voice brought me back to the moment. "Why have you stopped?"

I blinked and shook my head, shedding my thoughts about the immediate future. Dipping my head, I kissed her shoulder.

"Just letting you get your breath back." I eased out of her and turned her around. "Put your arms around my neck."

When she'd done as I asked, I hooked my hands under her thighs and lifted her. "Wrap your legs around my waist." I backed her against the wall and thrust into her again. "Tell me how it feels."

Her eyes were half-closed, cheeks flushed, water dripping down her face. "So good," she whispered.

I licked a path over her jaw, took her bottom lip between my teeth and sucked it into my mouth. Her body undulated against mine, breasts brushing against my chest, nipples hard and pointed.

"Can you feel me inside you?"

"Yes." The word was a sigh.

I adjusted my grip and brought one hand down between our bodies to run over her clit. Her lips parted.

"Do you want to come?" I flicked and pinched and toyed with her clit in time with my thrusts.

"So bad."

"On my dick while I come inside you?"

"Oh god," she groaned. "Yes, please."

My lips found hers. "Sing for me, Songbird," I whispered.

74

Eden

I woke up with the sun shining on my face and my body surrounded by warmth. My head rested on something solid, something which moved when I rubbed my cheek against it.

"Are you awake?" a rough voice whispered against my ear.

I burrowed deeper beneath the covers and wriggled backward into the heat of his body. I didn't want to wake up. Opening my eyes meant I would have to leave the safe space I was hiding in and face reality again.

The arms around me loosened, and I clutched at his wrist when he started to move away.

"Five minutes more."

"So, you *are* awake."

I sighed and rolled over. A finger ran over my bottom lip.

"You're cute when you pout, but we really need to get out of bed."

I forced my lids to lift and peered at him. "You mean we have to go to the police station, don't you?" And just like that, nerves twisted my stomach into knots. "They're going to arrest me."

"They won't."

"You don't know that. I *killed* him, Bishop."

"It was self-defense. Detective Flannigan was there. You saved his life."

My laugh was slightly hysterical. "Chester wasn't pointing the gun at *him*."

"No. He was pointing it at you. We all saw it. If you hadn't shot him, he'd have killed you." He sat up, tugging me with him. "So, what we're going to do is this. You're going to get dressed, have something to eat to settle your nerves, and then we're going to go to the station where you will give your statement and then we'll come home."

"But—"

"No, Eden." His voice was firm. "That's not how today is going to go. There's no buts, no maybes, and no way I'll be leaving there without you by my side. You're not going to be arrested, understand?"

I nodded. I wasn't convinced, though. I fully expected to be in prison orange by the end of the day.

***

"Ms. Marshall?"

I jumped to my feet. Bishop rose more slowly beside me and scowled at the officer standing near the door.

"*Mrs.* Chambers," he corrected.

The officer's eyes jumped from me to Bishop and back again. "I'm sorry, I … Mrs. Chambers, if you'll come this way? We have an interview room prepared."

"Where's Detective Flannigan?" Bishop asked.

"Because he was involved in the situation this morning, it'll be Detective Peyton who'll take the lead in the investigation."

Bishop's hand closed over my arm, stopping me before I walked through the door. "*Investigation?*"

"Into what happened."

"It's obvious what happened, Flannigan was there."

"I know but—"

Bishop lifted a hand to silence him. "One second." He pulled his cell out of a pocket and punched in a number.

"It's me." There was a moment of silence, while he listened to whoever was on the other end of the line. "It has. It's time … Are you still located in Glenville station?" His eyes held those of the officer in front of us. "We're downstairs with Officer …" He arched an eyebrow.

"Rafferty."

"Officer Rafferty, who is waiting to interview my wife with Detective Peyton, instead of Detective Flannigan … Yes, that situation this morning involved me … When? … Okay, good. We'll be waiting." He ended the call. "Captain Jenkins is on his way down."

Rafferty paled. "There's no need for the captain—"

"Oh, I think there's *every* need. Why don't we go through to that room you mentioned and wait for him?" His hand slid down my arm and he linked his fingers with mine.

The officer's Adam's apple bobbed as he swallowed. "This way."

He pushed open a door, and stepped back to let me enter first, then moved in front of Bishop.

"I'm sorry, but this is an interview with a suspect. You can't—"

Bishop's shoulder hit him on the way past, knocking him out of the way.

"Mr. Chambers, I must ask you to—"

"I wouldn't finish that sentence, if I was you, Rafferty." A new voice spoke up.

"Captain!"

The newcomer ignored Officer Rafferty and held out a hand to Bishop.

"Good to see you, again. I should have known that situation this morning had your fingerprints all over it."

"I'm surprised my name wasn't mentioned in Flannigan's briefing. Where is he?"

"Detective Flannigan is running late and he asked Peyton to stand in for him. Unfortunately, Peyton decided to ignore Flannigan's report and take a different route. I picked up the file on my way down." He turned to the other man in the room. "Detective, it seems you have some explaining to do."

"Sir—"

"Unless the next words out of your mouth are an apology

to Mrs. Chambers and her husband, I don't want to hear it. This poor woman was kidnapped last night and *you're* planning to interrogate her over a successful attempt to defend herself. Flannigan's statement is very clear. Dulvaney went for his gun, and Mrs. Chambers reacted."

"Do you know who her husband is, Captain? This man—"

"Has absolutely no criminal record." He turned to me. "If you feel up to giving us a statement about what happened after you were taken by Chester Dulvaney last night, then I'd appreciate it. But if you'd rather wait a couple of days, I understand that as well."

"Is he really dead?"

Captain Jenkins nodded.

I turned to Bishop. "It's over?" I whispered. "He's never coming back?"

"It is." His voice seemed to come from far away. "Eden? Fuck, *Eden*."

75

Bishop

I caught Eden as she slumped forward and swung her up into my arms. Nailing Detective Peyton with a glare, I strode past him to the low, hard couch set along one wall and lowered Eden onto it. Her face was pale, eyes closed. I brushed my fingertips over her cheek.

Behind me Captain Jenkins was reprimanding Peyton, but all my attention was on the woman in front of me. She wasn't out for long. Thirty seconds … a minute at most … and then her eyelashes fluttered, and her lids lifted. A small frown creased her brow.

"Wh-what happened?"

"I think everything finally caught up with you. Can you sit up?" I helped her up and then sat beside her.

"Here." A hand appeared in front of us holding a glass of water. I looked up at Jenkins.

"Peyton has gone back to his desk." He crouched in front

of Eden. "I must apologize. You were never meant to be treated like a suspect. The only reason you're here is to give a statement. Given the circumstances, I believe that can be taken via a phone call some other time. Chester Dulvaney's death will not be investigated as a homicide, and you are free to leave whenever you wish." He glanced at me. "Does this clear my debt to you?"

"As long as no one comes sniffing around again."

"You have my word."

I nodded. "Then we're good."

"I'll leave you here then. Take your time. You're free to leave whenever your wife feels ready."

He closed the door gently behind him, leaving us alone in the room.

"What did he mean?" Eden asked softly.

"About what?"

"He asked if this cleared his debt. What did that mean?"

"I helped him out with a situation a couple of years ago."

"What is he going to do?"

"Close the case on Dulvaney."

"Just like that?"

"Just like that," I repeated.

***

Leaving Eden alone so soon after what had happened wasn't something I was happy about, but there was something I had to do. And I needed to do it fast before the opportunity was lost. But I'd waited until we had been home for most of the afternoon and

Eden seemed more settled before I made a decision.

"I have to go out for a couple of hours. I'm going to call Rook and get him to bring Magdalena over to keep you company."

"You don't have to. I'll be okay on my own."

I shook my head. "It's not open for discussion. I don't want you here alone."

Ignoring her protests, I called Rook, who spoke to Magdalena and agreed to come over within the hour.

When Rook and his girlfriend arrived, I waited long enough to make sure Eden was comfortable being left with them, and then headed out. Rook caught up with me just as I reached my car.

"Where are you going?"

"To tie up loose ends."

"Oh?"

I glanced at him. "Did you want to come along?"

"I thought you'd never ask."

"You can drive then." I tossed him my keys and got into the passenger side.

"Where are we going?" Rook asked once he was settled behind the steering wheel.

I gave him the address of the hotel in town, tipped my head back against the seat and closed my eyes. "Let me know when we get there. I'm taking a nap."

"You're not taking a nap. You just don't want to explain to me what you're doing."

"Good. We're on the same page."

"I want to go on record that I think this is a bad idea."

"Noted. Now drive."

When we arrived at the hotel, I turned to my brother. "Wait here."

"I should come with you."

I shook my head. "It's best if you stay out here. If I'm not back in twenty minutes, then you can come and rescue me."

"I don't like this, Bishop."

"Nor do I, but it's necessary." And with that, I got out of the car and headed into the hotel.

I already knew what room I needed from Deacon's earlier report, so I bypassed the reception and headed up to the third floor. Room three seventy-two had a 'do not disturb' sign hanging off the handle. I ignored it and banged on the door with my fist.

"Open the door."

It swung open thirty seconds later, to reveal Susannah, dressed only in a hotel robe, which gaped open, revealing her naked body beneath it. She smiled.

"I knew you'd come back."

"I haven't." I pushed past her and shut the door. "What the fuck are you playing at?"

Her smile faltered at my snarled question. "I don't know what you mean."

"Don't bullshit me, Susannah. You know exactly what I mean. I know *everything*. Did you really think I wouldn't figure out that you were behind Eden trying to hire me. What I want to know is *why?*"

"Isn't it obvious?"

"Would I be asking if it was obvious? And close your fucking robe, I'm not interested."

Hurt flashed over her face, then her lips thinned. "You're such a fucking asshole, Bishop. I was *trying* to help you."

"Help me?" My voice was flat. "Help me with what?"

"Do you remember telling me that you were thinking about quitting, the same way Rook did? That you didn't see the point in what you did, anymore. The people you were ..." she paused and made air quotes with her fingers, "*saving* didn't deserve it."

I frowned. "I remember telling you that most of my clients were assholes."

"Exactly!"

"That wasn't me retiring."

She waved a hand, rolling her eyes. "The point is, I wanted you to have a client who really needed your help. So, I went searching. Eventually, I found Eden. She seemed like the perfect candidate to remind you that what you do is *good.*"

"How altruistic of you."

Her eyes narrowed. "But then you went and married her. What the fuck was that, Bishop? I *loved* you, and you went and married some nobody with an asshole ex-boyfriend."

"We were over months before I met Eden, because *you* lied to me. Which, incidentally, your husband knows about. He hired the same man that the asshole *ex* hired, only the job was to take me out."

"Don't be ridiculous. David wouldn't do that."

"You're sure?" I pulled out my cell. "Why don't we ask him?"

She glared at me.

"No?"

"Fuck you, Bishop."

"No, thanks. Been there, done that, didn't rate the experience all that highly."

76

Eden

"How are you feeling?" Magdalena tucked her feet beneath her and gazed at me over the rim of her wine glass.

"I'm fine."

"*Fine* fine, or *fine?*"

I frowned at her. "What does that even mean?"

Magdalena laughed. "Fine—as in healthy and well? Or *fine*—as in fucked up, insecure, neurotic and emotional? F. I. N. E."

"That's a thing?"

"Sure, it is. So, what's the answer?"

I considered it. "I think," I said slowly, "a mixture of both. I don't know if it's just because I haven't really had time to process what happened, or if I'm just relieved it's over." I licked my lips. "I'm glad he's dead. Does that make me a bad person?"

Magdalena shook her head. "Absolutely not. Rook didn't

really tell me much. He doesn't like telling me about the darker side of humanity, he says I've lived through enough of it." Her smile was warm and happy. "These men ... they're so ..."

"Bossy?"

She laughed into her glass. "*Very* bossy. But when they love, they do it with their entire being."

She thought we were in love, that it was the reason we got married so fast. I liked Magdalena a lot, and I didn't want to lie to her.

"Bishop isn't in love with me. Our marriage isn't real. It's just a business agreement. I needed his help and didn't have the money. He needed a ..." I didn't want to tell Bishop's secrets. "Well, it suited his interests to have a temporary wife. I married him and in return he promised to give me a new life."

Magdalena was silent for a long moment. "You know," she said eventually. "I told you that I met Rook because I hired a fake boyfriend to come to dinner with me. I went to the wrong table, and according to him when he tells it, he was bored and thought I was amusing, so he took the job anyway." She took a sip of wine. "But if he hadn't, I'd be dead now." She waved a hand. "The details don't matter, the point I'm making is that the men of this family, they don't like to admit to being human, to having feelings. It takes time to break through the walls they have around them. Walls they had to build to protect them from the lives they lead. But one thing I've learned, Eden, is that the kind of jobs you and I presented to them ... they're far too logical to just take that job unless something else is driving them."

"Something else?"

"Do you really need me to spell it out? I'm dyslexic, remember, so that could go horribly wrong." She grinned at my shocked laugh.

"You spelled *fine* well enough."

"Only because of the acronym. I read it somewhere and it stuck in my head. Stop changing the subject."

"I'm not!"

"You absolutely are. Answer me this. When this pretend marriage of yours is supposed to be over, what are you going to do?" She pointed a finger at me. "And look at that expression on your face! You don't want it to be over."

"I didn't say that." My protest was weak.

"You didn't need to; it's literally written all over your face. Have you slept with him?"

I sighed into my glass and gave up even trying to avoid her questions. "More than once."

"I knew it!" Magdalena reached down for the wine bottle and filled up both of our glasses. "If he's anything like Rook ... you're not going to experience something like that with anyone else."

I covered my face with one hand. "I can't believe we're talking about this."

"You like him."

"I wasn't supposed to."

"But you *do*."

"Fine, yes. I do."

She clapped her hands, spilling wine over her fingers, and laughed. "And *this* is why I don't often drink." She lifted her hand and licked her fingers. "I have an idea."

"What kind of idea?"

"A perfect one!"

"That doesn't fill me with confidence." I eyed her.

She grinned back at me. "You said you have a contract."

I nodded.

"Do you have a copy of it?"

"Upstairs. Bishop insisted on it."

"Of course, he did." She rolled her eyes. "Bishop won't make a single move without a contract detailing every step. You're going to have to break him of that."

"He said he wasn't spontaneous and that he likes to plan things."

"He does. But," she leaned forward, "he broke that when he decided to marry you, so there's hope for him."

"Does Rook like to plan?"

"Yes, and he still stepped up and pretended to be my boyfriend. So, you see, there's a pattern here ... and we can use it to our advantage. If you want to keep him, that is."

77

Bishop

"She told Dulvaney where Eden was out of spite?" Rook asked.

We were sitting in a bar on the opposite side of the street to the hotel I'd just come out of. After Susannah's admission that her plan was to give me a job to 'help' me feel good about my work and had expected me to go back to her out of gratitude when she told me she had organized it, I laid down a number of truths.

I wasn't in love with her.

I wasn't even in *like* with her.

Her husband knew about our affair, and I had no interest in making him think it was back on.

Then I'd raised the fact I *knew* she met with Dulvaney. *That's* when she started to cry. And I felt *nothing* other than irritation.

"Apparently, Eden was the reason I didn't go crawling back

to her. She decided that since she was responsible for putting her on my radar in the first place, she'd take responsibility for removing her."

"By contacting the violent ex-boyfriend?"

I nodded.

"And people claim *we're* the ones who are morally gray. At least we're honest about what we do."

"Did. You're retired, remember." I lifted an eyebrow.

Rook smiled. "Did, then." He took a sip of his drink. "What about you?"

"What about me?"

"Well, you have a wife now. Are *you* planning to retire?"

"It's not like that."

My brother snorted. "Of course, it's not. Lie to yourself, if you must, but you don't go to this much trouble for a woman *ever*. And must I remind you that you claimed you married her out of love. Are you now saying that wasn't the case, and I was right all along? That the marriage is a sham?"

I didn't reply.

"I knew it." He tipped his glass toward me. "What are the contract terms, Bishop?"

"Four weeks."

"When are they up?"

"Two weeks, give or take."

"How much thought have you already put into extending the terms?"

"If Dulvaney was still alive, that would be possible. But she doesn't need me to fulfill my part of the contract anymore."

"You must have something to bargain with."

My lips twitched. "Good sex?"

"You're sleeping with her, then?"

"It wasn't part of the plan, but yeah."

He looked at me, then threw back his head and laughed. When he showed no signs of stopping, I kicked him.

"Are you done?"

"Okay, fine. What are you going to do about it?"

"I think she's going to want to go back to New York. That's where her life was."

"*Was* being the keyword there. She could make a new life for herself here ... with you, if that's what you want?" He drained his drink and stood. "For what it's worth, I think she could be good for you. Just like Dally is good for me."

***

Rook's words stuck with me the entire ride home, and I was still thinking about them when we walked up to the house.

"I'll grab Dally and get out of here. You should talk to your girl and let her know what you want."

"What if I don't know what I want?"

Rook laughed. "Bishop, I've never known a time where you didn't know exactly what you wanted. You just don't want to admit it."

I didn't answer that.

We found Magdalena in the living room, curled up on the corner of the couch. She jumped to her feet when she saw Rook, staggered a little, then smiled brightly.

"How much of that wine did you drink?" Rook caught her when she swayed.

"Little bit." She pinched her thumb and finger together.

Rook's shoulders shook with his quiet laugh. "Let's get you home."

She nodded. "That's a great idea." She stopped beside me on the way past and leaned up to kiss my cheek. "You be nice to Eden. She's my friend and I like her."

"Where is she?"

"Kitchen. Looking for paper."

"Paper?" I turned toward the door.

"Yep." She popped the p.

"And that's our cue to leave. Come on, darlin', let's leave the newlyweds to work their shit out."

78

Eden

I couldn't find any paper in the kitchen because Bishop was obviously a monster and didn't have a junk drawer. That shouldn't have surprised me, not with how *prepared* for everything he was. I needed paper ... and a pen.

I chewed on the inside of my cheek, thinking.

His office! There'd be paper in there, surely.

My wine-soaked mind shoved away the tiny voice that told me he'd said not to go in there. It was only paper. There was bound to be some on the desk ... if there was a desk in there. He might be one of those crazy people who stood up to work.

I screwed up my nose.

No, he'd have a desk. I'd sneak in, grab paper and be out again long before he got home.

Home. When did I start thinking about the house I was living in as home?

I hurried down the hallway and turned the handle on the door to his office. It swung open silently and I stepped inside.

Paper. Where would he keep the paper?

Think like Bishop!

The thought made me snicker, and I slapped a hand over my mouth to muffle the sound. Drawing myself up to my full height, I adopted what felt like a stern expression and scanned the room.

There. A pile of blank paper on the corner of his desk. That was easy.

I snatched up a couple of sheets and a pen, then turned … just as male voices sounded. I couldn't make out what they were saying, but I recognized them both.

Bishop was home.

Oh no.

I looked around.

I could hide or …

I frowned.

What was that?

On the desk was a small pile of paper, with a photograph on the top. I edged closer. The image was blurred, so I squinted, waiting until it came back into focus.

It was me.

Pushing the photograph to one side, I looked at the sheets beneath to reveal the marriage contract we'd signed.

Why did he have it on his desk?

"Eden?" His voice echoed along the corridor, and I bit my lip.

"Eden?" My name preceded the door opening.

His head tilted when he found me beside his desk.

"What are you doing in here?" There was nothing other than curiosity in his voice.

I waved the paper I was clutching at him. "I need paper."

"Magdalena said as much. What do you need it for?"

"What kind of crazy person doesn't have a junk drawer in their kitchen?" I blurted the question.

"A ... what?"

"A junk drawer. You know ... somewhere to keep all the random things you collect that have no real home."

"I don't collect random things." He closed the door and leaned against it.

"You collected me," I muttered. "Why do you have our contract on your desk?"

"I just haven't put it away yet. Why did you need paper, Eden?" He took a step toward me.

"Because we need a new contract." My gaze shifted to the printed sheets on his desk, and I frowned.

"A new contract?"

I picked up the existing one and flicked through it, then lifted my head and looked at the man in front of me. He was watching me, his expression quizzical, and it struck me how easy I found it to read him now. Where once his features had been a study in blankness, now I could pick out the tiny micro-expressions hinting to his mood. And his mood right now was curious.

"What would you do if I tore this up?"

"Do you *want* to tear it up?"

I put down the blank paper and pen, took the contract between both hands and held it up. Holding his gaze, my heart hammering so much I was surprised it didn't break through my ribs, I tore it in half. Bishop didn't move, his eyes following the movement of my hands. When it was in two halves, I tore them again.

Tilting my head up, I met his gaze. "If you don't have the receipt, you can't return the goods."

One eyebrow shot up.

I tossed the torn-up contract into the air and watched the pieces fall to the ground.

"Eden, look at me." His voice came from directly in front of me.

I dragged my gaze away from the paper and found him less than a foot away from me.

"Are you drunk?"

I shook my head. "I've never been so sober in my life." And I was. The slight tipsiness I'd been feeling had gone, leaving me stone cold sober.

"You understand that tearing up the contract changes nothing. It's just a copy."

"There you go being all logical again." I shook my head.

"It's who I am." His fingers found my chin and lifted my head. "Is this your way of asking me to void the contract?"

"I want to live in your junk drawer," I whispered. Heat filled my cheeks. That had sounded less stupid in my head.

His brows pulled together. "Allow me to make a counteroffer."

"What kind of counteroffer?"

"How about you start your own junk drawer? You can fill it with whatever you please." He pressed a kiss to one corner of my mouth. "After all, you've already started your collection of random things."

"I have?"

His smile was slow and warm. My heart rate hiked, and butterflies took off in my stomach.

"You have." His arms looped around my waist, and his head lowered. "The first thing you can put in your drawer is my heart. You picked that up and pocketed it the day you married me. It just took me a while to realize." His lips brushed over mine. "I can't promise spontaneity, that's not who I am. But I can promise to protect you, keep you safe, and love you."

I blinked. "Love me?" The words came out as a startled croak.

"That's what this is, isn't it? Or am I reading it wrong?"

"You're not reading it wrong."

His mouth crashed down onto mine, sending the butterflies in my stomach into frenzied spins. When his lips moved from mine to track a path of kisses over my jaw, I let my head fall back and sighed in pleasure.

"Can I have it in writing?"

He chuckled against my throat. "Have what in writing?"

"That you love me."

"As soon as you confirm your response."

"Oh!" My eyes snapped open.

"I made an educated guess about your feelings from the way you aggressively tore up the contract. But I'd really like to hear it." His voice was a lazy growl next to my ear.

I placed a hand against his chest and gave him a gentle push. He took a step away, and looked at me, one eyebrow raised. I smoothed my hand down the front of his shirt, and the light caught the stone in my engagement ring, making it shine.

"I never expected to fall in love with my husband, but I did." I pressed my hand against his cheek and leaned up to find his lips with mine. "I love you, Bishop Chambers, and if you'll let me, I'd really like to bring some spontaneity to your life."

AUTHOR NOTE

Thank you for coming on a new adventure with me. I hope you enjoyed Bishop and Eden's story.

Special thanks must go to Shani, Ange, and Teresa for keeping me sane (mostly).

If there's anything you've read that you want to talk about—once again, we've opened a spoiler room specifically for this book. You can find it on Facebook, using the link below. Make sure you answer the questions, otherwise you'll sit there … in limbo … forever.

Chambers Brothers Spoiler Group

www.facebook.com/groups/chambersbrothers/

If you're not already a member, you can join me in my

Facebook Group

https://facebook.com/groups/lannsliterati

BOOKS BY L. ANN

MIDNIGHT PACK
MIDNIGHT TOUCH
MIDNIGHT TEMPTATION
MIDNIGHT TORMENT
MIDNIGHT HUNT
MIDNIGHT FURY

MIDNIGHT PACK FULL SERIES BOXSET

(ebook only - includes the short story "Midnight Link")

FORGOTTEN LEGACY
TATTOOED MEMORIES
STRAWBERRY DELIGHT - SHORT STORY
STRAWBERRY LIPSTICK - SHORT STORY
SHATTERED EXPECTATIONS
GUARDED ADDICTION
EXQUISITE SCARS
BROKEN HALO
NEGLECTED CONSEQUENCES

BLACK ROSARY
FRACTURED ANGEL

CHAMBERS BROTHERS
ROOK
BISHOP

CHURCHILL BRADLEY ACADEMY
DARE TO BREAK
DARE TO TAKE
DARE TO FALL
DARE TO LIVE

Made in United States
Troutdale, OR
04/23/2025